SHORT CUTS TO MURDER

13 tales about the macabre ways of men and women

BY DAVID MENON

AUTHOR'S NOTE

All of these stories have appeared before in three different collections, 'Kind of Woman', 'Losing Grip', and 'Sisters of the Moon'. I decided to put them all together in one volume to tidy things up and give you all a 'Short Cut'.

David

Paris, September 2016

CONTENTS

Some of these stories burst out of other tales I've written, like little bubbles of new worlds and different places, but most were inspired by my time in Finland a few summer's ago. The lakes, the forests, the wonderful people I met from Finland, Russia, and all over the world, and the peace and quiet of the magical places we worked in. It all conspired to get me writing. So I would like to dedicate this entire collection, including those tales that I didn't write in Finland, to all the Russian students, to Lena and all the staff of the Nordic school in St. Petersburg, to all of my fellow teachers from the UK, Canada, Kenya, and the USA, and to all of the local Finnish people who supported our efforts with their cooking and their general friendliness. It was a great time.

And of course, this is for Maddie and for the friends who stayed with me through some dark times and, finally, to the spirit of Rhiannon who always gets me through.Love and peace to all ... except to all the hypocrites ... they can all do one!

David
Paris, September 2016

DAVID MENON

David left a long career in the airline industry in 2009 to establish his writing career. He now lives in Paris and writes full-time including several stand alone titles plus the DSI Jeff Barton detective series set in Manchester and the Stephanie Marshall private investigator series set in Sydney. He also lived in Blackpool for a while which is where the inspiration for his 'DCI Layla Khan' series came from. He takes a keen interest in international politics and current affairs plus all the arts of theatre, film, TV, and music. He's a devoted fan of American singer and songwriter Stevie Nicks who he calls the voice of his interior world. He loves Indian food, a g and t with the emphasis on the g and not the t plus a glass or three of red wine. Well, it doesn't make him a bad person.

Also by the Author

DSI Jeff Barton series

'Sorcerer', 'Fireflies', 'Storms', 'No Questions Asked', 'Straight Back',' Thrown Down', 'No Spoken Word'. 'Landslide' will be the 8th in the series and will be out before Christmas 2016. 'Sorcerer' is also available in French as 'Le Sorcier'.

PI Stephanie Marshall series

'What Happened to Liam?', 'Could Max Burley Be a Killer?' The third will be 'Finding Answers for Stacey'

and coming soon.

DCI Layla Khan series

'In the Shadow of the Tower'.

Stand alone titles

'The Murder in His Past' plus 'The Wild Heart'.

Available through Amazon, Kobo, and e-sentral, amongst others.

ONE
Kathleen

Fergus Walsh was walking home from the big supermarket on Regent Road with a full bag of shopping in each hand. He'd taken this route down the old Ordsall Road in his adopted home city of Salford more times than he'd care to remember. It had been an industrial wasteland for many years until the local authorities finally got a hold of things and began the re-building of the district. Now there were fancy new flats going up all over the place, taking the residential makeover that had begun in the Salford Quays development all the way up the river to within sight of Manchester city centre a mile or so away. But they still couldn't clean it up entirely. A young Asian lad had been murdered along this very road earlier in the year. They still had some way to go to change the hearts of some of the people who lived here and Fergus prayed for them at Mass every Sunday. He had to take it easier these days owing to the arthritis he'd started to get in his knees and ankles, but he was determined that for as long as he could he wouldn't rely on his daughter Bernadette getting all his supplies in for him. She had enough to do looking after a house with a husband and four big strapping lads and he didn't want to burden her until he had to.

He'd been seventeen when he'd taken the bus from the village back in County Wicklow to Dublin and then the boat over to

England. He'd left his parents and half a dozen brothers and sisters behind. It was the year of the coronation of Queen Elizabeth, and his brother Dermot, the one who was always banging on about the oppression caused by the British Empire, accused Fergus of selling out by going to England. Dermot, on the other hand, had gone to America. He'd settled in Boston and become some kind of university lecturer. He'd always been the one with the brains but the family had rarely seen him since although he'd come over for both of their parents funerals accompanied by some Spanish looking chap called Eduardo. He'd never married.

Fergus turned the corner into the street in Ordsall that he'd lived in for forty years. He'd been part of the great Irish migration of labour that had crossed the Irish sea in the fifties and gone on to build the motorways, the hospitals, the schools, the shopping precincts, the housing estates across Manchester and other towns and cities in the northwest. He'd never been out of work since the day he arrived until the day he retired. It was an example he'd passed on to his family. Bernadette had worked from the day she left school until her eldest son was born and now that the youngest was fifteen she'd gone back to work. Her two eldest boys, who picked Fergus up every Sunday at 12 to take him for a couple of pints before taking him back to their house where Bernadette prepared Sunday lunch, had never had any problem getting a job and both had good ones. The younger two were a bit brighter than their older siblings and were staying on at school before heading for university. Fergus was so very proud of them all.

But despite the closeness Fergus still missed his dear wife Kathleen. It would've been their 45th wedding anniversary next week. But poor Kathleen had been taken by cancer two years ago and he didn't think he'd ever get over it. They'd met at an Irish association dinner and dance in Chorlton, South Manchester and Fergus had 'courted' her for a year before popping the question. They'd wanted to have more children but after the problems Kathleen had when giving birth to their daughter Bernadette they were told by the doctor that she wouldn't be able to have anymore. But they accepted that as God's grace and Bernadette was a very loved and treasured little girl though she was never spoilt. Both Fergus and Kathleen had come from the same working class Irish roots and had both grown up in houses where 'love' was often represented by Daddy's belt. Fergus had learned from that. He'd never laid a finger on either Kathleen or Bernadette and he would've flattened his son-in-law Dennis if he'd laid a hand on Bernadette or any of their sons. Violence was not the way although sometimes Fergus had been forced to take care of himself when he'd been out and about drinking in his younger days.

'Mr. Walsh! Mr. Walsh!'

Fergus turned to the call of the foreign sounding voice and knew instantly who it was. It was little Omar, the twelve year-old boy who lived next door to Fergus with his mother and two older sisters. They'd been refugees from Somalia and Fergus didn't know what had happened to the father. None of the family talked about it.

'Oh hello, Omar! How about you, young man?'

'Let me carry your shopping bags, Mr. Walsh' said Omar.

'Oh that's okay, Omar, thank you but we're near home now'.

'Please let me, Mr. Walsh' said Omar. 'My mother taught me it is the right thing to do with the elders of the community'.

Fergus smiled. 'Well then she's probably right, Omar' he said as he handed Omar one of his bags. He was fond of Omar's mother. She was a lovely, gracious woman who often handed him a pot of the traditional stew she makes with either beef or chicken. He'd grown to rather like it even though it was a little spicy for his usual tastes but he'd never risk hurting her feelings by refusing it.

'There you go now. That's the lighter one. Now tell me what you've been up to?'

'I came top of the class in mathematics!'

'Oh well done, Omar' said Fergus as they walked along. 'That's great. And are you still after becoming an accountant?'

'Yes, Mr. Walsh' said Omar who was dressed in jeans, trainers and a sweater. It's how his mother liked him to dress these days when he went out. 'Maybe I will look after the money of the players at Manchester United?'.

'Ah well, you'll earn a fortune doing that, Omar!

'Their attention was then taken by someone shouting at them from across the street.

'Oi! Nigger! Get away from him!'

'Don't you be calling this young boy disgusting names like that!' Fergus raged. 'And he's with me because we're friends'.

'You can't be friends with a nigger if you're a white man. It's against the rules'.

The two specimens in front of Fergus were in their early twenties. They looked like they hadn't had a proper wash for a week and they were covered in the most hideous looking tattoos. They were both in track suits and trainers and their heads were shaved.

'I know who you two are' said Fergus. 'You live up on Mercian street, don't you? You're the two Dixon brothers and you look like the older one so you must be Tommy and he behind you must be George. I know my neighbourhood. And I know you've never done a day's work in your sorry, little lives'.

'Whose side are you on, Paddy?' asked Tommy Dixon.

'My name is Mr. Walsh to you!'

'Listen, you don't tell me what to do in my own fucking country. Alright?'

'And if you'd anything about you then you wouldn't swear in front of a minor'.

'You don't get it, do you, Paddy?' said Tommy who came right up close to Fergus. 'I can't get a job because of all these foreigners coming in'.

'That's rubbish and you know it' said Fergus who wouldn't be intimidated by the likes of this idiot but he was fearful for Omar.

'Oh you think so, old man?' Tommy sneered.

'You're just too bone idle to show any initiative'.

'Hey, steady on, Paddy, that sounds like fighting talk to me' said Tommy. 'I believe in England for the proper white English and that means no niggers and no Irish bleeding us dry of everything that belongs to us'.

'Is little George here mute or something? He doesn't seem to speak'.

'He agrees with everything I say'.

'Christ, it must be like the blind leading the bloody blind'.

'Now I'm warning you, Paddy'.

'Oh stop trying to act the big man and let us pass!'

'No' said Tommy. 'Are you going to make me?'

'Omar, go inside to your mother now son, go on' said Fergus.

'No, Mr. Walsh, I'm staying here with you' Omar insisted.

'Go inside, Omar, I'll be alright here'.

'Do as you're told, nigger' Tommy sneered.

'I've told you before not to call him that!' Fergus raged.

'And what are you going to do if I carry on, Paddy?

'Fergus threw a punch at Tommy that landed right on the end of his nose.

'Fuck's sake!' Tommy exclaimed, his hand over where the blood was coming from and his eyes full of shock and then anger. 'You fucking Irish cunt!'

'Now are you going to let us pass, Dixon?' Fergus asked. 'Please'.

All of a sudden, George Dixon came leaping out from behind his brother and stabbed Fergus. He stabbed him repeatedly whilst Omar screamed for him to stop. Then he and Tommy ran off and Omar tried to help his dying friend. Omar's mother came out of her house and tried to stop the bleeding by applying pressure to the wounds but there were too many of them. She cried. Omar cried. Their only real friend in the street was dying.

'We must call an ambulance' said Omar, frantically, sobbing his heart out. 'He was defending me!'

'I know, my child, but it's too late now' said his mother who could see that it was too late for anyone to save the life of poor Fergus. 'All we can do is to give him peace as he goes on his way. Then we will call an ambulance'.

Omar's mother held one of Fergus' hands and Omar held the other as their friend the Irishman who'd helped build England's motorways, hospitals, schools, shopping precincts and housing estates, went up to be re-united with his dear, sweet Kathleen who he could see had her arms open wide for him.

'Thank you to everyone for coming' said Bernadette, in a faltering voice. She was flanked by her husband and four sons at the memorial service for her father in St. Mary's church. It was packed to the rafters with many of Fergus' old pals but also with complete strangers who wanted to pay their respects to a man who'd lost his life so violently at the hands of cowards. The Dixon brothers had been picked up and charged less than twenty-four hours after the murder thanks to the co-operation of a neighbourhood that had been sickened by their crime.

'My father was murdered because he'd befriended a family from Somalia and because he was Irish instead of being English. Now, my husband's Uncle Brendan, God rest his soul, was a policeman in Birmingham during the seventies, just after the pub bombings there. He would say that, as a matter of course, drunken Irish men would be picked up off the streets and beaten up until they confessed to being members of the IRA. It was wrong and it was one of the reasons why he left the police force but my father came from the same generation as the men Brendan described. They had nothing in the way of paper qualifications but they worked damn hard on the reconstruction of Britain after the Second World War. They didn't deserve to be treated that way after all they'd done for this country. My father befriended a family from Somalia who'd come here for a better future, just like he'd done all those years ago, and it cost him his life. Now that's not the kind of Britain I want to live in today and it's not the kind of Britain I want my grandchildren to grow up in. If my father's murder can mean anything it should be that as a community we should come together and fight those who want to divide us on the grounds of race. My father didn't care where anybody came from as long as they were honest and hard working. We owe it to him and we owe it to his friends, little Omar and his mother, to make sure that nothing like this ever happens again. My father would've been proud to see so many of you here'. Her husband then put his arms round her. Everybody held up the candles they were holding. Silence fell on the gathering despite the whirring sound of the TV cameras that had come to capture the event for the local and national networks. But the reporters kept a discreet distance. Even they knew when respect had to be shown.

TWO
Adam

Adam Taylor lived in one of the kind of flats on the edge of Manchester's city centre that had been purpose built for young professionals. But none of that was his primary concern as he got ready to go out on the town. He was a newly qualified English teacher and was starting his first post on Monday at a north Manchester comprehensive. He was looking forward to the challenge and by all accounts it was going to be a definite challenge to get some of the kids to feel motivated into believing in anything other than unemployment, benefits, and too many kids they couldn't financially support. But he was keen and eager and desperate to get started and to try and 'inspire' the kids who came through his classroom door. He'd always wanted to be a teacher on the rough end of the education stick. He'd grown up to believe that a good education was a right for all kids and not just the privileged few at the top who were educated in the private sector. Thanks to the influence of his father who was a self-confessed 'old fashioned socialist' and who was also a teacher to whom Adam had always been very close, he'd come to believe fervently in the comprehensive system and not just because of his father's subtle indoctrination. He'd vowed never to sell out to whatever fad like initiative that any government of the day brought forward that might dilute the basic principle of a comprehensive education available to all. He'd rather eat shit than take a job in one of the new free schools. As far as he was concerned free schools were just another example of the already bloated number of privileges extended to a vocal and self-obsessed middle class.

'Come on Adam! Have you finished in the bathroom yet you big girl!'

Tonight was Saturday and it was party night. Adam, his flat mate Dylan who was also starting as a teacher on Monday and who'd so delicately tried to hurry Adam along, and a few of their other mates were heading to the Rice Bowl Chinese restaurant on Cross Street for something to eat before hitting the bars and clubs. Nobody was allowed to go home before they'd either pulled or were incapable of standing up. This was to be their last big night before they got down to their new and cherished careers.

Adam spotted her as soon as they walked into the club at the bottom opposite Deansgate station. She was standing with some mates and wearing a short white chiffon dress with a line of white fur round the hem and a low cut neck. Her white lace bra and pants were clearly visible underneath and her dark brown hair was folded up in a kind of bun. She wore white high heels and her handbag was small and white with a shoulder strap. Urged on by his mates and the beer he sidled up to her and could've dropped dead with shock when she actually started talking to him.

'Hiya!' she breathed. 'I saw you looking and was hoping you'd come over'.

'You were?'

'Yeah? You look like the kind of nice guy I'm looking for tonight. I'm Lucinda'.

'And I'm Adam'.

'Well then Adam, tell me something about yourself'.

The conversation was full of Lucinda's smiles and the kind of looks that any man in Adam's position would feel in his pants. To think that a beautiful girl like her might be interested in him was a test for all his liberal equality instincts. But he wasn't doing anything wrong. He was chatting her up and she wasn't objecting. They were finding out about each other. She worked in the administration office of a building firm in Oldham and she hated every minute of it. She said it was so dreary she sometimes thought she might die of boredom. He told her that he'd just graduated from university. She didn't have a boyfriend. He didn't have a girlfriend. Thank you, God! If he could have sex with her then he would do. She took his breath away. After an hour or two of talking during which there were no awkward silences Adam took the plunge and invited her back to his place. He still thought she was way out of his league but he asked her anyway. What did he have to lose and besides, he liked her and she seemed to like him.

Lucinda smiled promisingly and said 'I thought you'd never ask'.

Adam was lost for words for a moment but then blurted out. 'You are beautiful'.

'Thank you. And you're pretty fit'.

'We can walk back to my place from here'.

In the hallway of his flat she urged him gently against the wall and her kisses were as tender as anything. She had his t-shirt off in no time and the feel of her soft warm hands on his skin was like magic. She unbuckled the belt round his trousers and let them fall to his ankles. Then she slid her hand down the front of his boxer shorts. He groaned and sighed at the way her fingers were handling his cock.

'I had a feeling you'd be a big boy and I'm not disappointed, Adam. I'm going to have a lot of fun with that inside me'.

This was like a dream come true. She was only nineteen but she seemed to know her way around a man who was nervous and keen to please. During the night he found out that she was sexually experienced way beyond her years and way beyond anything he'd known before. She was the best thing that had ever happened to him sexually.

The next morning was when the scales fell from her eyes.

'How are you?' he asked after she'd woken up. 'Do you want some tea or coffee? I'll make us some breakfast in a minute too if you like'.

'I don't like' came the curt reply.

'What's wrong?'

'Adam, you're fit as fuck and I fancied the arse off you. But in bed you need more practice love, sorry'.

Adam felt like he'd really had the wind knocked out of his sails. 'Oh'

'But that's not what I need to talk to you about'.

'What do you mean?' They were still in bed but all of a sudden Adam had a dreadful sense of foreboding. 'Lucinda, what's going on here?'

'I'm fifteen, Adam'.

Adam could've been sick. 'What?'

'I played you. I saw you in the club last night and knew you'd believe anything to get into my knickers'.

'You can't mean it' he said.

'I mean every word, Adam. I trapped you last night and now you're going to have to do as you're told if you want to stay out of trouble'.

'But last night you told me you were nineteen and worked in some admin office?'

'The building firm in Oldham is where my Dad works. I lied to you. Now get over it, get down to the cash machine and get me a grand. If you don't then you really will wish that last night had never happened'.

Adam was in a panic. He'd been stupid to believe her but what reason would he have had for not believing her? 'You've done this before'.

'You wouldn't believe how many idiots there are like you out there. How do you think I get to wear such lovely clothes?'

'Do your parents know you do this?'

'Just go and get me the grand, Adam, I'm running out of patience. And then call me a cab. There's a good boy'.

Against his better judgement Adam did as he was told. He went down and got her the thousand pounds. It meant that he only had twenty-seven pounds left in his bank account but that was the least of his worries potentially. He was a newly qualified teacher who'd slept with an underage girl. He didn't know that she'd been underage but how much worse could it fucking well get? What if she came back for more money? She was clearly no innocent.

'How many times have you done this before?'

'I've lost count to be honest'.

'Why do you do it?'

'Because I can' she answered matter of factly. 'Call it girl power'.

She left his flat shortly after ten and he spent the rest of the day throwing up and going out of his mind with worry.

Monday morning.

9.13 am, Parkview Comprehensive school, Manchester.

Adam was excited and more than a little nervous as he went to start his first day. He had a meeting with the headmaster, the head of his department and then he was introduced to the rest of the teaching staff. Everybody seemed great. Now all he needed were some students to start working on. He'd heard nothing from Lucinda since yesterday morning and he was slowly starting to let go of the whole experience. She'd conned him. He'd acted in good faith. She'd used her body to get money out of him just like any prostitute. He had to put it behind him and forget about it. What else could he do? Go to the police and confess he'd been tricked into sleeping with an underage girl?

But then his first class filed into the classroom.

There on the front row was Lucinda.

And from the look on her face the nightmare had only just begun.

12.01pm

She waited until the start of the lunch break. She watched the rest of the class file out and then it was just her and him.

'You stay away from me' said Adam.

'I could click my fingers and it would be all over for you'.

The smirk on her face made Adam want to smack it right off. 'Look, I gave you the money so what more do you want?'

'Oh well, I could tell them that you gave me the money to stop me telling the truth about how you sexually assaulted me'.

Adam felt the floor beneath him move. 'You wouldn't?'

'Wouldn't I?'

'You'd be telling them a complete pack of lies'.

'And that's a concern of mine because?

'He begged her not to do that for the sake of his career but she said she didn't give a fuck about his career. She wanted to be a celebrity and a teacher having sex with an underage student would get her all over the tabloids and get her loads of money from selling her 'sob' story to the papers and all the gossip magazines. It was too good an opportunity to miss and she'd be mad to let it pass. She then went straight to the head of the school and told her 'story'. The head then called the police.

The teaching career of Adam Taylor ended on the same day it had begun. Lucinda claimed in court that she'd told him right from the start that she was only fifteen and when he asked her back to his place she thought she was safe because he'd been so charming. But instead he seemed to change and he forced her into his apartment where he sexually assaulted her. She claimed that she'd been terrified by him and she'd feared what he might do to her if she said no. When Adam came to the stand he tried desperately to get the court to believe him. He'd asked her back to his place, believing she was nineteen, and she'd said yes without question. He insisted to the court that the time they'd spent together had been entirely consensual. He said that he wasn't the sort of man to force anybody into doing anything and that he'd been brought up to respect women when it came to sex. He was in tears as he repeated over and over again that she'd told him she was nineteen and she worked in an administration office. He said that none of it would ever have happened if he'd known she was only fifteen. He also told the court about how she'd boasted about extorting money out of other men in this same way by lying about her age. But the court believed Lucinda. She was underage after all. She was just a child. How could she have been manipulative enough to do what Adam Taylor claimed? She told the court that Adam had given her the thousand pounds to 'keep her mouth shut' about the 'assault' and why would a nice young girl from an ordinary working-class family like her lie about what had happened? So the court believed her again when she claimed to want justice, not money. She was good at playing the victim right down to her dramatic 'faint' whilst being cross examined. He'd broken the law even though he hadn't known he was breaking it at the time. He couldn't go unpunished and the court believed Lucinda's claim of total innocence.

Adam Taylor joined the ranks of the unemployed with an entry on the sexual offences list. Four years of studying at university so that he could inspire kids to broaden their knowledge and therefore their opportunities had gone down the pan on the word of a fifteen year old girl who'd told a pack of lies. He was a broken man.

Lucinda Davies took her Mum on a luxury holiday to Barbados with all the money she made from selling her 'story' in an exclusive deal with the Daily Mail that ran into six figures. And she still had plenty of it left to buy loads and loads of clothes from all the best shops in Manchester.

Three years later.

Lucinda Davies was managing to achieve everything she'd set out to. As lead singer with the girl band 'In Your Face' who were storming their way up the charts all over the world, she had stacks and stacks of money and all the attention she'd ever dreamed of. And now she also had the final piece that would complete the picture of a modern, young famous lead singer with an up and coming girl band. She had the premiership footballer boyfriend.

Lee Smith had been talent spotted by Manchester United when he was only thirteen and now he'd been on the first team for a whole season. He was still only eighteen but he was the player with the second highest number of goals scored in the last season and they were talking about him as the new Wayne Rooney. His agent was also pushing the 'Lee and Lucinda' brand as the new 'Posh and Becks' and Lucinda was more than happy with that. Victoria Beckham's autobiography was the only book she'd ever read although she now thought she should read something that would make her think about stuff so she'd sent someone out to buy the latest blockbuster by Katie Price. This was also going to be useful because the marketing team behind 'In Your Face' said that a novel with Lucinda's name on it but written by a ghost writer would be highly profitable in today's market. So Lucinda had decided to read Katie Price to see what a novel actually was and what it was all about. But she was finding it difficult. She'd only read the first three pages but already she'd come up against loads of words she didn't know. Like 'seldom'. She hadn't had a clue what that meant. And she'd never heard of 'shallots' even without trying to pronounce it. Were they Indian or something? Her Mum only ever used onions in her good old English cooking. That was one thing she wasn't getting used to about being a celebrity. Some of the receptions she had to attend served up the most horrible so-called food, like bits of smoked salmon on bits of brown bread. What was that all about? Salmon came in a tin and you only had it on a Sunday when Grandma and Granddad came round for tea.

Lee went to meet Lucinda in a country hotel in Cheshire. Lucinda had bought her parents a new house in Bowden, south Manchester which she also used as her home base. Her Mum liked Lee and thought he was perfect for Lucinda but she didn't like them having sex under her roof. So for a bit of a random change from Lucinda staying over at Lee's penthouse in Manchester city centre, they sometimes sneaked out to this hotel where Lucinda went in through the back door and Lee went in the front wearing a baseball cap and sunglasses to deter being recognised. However, when you pull up in a brand new red Ferrari with a number plate that read 'ACE LEE' not only did it mean you got noticed but it didn't take long for other patrons of the hotel to put two and two together, especially if they were Manchester United fans.

'Sorry about that, babe' said Lee once he got to the suite they'd hired and put the chain lock on the door behind him. 'I got recognised and had to stop for some autographs and pictures and that'.

'Me too, babe' said Lucinda who was concentrating on the

messages on her mobile phone and didn't even look up to greet her boyfriend. The messages were from Alfredo who was the manager of 'In Your Face'. He was a Spanish entrepreneur who'd put together boy and girl bands in several different European countries. 'I came up from London on the shuttle from Heathrow and I was surrounded. There was a bloke in a wheelchair and I made a beeline for him so that a picture would be taken for the sake of the image and that. I didn't speak to him though. I don't know what to say to spastics. I mean, they give me the creeps really'.

'What are you doing, babe?' asked Lee. 'Are they from your Mum?'

'No they're from Alfredo' groaned Lucinda. 'The bloody nerve of the bastard'.

'Why, what's he done now?' asked Lee who was well used to Lucinda having fights with her manager. His own manager wouldn't stand for it if he acted like that with him. Christ, he'd be well out on his ear.

'You know the tour he's organising for us for the autumn?'

'Yeah?'

'Well he only wants us to sing live with a band on it!'

Lee was a little perplexed. 'Isn't that what you do on tour, babe? When I went to see Mumford and Sons at the Apollo last year that's what they did I think'.

'I'm not giving away half the proceeds from the tour to a band of bloody musicians! No fucking way! I want all the money. It'll just be the three of us on stage miming to a backing tape with the microphones switched off. This isn't about music or what Alfredo calls creative integrity, whatever the fuck that means. This is about celebrity and I thought Alfredo understood that'.

'How did this come about then?'

'Apparently we've been bad mouthed in some so-called music magazine or other because we've never sung live. Alfredo wants to pander to that but I told him that I never joined to sing live. I just wanted to be the lead singer in a band. That's what I signed up to, not all this musician crap'.

'What do Candy and Beth think?'

'They agree with me'.

'Do they know yet about the money?'

Lucinda had managed to negotiate a secret deal with Alfredo which meant that she was going to get two million for the tour and her band mates, Candy and Beth would only be getting five hundred thousand each.

'No and they're not going to. Besides, I can justify the difference. I am after all the main talent of the band. Everybody knows that. Anyway, I could always get pregnant and then I wouldn't have to do Alfredo's stupid tour because my clause in the contract says that he'd still have to pay me the two million'.

'And Candy and Beth would still get nothing?'

'Yeah' said Lucinda, holding up her finger to emphasise her point. 'But don't ask me to care because I don't'.

'Weren't you working on some new songs down in London, babe?'

'Yeah and we've settled on two titles both of which I came up with'

'What are they then babe?'

'Do it to me like you did it to me last night' and 'It's not always about money'. I don't know why but they all laughed when I came up with that second one. Anyway, the writers are setting to work on them both and they should be ready when I get back down there tomorrow. Candy and Beth have stayed down there. They like fiddling about in the studio and all that rubbish. They both want to be writers and producers one day whereas I just want the house, the money, the celebrity and the premiership footballer husband who earns millions'.

'Sounds good to me, babe' said Lee as he fell onto the bed beside her and they started kissing. 'Let's start practicing now'.

'And that sounds good to me, babe. Get those boxers off and start scoring some goals in the back of my net'.

Lucinda's father was driving her home from the BBC's Media city studios in Salford where she'd done an interview for the BBC Breakfast programme to promote the new single by 'In Your Face' which was called 'Come and Get it Boys'. She'd struggled during the interview when the presenter asked her if she didn't think the lyrics were a little bit explicit and inviting men to see women just as sex objects. Lucinda didn't know what explicit meant.

She asked her father to go via the hotel in Cheshire where she'd spent the night with her boyfriend Lee because she'd left her tablet computer there and she didn't want it falling into the wrong hands. It meant a thirty mile detour but Lucinda's father had grown used to the family dynamics being focused around whatever Lucinda wants Lucinda gets. It had always been the case since the day his daughter was born. His wife had let their daughter rule the roost. And it had gone too far for him to be able to grow a backbone now.

'Do you want me to go in for you, love?' her Dad asked.

Lucinda thought about it. She wasn't in the mood to be recognised or even mobbed this morning and yet she couldn't resist the temptation to stir people's interest and make sure people did recognise her.

'No, you're alright, Dad. I'll put my sunnies on and my baseball cap' said Lucinda. 'Park up as close as you can to the door though'.

'The closest spots are reserved for the disabled, love'.

'So?'

'Well they're reserved for the disabled'.

'Oh look I do enough charity work for spastic this and spastic that and there's absolutely no money in it. Well I want some payback. Park in one of those spots and if anybody kicks off I'll just put on my best pop star tears and say I was being hounded by the press'

Lucinda put her baseball cap and sunglasses on and strode purposefully into the hotel. She looked down constantly at the messages on her mobile phone but was also aware enough to be able to pick up any whispers from anyone who might've realised it was her. She stood in line at the reception desk behind all the other guests who wanted attention and got into an internal strop because nobody had seemed to have realised it was her. It was all part of the game. She wanted to be recognised so that she could then pretend to be frightened by not even being able to go into a hotel without being hounded and that's what would get all the press attention and attract sufficient public sympathy to see the new single go up the charts. But it didn't seem to be working on this chilly Tuesday morning. She was about to take her sunglasses off to aid the process of recognition when the sight of someone down a corridor made her feel like she'd been handed a penny from Heaven. She walked up behind Adam Taylor who was servicing a room.

'Well, well, well' she said. 'Look who it is'.

Adam Taylor heard Lucinda's voice and it sent a shiver down his spine.

'Of all the hotels I could've gone into I walk into the one where you're having to work' said Lucinda with a giggle. 'How's life, Mr. Taylor?'

'Get away from me'.

'Now that's not very friendly. I mean, what does it say on that badge you're wearing? 'Let me help you'. Oh but what a come down. All that time studying to be a teacher and here you are dealing with everybody's dirty sheets in a hotel. You really shouldn't have been a naughty boy'.

'I wasn't' he insisted. 'You were a liar'.

'Yes, but they believed my lies'.

'You played an evil game with me'.

'Yes, and I won'.

'You destroyed my career'.

'And my career has gone from strength to million pound strength. You know I've got so much money coming in that my accountant has to put it all in a country called offshore so that I don't have to pay all the tax they want here. And what do you get? Minimum wage? All that so-called study and education and I took it all away with one opening of my luscious legs. What a world we live in, eh?'

Adam had dreamt of the moment when he might bump into

Lucinda Davies. He looked at her and felt such a surge of pure hatred that it was taking all he had to not go for her throat. Why should she have got away with it? Why was he stuck in the arsehole of life when she was gliding round the world with all the money and attention she wanted? It wasn't fair. He should've been well into his teaching career by now. And yet there she stood looking as pleased as anything about what she'd done and virtually goading him to react. It just wasn't fair.

'What's the matter, Mr. Taylor? Oh, have you lost your tongue? I'm glad I didn't lose mine when I was telling all those lies about you and getting you the sack and a criminal record'.

'Just leave me alone'

'What, before I've had a little fun? No chance'.

Lucinda then grabbed the service trolley that Adam was working from and turned it over onto its side. It sent all the stock of towels and toiletries all over the floor.

'Oops! I think you'd better pick all of those up. I hope they don't stop it out of your wages. Anyway, got to dash. I've got more millions to make'.

'You make me sick'.

'Oh and once the band is over I'll not only have millions in the bank but I'll also be married to my Lee so we'll always have millions. I'd like to say I'll see you around but we don't of course mix in the same circles and never will do. You're only one step up from the underclass now. Enjoy the rest of your life in the dead end zone'.

Splashed across the newspapers the next morning was a story of how 'dreadfully upset' Lucinda Davies had been to walk into her 'absolute favourite' Cheshire hotel, one to which she'd come to see as a second home, only to find the former teacher who'd sexually assaulted her when she was only fifteen working there.

'It was like seeing the devil right in front of me' Lucinda told the Gazette whilst sobbing as she recalled the experience. 'This is a place I see as a sanctuary when I need to find some peace and quiet and some privacy for me and Lee. It was like it had been invaded seeing Adam Taylor there. I had this really bad panic attack and I couldn't breathe. It brought the whole assault right back to me and I had to relive it all over again which was just horrible. I'm still shaking as I think of it'.

Adam threw the paper down on the ground as he walked into work. She was telling a complete pack of lies again and yet he knew that the court of public opinion would no doubt believe every single fucking word because she's one of the modern off the peg celebrities who just wants to be famous. And the mass of people out there seem to love the shallow, meaningless, pointless shit of it all.

He started the working day at seven and at ten past nine the manager, Alison Roberts, called him to her office. When he walked in she looked grave.

'Sit down, Adam'.

'Sounds like I'm not going to like what you're about to tell me'.

'Adam' she began with as much sympathy in her voice that she could muster. 'These things are never easy even when you've been in the job as long as I have. And as you know we do take pride in this company at giving people with backgrounds like yours a second chance'.

'Backgrounds like mine?' he questioned even though he of course knew exactly what she meant.

'Adam, do I really have to spell it out?'

'You do if we want clarity in this conversation which I assume you do?'

Alison took a deep breath. 'I've been talking to head office this morning and I'm afraid that due to the adverse publicity for the hotel in today's press, I'm going to have to dismiss you with a month's notice. I personally insisted to head office on that'.

'Do you have a problem with my work?'

'No, Adam, you … '

'… have I ever been late or taken endless days off as sickies like some of the others do?'

'Adam, you know that your work record is exemplorary and that you're well thought of here'.

'Then?'

'Adam, don't make this anymore difficult than it needs to be'.

'So let me get this straight' said Adam. 'You're dismissing me because some two bit pop star doesn't want to see me working at this hotel and because she's a liar and I'm supposed to somehow make that easy for you?'

'Adam, if it was up to me … '

'… oh yeah, sure'.

'Adam, you know we've always got on and if it's any consolation I don't believe Lucinda Davies but this is not my decision to take'.

Adam stood up and began pacing up and down the small room. He put his hands against his head. 'I'll never be free of this'.

'Adam, my advice would be to go abroad' said Alison. 'Start a new life somewhere else where nobody knows you or Lucinda Davies' allegations'.

'But why should I have to do that when I'm an innocent man!'

'Adam, I know it's unfair'.

Adam began to cry. 'She destroyed my career and everything I'd worked for. I can't go abroad Alison because I've got a record as a sex offender which means that most countries won't let me in and yet it's all a lie Alison. She entrapped me and my life is finished whilst she's raking in millions and there's nothing I can do about it'.

Alison stood up and walked round from behind her desk. She put her arm round him and tried to offer him some comfort but she could see that he'd gone beyond that. Adam clenched his fist and was hitting it on the top of a filing cabinet.

'Adam, I'm worried about you' said Alison. 'I hate seeing you in this state'.

'I'm sorry' said Adam before turning on his heels and running out of her office.

'Adam, come back!' she called after him from the door. 'Come back and we'll talk!'

Lucinda Davies entered the hotel in her usual way through a back door and disguised in a baseball cap. She was shown to her usual suite by the owner of the hotel chain who'd come down from company headquarters in Manchester specially. Lucinda lapped up all the fuss and attention but then after she'd closed the door behind her she stuck two fingers in her mouth in a mocking gesture. She'd agreed to the hotel bestowing her with love as long as it was kept secret. She was here, after all, to escape a stalker.

She threw her bag on the bed and couldn't wait for Lee to arrive. They were so loved up with each other and besides all that she wanted to shag him. She was desperate to get pregnant so she could get out of doing the upcoming 'In Your Face' tour. Rehearsals had not been going well. Several musicians had walked out claiming that Lucinda just couldn't cut it live and the other two girls in the 'band' were much better and more credible singers. It had really upset her but she had a rare day off tomorrow from band activities and was planning on going shopping with her Mum which she knew would make her feel better.

She went into the bathroom and laid out all her toiletries on the side next to the wash basin. She threw some water over her face and walked nonchalantly back into the living area of the suite. Then she was stopped dead in her tracks. A middle aged man was standing in the middle of the room. His head was shaved and he wore a denim jacket over jeans. He also had a gun in his hand.

'Have you been stalking me?'

'There's no need to be afraid, Lucinda'.

'You've got a flaming gun!'

'Don't scream' he said. 'Don't even raise your voice. I'm not going to hurt you'.

'Oh my God!' Lucinda wailed. 'What do you want?'

'I just wanted a bit of time with you' he said. 'My name is Steve. I never wanted to hurt you. It's just that I don't think you should marry Lee Smith. He's no good for you. He'll be off shagging other women and break your heart. I know his type. He's only out for what he can get'.

'You're mad'.

'Don't say that'.

'Well you are. You're stark raving mad!'

'I said don't say that! You've been used, Lucinda. Used by men who've told you that you've got talent when you haven't. My daughter, my beautiful little Nicole, she was told she had talent. She was told she could sing and that recording contracts would be flying through her window. But then they got her into drugs. There was no going back from there'.

'I'm not on drugs' Lucinda whimpered.

'No but you soon will be' said Steve. 'And I've got to save you. I'd been a good father. I'd given her everything she ever needed but it still wasn't enough. I can't let you go the same way. It wouldn't be right'.

The door opened and Lee walked in. 'Babe!' he cried. He saw what was happening and at the same time he and Lucinda lunged at Steve. Lucinda managed to wrestle the gun off him. But then in the madness of the moment the gun went off and Lee dropped to the floor. Steve panicked and ran. Then Adam, who only had a week to go to work out his notice, came in. He never expected to see Lucinda there or the scene that presented itself.

'I heard shots being fired' he said. 'What the hell have you done?'

'I swear it was an accident' Lucinda pleaded frantically. 'I didn't mean to do it. How could I have meant to shoot my baby?' She fell to her knees beside Lee's body. 'I loved him. I really loved him. Adam you've got to help me'.

'I've got to help you?'

'Please tell them it was the stalker who shot Lee'.

'The stalker?'

'Didn't you see that guy running out of the room?'

'Yeah, I saw him'.

'We were wrestling for the gun and it just went off'.

'A terrible accident'.

'I'll pay you. I'll give you anything you want'.

'Hold on a minute' said Adam. 'Your fiancé is lying dead on the floor and you're negotiating about how he died? You really are a piece of work'.

'Adam, I'm desperate!'

'But your prints are all over the gun' he reminded her. 'And I really can't believe you're asking me for help with this'.

'I'll admit it' she cried.

'You'll admit what?'

'I'll admit I was telling lies when I got you done for assault'.

'If I do what exactly?'

'If you say that the loony stalker shot him'.

'You'd do that to an innocent person?'

'I'm a survivor' said Lucinda. 'You help me and I'll help you'.

Adam stared into her pleading eyes and then said 'No'.

'What?'

'I said no'.

'Are you mad?'

'You're going to have to take some responsibility for your actions, Lucinda'.

'Then I may as well shoot you whilst I'm at it' said Lucinda who then pointed the gun at Adam. 'I'll say I had to shoot you in self defense'.

Adam held up his hands defensively. 'Calm down, Lucinda. Do you want to go down for a double murder?' He heard police cars come to a screeching halt outside.

'This is your last chance' said Lucinda. 'I won't ask again'.

Three months later Lucinda and Adam were sitting alongside each other in the Manchester crown court at the trial of Steve Anderson for the man slaughter of 'footballer and fiancé of pop star Lucinda Davies', Lee Smith. Lucinda had confessed to a 'complete misunderstanding' over the assault charges she made against Adam and that she had lied to him about her age. She blamed it on her 'youth and inexperience'. They believed her again but this time they also believed Adam and his conviction was quashed. To be removed from the sex offenders register had been more difficult and he'd had to go to appeal, but he won that battle too in the end.

Lucinda had been all over the press 'pouring out her heart over the loss of her beloved Lee' and claiming that 'she'll never get over it'. It did however give her the excuse to get out of the 'In Your Face' tour and go on more shopping trips with her Mum.

She and Adam hadn't exactly become best mates during this period but they were speaking with civility to each other. Adam had given no interviews at all. He'd been waiting for his day in court.

He was called as a witness for the prosecution and Lucinda smiled gratefully at him as he took the stand. But then the smile dropped from her face when he started talking.

'I want to state here and now, and whilst I'm under oath, that Steve Anderson did not shoot Lee Smith' he declared to gasps of shock from those present in the court. 'Lucinda Davies shot Lee Smith and I only said it was Steve because Lucinda threatened not to admit she'd told lies about the assault charge she'd made against me all those years ago if I didn't. I've waited a long time to clear my name and I couldn't miss the opportunity'. He then looked up at Steve in the dock. 'I'm sorry, Steve. But I'm putting it right now for both of us'.

Lucinda lunged at Adam and tried to strangle him. She was pulled off by court security guards and as they took her away she screamed 'you fucking Judas! I'll have you for this, Taylor! Look over your shoulder from now on because I'll get you!' She was charged with the man slaughter of Lee Smith the next day.

Adam was charged with perverting the course of justice but when it came to court the circumstances of the case led the judge to give him a suspended sentence.

At her trial Lucinda was sent down for seven years.

Adam brought a civil claim for compensation against Lucinda and when he won it relieved the former pop star of a six figure settlement sum. Adam kept a third of the money for himself, he gave a third to Steve Anderson, and he gave the remaining third to a charity that helps people who've been the victims of malicious and false allegations.

He then sat down and tried to work out what he was going to do with the rest of his life.

THREE
DEAN

'Have you been in the bath yet our Dean?'

Dean Ellis was so infuriated by the way his mother always barged into his room without knocking. It was a good job he'd put his pants and trousers on. He was a man now for God's sake. He wasn't a boy anymore. He went to the gym three times a week. He could lift dumbbells almost half the weight of himself. He had pecks. He had a firm, flat stomach. He didn't look like he'd been pumped up, he'd have hated to look like that, but he looked fit and able. He was happy with that and he didn't want to go any further. He didn't want to become obsessed. But, whatever, he was twenty and his mother should respect his privacy.

'Mum, could you please knock before you come in?' he asked. She was standing there in her standard knee length blue overall that was buttoned all the way down and which she'd worn forever. She looked way older than her mid-forties. She was an agoraphobic. She hadn't been out of the house since his father left when Dean was a baby. Various doctors and home nurses had tried to help her but she'd thrown it all back in their faces, just like she'd pushed all of her family away. It had made Dean's life difficult to say the least. His mother never took any pleasure in a sunny day. They'd never been on holiday or even on a day out. Nobody invited them round at Christmas or came round to see them. Life had been conducted entirely within the home he'd grown up in and it had made her desperately possessive and controlling. She was paranoid of anyone on the outside. One day he'd leave her behind in her own little world with nobody for company except the empty space inside her own head.

'I don't knock on doors in my own house, thank you very much' came Yvonne Ellis's swift and indignant reply. 'Now have you been in the bath?'

'Yes, Mum, I've been in the bath and I've hung up my towel' said Dean as he reached for his shirt and started putting it on.

'You can't have been in the bath, our Dean, I didn't hear you'.

Oh Christ, thought Dean. Here we fucking well go again. 'Mum, I've had my bath and that's that'.

'No you haven't had your bath, Dean because if you had I would've heard you' Yvonne shrilled, adamant that she was right. 'Now get back in that bathroom and run a bath now!'

'For crying out loud, Mum, don't talk to me like that! I've had a bath and I'm now getting ready for work. So if you don't mind'.

'Oh you think that just because you work in some swanky hotel you can laud it over everywhere' she scoffed. 'Well you can't! In my house it's my rules and mine only!'

'Mum, I'm twenty years old'.

'Meaning what exactly?'

'Meaning you can't talk to me like I'm a child anymore!'

'Dean, I'm your mother! I can speak to you how I see fit'.

'Oh no, Mum, you can't' said Dean. 'I won't have it. Not

anymore'.

'Why do you always have to fight me, Dean?' she pleaded, wiping away what Dean called her 'ever ready' tears because that's what they were, always on hand to add another layer of drama to proceedings. 'Why do you seem to like upsetting me?'

'Mum, I don't like upsetting you and there's no need for you to get upset' said Dean. 'I'm just trying to get ready for work'.

He was so pissed off with all this. Every time he went to work she started a confrontation over nothing and he'd worked out why a long time ago. She wanted him to go out in a bad mood and reflect that on those he met when he was outside. She didn't want him to be popular with people. She wanted him to be solely dependent on her. She may have some severe emotional issues but she was also fucking devious and he'd had a lifetime of it. She was his Mum and he loved her but she was such hard work. She wanted him to remain a child so she'd have a purpose in life. Well he couldn't do that. He wanted the normal life he'd found with his friends. He wanted to meet someone and fall in love one day. He didn't want his life to repeat hers.

'But all I've got is you' said Yvonne, still crying.

That was how she always got him. If all else fails then go for the sympathy vote.

'And whose fault is that, Mum? You've driven everybody away and I can't exist just to meet your emotional needs. It's not fair'.

'You'll always be my little boy' she whimpered. 'And yet when you go off with your friends you're rejecting everything I've ever done for you'.

'No, I'm not, Mum' said Dean, who resented having to deal

with all this. And what had she done for him anyway? Whatever she'd done for him was all about whatever she needed to do for herself. 'That's a stupid thing to say'.

'No it isn't!'

'Yes it is' said Dean, firmly. He never used to fight back but he'd learned that there was no other way to avoid getting sucked into her self –imposed abyss. 'Wanting to lead my own life is normal, Mum. It's just a normal part of growing up'.

'You are so like your father' she sneered.

'Well out of the two of us you'd be the only one who'd know about that because you're the only one who's met him'.

'He humiliated me! He left me for another woman!'

'Yes, Mum' said Dean, wearily. He'd heard this refrain so many times. 'It happens to women all the time but they get over it and they get on with their lives. They don't hide themselves away for nearly twenty years'.

'Well I'm not like those other women!'

'Don't I know it' said Dean who'd wished to God so many fucking times that his mother had been a normal woman and he'd grown up in a normal family. He'd tried soft soaping her. He'd tried doing the whole understanding thing. But it had got him nowhere. It had only made her worse.

'Why do you want to hurt me, Dean?' she pleaded.

'I don't want to hurt you, Mum'.

'But why can't you just do as you're told and then we'd have none of these arguments?'

'Because I keep telling you, Mum, I'm not a child anymore' said Dean as he packed his MP3, which he'd set up to listen to Ed

Sheeran once he was out of the house, and his mobile phone into the canvass bag that he threw over his right shoulder. 'Now I've got to go or else I'll miss the tram'.

'Don't go like this' pleaded Yvonne, still sobbing. 'Throw a sick day and stay with me'.

'Mum, I'm not throwing a sick day when I'm not sick' said Dean who'd missed so many days at school because of his mother's emotional pleading. It had almost cost him his entire education. 'I've never done that and I never will. I'm going to work'.

Dean liked his job as a bell boy on the concierge desk at the five-star Claremont hotel in the centre of Manchester. To get there he caught the tram to St. Peter's square, right in front of the hotel, and then crossed the road and ran up the steps of the grand Victorian era building. He worked a shift rota with a dozen other guys, some of whom were hilarious to be with, others were more serious, but he got on well with them all and for those hours of his shift he was able to forget all about the tension at home. His mother didn't know that he was saving up to get his own flat. He had his eye on a studio in Salford Quays, in one of the brand new blocks made out of steel and glass and thick, light grey concrete, with a pull down bed at one end, a 'station' in the middle with a bathroom and kitchen, and a lounge area at the front with a floor to ceiling window offering a fuck off view. That's where he wanted to be. In that long oblong shape that was testament to modern living in the city. God knows what his mother will do when he tells her he's moving out. She'll probably commit suicide and then he'll feel guilty for the rest of his life. That's what needy people like her do. They try and pull at your heartstrings even from beyond the grave and yet from the outside they always appear to be the victim. Nobody thinks of the poor bastards who have to live with them.

'Oh go on and get off to your so-called work and see if I care if you get knocked down and smashed up'.

'Mum!'

'Well you think your so-called friends want you but they don't. They're laughing at you behind your back. They're just using you. Your friends are all liars. You mark my words. They don't want you. Why would they want you?'

'Mum, please!' Dean exclaimed.

'I'm only trying to save you from being hurt later on' she said. 'They'll drop you when they don't need you anymore. That's what people are like. That's why I've stayed in all these years because everybody is a liar, just like your father, and they'll all end up dumping you just like your father dumped me'.

'Mum, my life is never going to mirror yours. I'll make bloody sure of that'.

'Well let me tell you this' said Yvonne. 'I'm your mother and nobody will love you like I do! Do you hear me? Nobody!'

'Well thank God for that' said Dean. 'More than one of you in a lifetime would kill me'.

'Ungrateful bastard'.

'Mum, right across the world there are people dealing with real tragedy, real loss, real suffering. People who've lost loved ones, soldiers who've lost an arm or a leg in some foreign land. But you ... you've locked yourself away for twenty years because a man walked out on you and you can't stand to lose face. You make me sick'.

Dean had always been aware of his power to please men. When he was fourteen he'd opened the wrong door by mistake and wandered into the teachers changing room at the gym in his school. Onc of the teachers, Mr. Grainger, was in the middle of getting changed and was stark naked. Dean was initially shocked but he couldn't take his eyes off Mr. Grainger. It was the first time he'd seen a naked man and he couldn't help but feast his eyes. He liked the hairs on Mr. Grainger's chest and arms and legs. He liked the shape of his shoulders, his stomach, and his thighs. He liked the way his cock was getting hard. No words were spoken. Dean stepped closer and Mr. Grainger didn't move. It was all in the look. It was all in the eyes that said yes without saying yes and that's the biggest lesson Dean would learn from the whole experience. Then he was on his knees and sucking on Mr. Grainger's manhood. He liked the taste of it. He liked the feel of it in his mouth. He liked the explosion that hit the back of his throat. He liked the look on Mr. Grainger's face. He liked the touch of his hands.

Dean carried on pleasuring Mr. Grainger, the married father of two young kids, on regular occasions until he finished school. After that he'd enjoyed a lot of sex and then one night at the hotel he'd taken the bags up to the room of a guest who was a businessman from Plymouth. The man, an okay looking guy in his late thirties, asked Dean if he knew of any male escorts he could try. Dean said that he didn't. Then the man asked Dean if he'd perform oral sex on him for fifty quid. Initially he was taken aback but after a moment or two of thinking about it he couldn't think of a reason to say no. Where was the harm? Nobody would know. Nobody controlled him and if he could get into this regularly he'd have enough money saved to move into his own flat in no time. So in a matter of seconds the offer the man had made had turned into the beginnings of a plan. He obliged him that night and the night after. They had fun. He teased the man about his West Country accent. The man explained that he was married with three kids and only indulged his taste for men when he miles away from home. He was now one of Dean's regulars whenever he was in the northwest.

After that Dean took some pictures of himself and uploaded them and a profile of himself onto a website advertising 'lads' for hire in Manchester. The bookings started coming in almost straight away and the cash followed them. It was exciting and getting paid to pleasure men was the best thing about it. There were some really ugly bastards out there who presented Dean with something of a challenge when it came to putting on a smile for the money. His trick in those situations was to close his eyes and think of Harry Judd. But most of them were just blokes who were clean and average looking, business types, mostly married, mostly straight, mostly taking advantage of being miles away from home to indulge their curiosity about sex with men. They came from all over the UK and elsewhere in Europe. Some were quiet and nervous and he usually massaged them first to get them relaxed. Some were heaps of fun, and some of them were actually pretty hot. The work gave him a glimpse into worlds he'd never have seen otherwise and it was better than stacking shelves at the local supermarket to earn extra cash.

Working at his 'day' job in a hotel meant that it was an environment he was used to and didn't look conspicuous in. That was useful in his line of 'other' work considering that much of the time he conducted his trade in places like the one he was walking into now. It was one of the new boutique style hotels with dark velvet upholstery and art deco furnishings. Dean liked this particular place. He liked the decor. One day he'd have a house that would be decked out like this. It was warm and it was lush and it had a touch of mystery about it. He could imagine all kinds of people from parallel universes sitting around watching what was going on whilst doing their own thing. All kinds of people he couldn't see but who could see him. It had been no surprise the last time he came to meet a client here to find that it was hosting a magic circle convention. It just suited the place.

He knocked on the door of room 256 and a few seconds later the familiar face of another of his regular clients opened it. He stood there with his shirt sleeves rolled up, open necked and outside his trousers, one of those thin cigars between his fingers and clutching a glass of scotch.

'Come in' he said.

This was the fifth time Dean had been to see Charles. He was tall, well over six foot with short black hair peppered with flecks of grey, blue-grey eyes, a dimple in his chin, big hands. He had a very Southern England upper class accent that spoke of having been given every advantage his place in the social order would afford him. Dean wasn't quite sure what he did for a living exactly. He did know that he was some kind of international businessman but he didn't know anymore and didn't especially want to.

Charles caressed the side of Dean's face with his hand. 'I wish you lived closer to home. I've actually been missing you lately'.

'I didn't think that was part of the deal'.

'I was even thinking of seeing if you'd agree to moving down to

London?'

'What?'

'Well think about it' said Charles as he wrapped his arms round Dean and held him close. 'I live in Richmond. I've got enough money to set you up in a small flat nearby. It wouldn't be huge, just one bedroom but I'd give you enough to furnish it the way you want it. All I'd ask in return is that you give up the escorting and devote yourself to me'.

Dean was somewhat stunned. He'd never even thought of moving away from Manchester. He'd only ever got as far as moving away from his mother. And he had his own plans to get a flat and be independent. 'I don't know, Charles'.

'Look, I couldn't promise you anymore than that. My wife and my kids would always have to come first. I know you've been saving up to get your own place so why not make a break for it and a fresh start somewhere else?'

'But all my friends are here'.

'You'd make new ones and besides, you could have all your friends from up here to visit'.

'But what about my job?'

'There are hotels in London, Dean and I've got plenty of contacts'.

'I couldn't ask all this of you'.

'You didn't' said Charles. 'I wouldn't be the first man to fall for his concubine. I'm smitten with you, Dean and I haven't felt like that about a man since before I got married. I let him slip through my fingers and I'm not going to let you do the same'.

Charles then kissed Dean with the usual intensity that Dean was used to from him. Charles's mouth tasted of the scotch and the cigar and Dean rather liked it. It was a masculine taste. The flavour of the pleasure to come but now there was a greater need to be answered.

'All I'm asking is that you'll think about it' said Charles. 'I'm not going to withdraw my offer and I'm not going to stop seeing you. I want you in my life and I want you to say yes'.

Dean started to unfasten the belt on Charles's trousers. 'Let's not talk anymore for a while'.

Canal Street in Manchester on a Friday night was always packed with revellers. Dean and his friends were having a good night. They'd been for something to eat in the El Runcon Spanish restaurant near Granada studios and done a couple of bars before arriving on Canal Street. They were in a crowd of about a dozen but as was always the case it filtered down to Dean and his best friend Robbie. For Dean it was just because he didn't want to go home. Robbie was desperate to meet the man of his dreams and liked to stay to the bitter end just in case his chance came by. Dean didn't really want a partner at the moment. He was too busy at night with his other activity and that would be hard for any boyfriend to take. Besides, he couldn't very well take anyone home to meet mother, so he'd decided he was happy to stay single until he was in his own flat and master of his own ceremonies. But he'd not been able to get the offer Charles had made him out of his head. It was certainly tempting. Charles was a sweet man and he was handsome, no doubt about that. He probably would take care of him. But was it what he wanted? He wouldn't mind if Charles was free to love him and be with him all the time. But this wasn't going to be anything like that.

This was about Charles getting everything he needed without compromising anything for what Dean might need.

'So come on?' said Robbie as he sidled up to Dean who was standing with his back leaning against the bar. 'What's swimming about in that think tank of yours?'

'I've had an offer to be a kept man'.

'Who from? You haven't even got a boyfriend?'

'One of my clients'.

'Should I start calling you Julia Roberts?'

'What?'

'Pretty Woman?'

The penny dropped and Dean laughed. 'I haven't got the hair or the legs for it'.

'So who's the Roy Gere?'

'Charles, you know, the guy from London? He wants to set me up in a flat and I can do what I like as long as I don't see other men'.

'I take it you haven't given him your answer yet?'

'I don't know what the fuck to do, Robbie'.

'Is the sex good with him?'

'Yes, it is' said Dean. 'And he's kind, sweet, and I can't say he's ugly. He's handsome in that very upper class English way like Hugh Bonneville or Colin Firth. And he makes me laugh. It wouldn't be easy to turn down his proposal'.

'Then why are you even thinking about it?'

'Because I'd always be second fucking best! Robbie, I want a man who can truly share his life with me. I don't want to be somebody's secret. I want us to get a place together, live in it together, do the Friday night shop together. I want a normal relationship, Robbie. Christ, I've had a lifetime of putting up with an abnormal one in the shape of my mother and I can't go from that to being somebody's affair'.

'Dean, look at me' said Robbie. 'I'm twenty-four and I still haven't had even a sniff of a proper relationship. I come in here every weekend and nothing ever fucking happens. I'm not ugly, I take care of myself and I'd welcome someone with open arms. Maybe they catch the desperation and it puts them off, I don't know, but the planets never seem to align in my favour. Maybe I need a fresh start somewhere else too. I'd move down to London with you, get my own place of course, but then you wouldn't be on your own down there'.

'But you're just starting out in your career?'

'Yes, as a nurse. I could probably get a job down in London without too much trouble. What I'm saying to you, Dean, is this. You could get your own flat in Salford Quays and carry on with your escorting and I could carry on at Stepping Hill hospital and in ten years time we could still be stood here wondering where the last ten years have gone and still as single as Cliff fucking Roy. It may not be ideal with this Charles, but he wants you in his own way and you never know where it might lead'.

'You think I should take the chance?'

'I so do, yes. And like I say, I'll come down with you so you won't be spending every spare moment waiting for Charles to see if he can get away. We'll be two Northern lads in the big smoke, off on an adventure. That's got to be better than standing still round here'.

'But this is Manchester. This is where it's supposed to be all happening'.

'And it is but it's like any sort of development. There are always some who are left behind. That's why there are still millions of poor in China'.

Dean woke up in a sweat. Every now and then his dreams were visited by what he called the 'black death'. It took him back to a time when his mother's care was tantamount to that of a prison guard. He'd set his alarm for seven and when he looked across at his bedside clock it was still only half five. He pulled the duvet back over him and tried to go back to sleep but he couldn't stop his sub-conscious from taking him on a journey back through the years.

When Dean left school he didn't have any friends. His mother had seen to that. She used to make him come home every day for his lunch even though it was a fifteen minute walk each way and he only had an hour. And even when he did get home he couldn't just sit down and eat something. She would have jobs for him to do. If he protested then she'd accuse him of being selfish. She was even worse when he came to do his exams. If he retreated to his room so he could study she would constantly interrupt him, telling him there were jobs around the house that she needed him to do. It was all meaningless stuff that could've waited but that didn't matter to his mother. He wasn't allowed time to himself for any purpose. She was so emotionally needy that she had to have him in the same room as her when he was at home or else she felt rejected. If any of his class mates called round, or any of the other kids in the street who were of a similar age, she would always tell them that he didn't want to come out. When he protested that she hadn't even asked him she'd get upset. She'd accuse him of wanting to make her worry because she wouldn't know exactly where he was if he went out with children she denounced as 'street urchins'. Then she'd want to know why he wanted to go out with strangers when she provided the best she could for him at home. Then the tears would start flowing. Then she'd put the door key in her pocket so he couldn't unlock it to get out. Every evening, every weekend, every school holiday he stayed indoors with his mother and even if he stopped to speak to someone in the street when he went to get the food shopping, there was trouble. She'd want to know why he wanted to talk to a stranger instead of her. So in the end he gave up. He did it her way. He declined every invitation. He didn't go to any of the parties to do with leaving school. He stayed in with his Mum and she cooked him his favourite tea and they talked the same conversation they'd talked at every tea time for as long as he could remember.

She then tried to stop him from getting a job. She contacted social services to explain that she needed him to stay at home to take care of her because she was 'disabled' with agoraphobia. She said she wanted them to give him benefits but pay them to her and she would give him whatever 'pocket' money she thought he should have. She told them she couldn't be left alone all day whilst he went to work. But to Dean's immense relief the social worker who came round said that they couldn't do as his mother demanded. Instead he offered her medical help and counselling to help her deal with her 'condition'. She refused it. She wouldn't even let the professionals through her door when they came round. She told them they should be ashamed for helping all the 'black scum' in the country but not her. She was so furious she hadn't been able to get her own way that for weeks on end she accused Dean of having colluded with social services against her. But then he fought a battle with her and won. He went out and found himself the job at the hotel even though she was dead against the idea. But it was the first step of him freeing himself. He made friends. He started going out. He got himself a social life. He went out no matter how much of a scene she caused about it. It was bloody hard but he managed to stand up to her through sheer determination. It wore him out emotionally. Sometimes his whole body ached with all the locked up tension. But still he went places. He went places with people who wanted him to be with them. He ate at restaurants and drank in bars. He did his shopping with a credit card. He was like other normal people. It still felt like he was living through one long row at home, but he now managed to exert his own will. She'd continued to put his clothes out for him each day but each day he deliberately found other things to wear. She'd continued to order his clothes from a catalogue but he bought his own stuff and gave what she bought for him to the Oxfam shop. He hated acting like they were at war but there was no alternative. She insisted on doing all his washing and ironing but it was strange what happened to some of the clothes he'd bought for himself. Either she'd got the temperature of the wash too high and they'd shrunk, or she'd been distracted whilst ironing and left the hot iron face down on the fabric. He caught her one day deliberately pouring a mug of coffee over one of his shirts, a pretty expensive Italian designer shirt he'd bought from one of the more exclusive shops in Manchester. He went mad but as usual she'd turned on the tears and managed to turn the situation into something he should apologise to her for. He now kept the clothes he bought in his locker at work and had them laundered there too. He shouldn't have to go to those lengths to ensure his free choice over what he wears. But he did have to until he was able to get his own place away from her. Charles was offering him a way out. To some it would seem like a real chance. But he'd be swopping one person's control of him for another. His life would be lived permanently on stand-by for Charles who'd be able to pull all the strings. The situation would of course be vastly different but it would still amount to the same thing of his life not being held in his own hands.

'Get to the table for your lunch now, Dean!' his mother commanded in a shrill voice up the stairs.

Dean was in his bedroom and breathed in deeply. How many times did he have to tell her that when he was on late shift he didn't want any lunch? He had to leave just after twelve and that meant eating way too early. To confess that he'd have something at work later on in the afternoon was tantamount to confessing to treason in his mother's book so he just kept silent.

'I did say I didn't want anything to eat, Mum' said Dean as he walked into the kitchen where everything was laid out on the table. 'Like I always do when I'm on late shift'.

'And you don't tell me what to do in my own house, Dean, and you'll sit there until you eat it all, work or no work' said Yvonne.

Dean stared out at the table. She made him so angry with the things she said to him like he was still some recalcitrant little boy who needed discipline. She'd made a ham salad and he thought he may as well eat some of it. It would certainly keep her quiet and it didn't look like she was eating with him which was a bonus because he found his mothers eating habits absolutely revolting. She put brown sauce, tomato ketchup, and salad cream on absolutely everything, even on her toast in the morning. The sight of it made him feel quite sick at times and what made it worse was that she tended to eat with her mouth open, chomping on her food rather than chewing it round her closed mouth before swallowing it. And Dean detested the sound of all that chomping. So if he was going to be eating on his own then it was a small mercy.

'Are you not eating, Mum?' he asked as he tucked into the salad.

'It's far too early for me, Dean' she asserted.

'But that's just what I said about me but … oh never bloody mind'.

'Just because you've got some swanky hotel job doesn't mean you can dictate to me about when you want your meals, Dean' said Yvonne. 'I've got a duty as your mother to provide you with at least one full meal a day and I'm not letting the shifts they put you on disrupt that, oh no. Not when it's my duty'.

Dean pushed his plate away. 'I've had enough'.

'You'll sit there until you finish what's on your plate' said Yvonne, firmly.

'Oh just shut up, Mum!'

'I said sit there until you've finished, Dean!' his mother bellowed. 'Don't keep challenging my word. Do as you're told!'

'You really do need help, Mum'.

'No I don't. I just need my son to do as he's bloody well told'.

Dean just shook his head and went up to his bedroom. When he went back downstairs a couple of minutes later he was almost ready to leave. His mother was sitting at the kitchen table drinking a mug of tea and looking like Margaret Thatcher must've looked before she ordered the sinking of the Belgrano. But Thatcher had a purpose to what she did. An evil, destructive purpose as far as Dean was concerned, but a purpose nonetheless. But what purpose did his mother have?

'Leaving me again?'

'I'm going to work, Mum' said Dean. 'And it's about time you took some responsibility for yourself. You've been wallowing in all this self-pity shit for too long'.

'He humiliated me!'

'He left you for another woman! It happens, get over it!'

'She was black!'

'And what's that got to do with anything?' Dean asked. He'd never heard that from her before. Then it started to dawn on him. 'So are you telling me that you've based twenty years of racism on the fact that my father left you for a black woman? You've stayed indoors all these years because of that?'

'I couldn't face people with the shame of it'.

'So if she'd been a white woman then that would've been okay?'

'Well at least he would've stayed within our own kind'.

'Oh this is more bloody twisted than I could ever have imagined!'

'What do you mean? You wanted the truth and now you've got it'.

'Mum, I've spent years wondering if my Dad was a murderer, a bigamist, a con man of some kind who was in prison, a waster, a no mark. I thought it must've been something that terrible for you to have reacted in this way for all these years. But now on this calm, sunny day you think I'm going to understand your bizarre actions because the woman he left you for was black? Like I said, Mum, you're twisted!'

'Dean, I …. '

'…. no, Mum. Just stay out of my way until I've calmed down'.

'But why are you angry with me?'

'You mean you really don't know? Unbelievable!'

'But I'm the victim!'

'No, you're not, Mum' said Dean. 'You just enjoy playing the bloody victim!'

When Dean got home that night he was struck by the silence in the house. He stood in the hallway and looked upstairs but there were no replies to his calls. Then, to the right of where he was standing, his mother came out of the living room and attacked him. She struck him across the face and then across his head. She grabbed a clump of his hair and was yanking his head around with it like he was some kind of toy. He brought his hands and arms up and wrapped them round his head to protect himself but she was relentless. It was like she was possessed.

'Get off me!'

'You don't tell me what to do, Dean! Oh no, you need to be reminded who's boss around here, young man! You stay out all hours of the night making me worry myself sick about where you are and then you turn round and accuse me of enjoying playing the victim after your father left me for that black bitch! Well there are consequences for your bloody cheek! Now go to your room and stay there until I say you can come out again!'

It was that last sentence that fired all the resentment and anger inside him. She'd done it all his life. Every time he'd tried to hold his head up high she'd come along with an axe and try to behead him. But he was stronger now. He could pull the axe out of his flesh and not feel the pain anymore.

He managed to grip her shoulders and push her back but she started biting his wrist and spitting in his face. She really had lost it. He could think of nothing else to do but slap her across the face. For a moment she stood there, startled and unable to believe he'd hit her. An excruciating silence fell on them and then she began to rub her face.

'You evil animal' she cursed.

'Oh and what were you when you were lashing out at me?'

'I'm trying to protect you from all the evil out there!' she cried, her tears now flowing down her cheeks. 'You're my darling, darling boy and I can't lose you'.

'You hit me first, Mum' said Dean. 'You started it. Or is it because you're a woman and I'm a man and therefore you can assault me but I'm not allowed to defend myself or retaliate? Well mother or not, you hit me and I'll hit you back'

'I didn't know where you were!' she cried.

'That's a lie! I told you I was going out with my friends for a drink after work' said Dean, who was rapidly losing it. 'But you don't listen! And it's not even late. It's only just gone midnight for God's sake!'

'I was lonely' she blubbered. 'I've got nobody but you'.

'And that's nobody's fault but yours, Mum! I've got to have a life. I can't shut myself away in here'.

'You don't really want to be with all those other people' said Yvonne. 'You don't need them and deep down you know that. Deep down you know that you only need me. We could have a good life the two of us. We don't need anybody from outside'.

'Oh God!' Dean bellowed. He couldn't stand it when she spoke about them as if they were a couple. She couldn't use him as a replacement for a husband. He punched the wall with his fist. 'It's not all about you!'

'Oh no, I'm just your mother who brought you up and made sure you had nice things to eat and nice clothes to wear'.

'But you didn't, Mum. Someone else, namely me, goes out and gets all those things to eat whilst you got all the clothes from a mail order catalogue'.

'I can't go out! Your father humiliated me'.

'Oh change the fucking record!'

Dean fell back against the wall and slid down to the floor. He looked across at his mother who was weeping. This can't go on. He felt like he was living like Alice in wonderland on either side of some dividing mirror. On one side was the time he spent outside his home. On the other side was the time he spent at home with his mother. He'd let it all carry on regardless of the affect it had been having on him.

'Mum?'

'Don't speak to me'.

'Mum, you need to get some help'.

'Oh it's all so convenient for you isn't it! Paint me as some kind of mad woman when the only thing wrong with me is a broken heart.

A heart your father broke'.

'But Mum' said Dean, softly. 'We both know its gone way beyond that'.

'Oh and you want to fly off and forget about me? Is that it? You want to leave me just like your father did but you want to somehow save your conscience'.

'Mum, calm down and let's just talk'.

'I've been trying to save you from becoming your father' said Yvonne. 'But it looks like I'm failing. So why don't you piss off now just like he did'.

'Mum, I'm trying not to give up on you'.

'Give up on me? What the hell are you talking about? That's what he always says about you'.

'What did you say?'

Yvonne went very quiet and sheepish. She hadn't planned on saying that much. 'Nothing. I didn't say anything'.

'Yes you did' said Dean. 'You said that's what he always says as if he's a current part of your life?'.

'I didn't mean anything by it' Yvonne insisted. 'It just ... came out'.

'Rubbish! Have you been keeping him from me?'

'How could I have done that?'

'I don't know' said Dean. 'You tell me'.

'You think that ... '

'... just tell me, has my father ever tried to get in touch with me?'

'Yes, he has! And do you know what? I told him where to get off every time!'

Dean looked at her as she spat the words out. It was as if she was a child who was proud of the fact that she'd deliberately thrown his favourite toy away.

'What are you telling me?' asked Dean, aghast at the connections he was making in his head. 'You've spent all these years destroying any chance I had of having a relationship with my own father?'

'He left us! I had every right!'

'You had no right to stop me seeing him! He left you, not me!'

'Every couple of years he's turned up' said Yvonne as if it really didn't matter at all.

Dean was utterly distraught. All these years of feeling the pain of his father being absent from his life and she could've fixed it. It was almost too much to take in.

'Every couple of years and you never told me? And when was the last time?'

'When you were eighteen' she announced, like she'd really got one over on him and was absolutely loving it. 'Just think of it. He was so near and yet so far'.

Dean tried his level best to stay calm. The temptation to batter her senseless was almost overwhelming. Everybody talks about having to keep your anger under control. But nobody ever talks about people needing to keep their extreme provocation under control. Those who push and push and push until the other person snaps need to be treated as well as the one who lashes out with their fists. Because Dean knew only too well, after twenty years of living with the emotional time-bomb that was his mother, that there's only so much a person can take before they can't take anymore.

'Do you have an address for him?' Dean asked.

'I might have, I might not'.

That was when he saw red. He grabbed a vase from on top of the hall cabinet and smashed it against the wall. It shattered into tiny pieces. His mother cowered.

'You've gone mad!'

'Give me his address, Mum, or so help me I'll walk through that door and you'll never, ever see me again!'

His mother completely capitulated. But there was still a look of triumph on her face.

'Very well' she said. 'I'll give you the address. But I'm warning you, it's too late'.

'What do you mean it's too late?'

'He died a year ago of cancer' Yvonne announced. 'You had an invitation to the funeral but I tore it up'.

Dean had barely been able to even look at his mother since she'd made her announcement that his father, a man she'd kept from him, had died. She finally gave him all the details of David Ellis Clarke and he went to the address in Cheadle Hulme where he'd been living the last twenty years. Removal men had just moved a young couple and their little daughter into number 23 and he was about to give up when one of the neighbours, a middle aged woman with light brown shoulder length hair and dressed in the uniform of an air hostess, came running out and told him that if he wanted to contact Marcia Clarke then she'd be happy to pass on any note. Marcia had moved with her two teenage daughters to a new house on the coast at Southport to make a 'fresh start' after her husband's death. The neighbour asked Dean who he was and when he told her she explained that Marcia had tried to get in touch with him after his father's death but all attempts had been thwarted by his mother. She said that Marcia would still like to talk to him because, apart from anything else, he was due something from his father's estate. He asked the neighbour if she'd known his father well. She said that yes, she and her husband had been good friends with Marcia and David and that he was a 'lovely man'. He wanted to ask if he ever talked about him but thought that might be a bit too much. He gave her a note for Marcia, his step-mother, with his mobile number on it. Then he thanked the neighbour for her kindness and walked back to the station to catch the local train back into Manchester with the heaviest heart he'd ever known.

Despite his despondent mood he still went into work that afternoon. He was never going to forgive his mother. She'd taken from him one of the most precious things in life and it was something that could never be replaced. It was all lost now. It was all gone and the only hope was for a healing of the pain in the next life.

He'd just taken some bags up to a guests room and returned to the concierge desk just inside the hotel main door, when he was approached by a tall, desperately thin white woman with clearly expensively maintained shoulder length hair and wearing a knee length fur coat. She wore black leather boots and Dean didn't know what it was but there was something pretty spiteful in those eyes.

'Are you Dean Clarke?'

'Yes? But forgive me, I don't think we've met?'

'We haven't met' said the woman. 'But you have met my husband. His name is Charles. I'm Geraldine, his wife. Could we go somewhere and talk?'

Dean's mood hardened. This was the last thing he needed today. He hadn't thought much about Charles' proposition these past few days. He'd been too preoccupied with the revelations about his father. But how had she found him?

'I'm on duty' he said, flatly.

'It wasn't a request'.

'I've got nothing to say to you'.

'Well I've got plenty to say to you so unless you want all your work colleagues knowing what you get up to then I suggest you find some time to listen to me'.

Dean managed to get twenty minutes off and 'took' Geraldine walking down Quay Street towards the Granada studios.

'Are we walking with any kind of purpose in mind?'

'You wanted to talk' said Dean. 'So talk?'

'You're an off -hand little bastard'.

'I just don't know what it is you want from me'.

'What do you think I might want?'

'Look, I've had a very difficult few days and I'm in no mood to be messed around with. So just say what you've got to say and then leave me alone'.

'Alright' said Geraldine. 'But just stop and listen'.

Dean stopped and turned to her. 'Well?'

'If you think you know my husband then you're very badly mistaken' said Geraldine. 'And if you think you can somehow be part of his life in some glorified brothel he sets you up in then you're making the biggest mistake of your life'.

Dean folded his arms. 'And why might that be?'

'You're not the first and you probably won't be the last'.

'Can't you think of anything more original than that?'

'I don't think you're in a position to question what I say'.

'Oh cut the melodrama, I'm really not in the mood'.

'How much do you want?'

'To do what?'

'To tell my husband you won't be going along with his dirty little plan to keep you in a style I'm sure you'd love to become accustomed'.

'What's this? Wheel out the cliché week? I'm not taking your money'.

'You're quite prepared to take his'.

'That's different'.

'How so?'

'Because ... '

'... oh don't tell me you've got feelings for him? You stupid little bastard. Do you really think I'm going to let you threaten everything I've got?'

'Don't be absurd'.

'Oh didn't he tell you? He's in love with you and he's trying to work out how quickly he can move you out of the dog kennel and into the house. And there's only room for one of us there'.

Dean felt a sudden joy leap into his heart at the thought that Charles thinks of him as more than just a carnal business transaction. He knew that Charles was fond of him but he didn't know that he had it in his mind to break up his marriage over him. He hadn't realised that he felt that strongly. But now that he did know it certainly helped him to make up his mind.

'Then I look forward to getting the decorators in and removing all traces of you'.

Geraldine laughed sardonically. 'There you go again thinking you can get one over on me! I've given him three children, I've been there whilst he's built up his business from scratch. If you think that I'm just going to hand all of that over to you without a fight, then think again!'

'Yes, but you've also got other issues of your own, haven't you? Your anorexia? Or as I call it, the hypochondria of the self indulgent spoilt brat. He told me that making love to you was like trying to fuck a skeleton'.

'Oh boy you've gone way too far with that one'.

'Really? Well like I said, sweetheart, I'm not in the mood today so if you've finished with your little attempt to pay me off then get out of my fucking face and do one!'.

'I'll see you in Hell!'

'Not if I see you first'.

Six months later

Robbie wasn't looking forward to going round to see Dean. What could you say to your best friend who's been paralysed from the neck down at the age of twenty-one and couldn't even kill himself if he felt like it? What do you say when you know it was his mother who told Geraldine where Dean was on that fateful night when Geraldine took out a contract on Dean to stop him from proceeding any further into her husbands' life?

'Has Charles been in touch?' asked Robbie.

'No' said Dean. 'Did you really expect him too? I'm hardly in a position to perform the same kind of service on him that I used to, am I?'

'I didn't mean that'.

'I know what you meant, Robbie' said Dean. 'And my heart breaks constantly because of it. But he's lost me and now he's lost Geraldine too because she's bound to be sent down, especially now that the guy she hired has confessed that it was her'.

'She should go down for life'.

'Yeah, well, she probably won't'.

'Dean, about your Mother ...?'

'... I'm not telling the police that she told Geraldine where to find me, Robbie. I'm just not going to do it. I can't. She wouldn't have known what Geraldine was planning to do'.

'Okay, but please don't tell me you're wasting any sympathy on Charles when he's been nowhere near you since this happened'

'No, I'm not' said Dean. 'But at least I know that he was planning to make me an open part of his life. That's all I've got to hold onto. He loved me before I turned into this and he was going to divorce Geraldine because of it. That's what might've been, Robbie, and that's what keeps my dreams at night happy'.

'It breaks my heart to see you being this brave'.

'I don't actually have a lot of choice, Robbie'.

Dean would never be able to forget the car that came screaming up behind him before sending him flying into the air. He'd never be able to forget the doctor telling him the good news that he was alive and would survive but that he was paralysed from the neck down and wouldn't be able to do anything for himself at all. The money from his father's estate was used to make the necessary alterations at home so that his mother could take care of him. But his dreams were over now. His life was finished. He would never see anything else except the view he now had out of his bedroom window of life going on for other people.

'By the way, where is your Mum today? 'asked Robbie as he sat in a chair by the side of Dean's bed. 'It was Sonia the nurse who let me in'.

'Gone to her latest session with the psychologist over her agoraphobia' said Dean. 'She can't get out of it now she's looking after me. She has to accept treatment finally'.

'Dean?'

'What?'

'I've got something to tell you'.

'You're not pregnant, are you?'

Robbie laughed. 'No. I'm moving'.

'Are you? Are you moving in with sexy Doctor Todd Manning then? I'm made up for you, lad'.

'Well I am moving in with Todd, yes' Robbie explained.

'Well it's about fucking time' said Dean. 'You've been seeing him for weeks now'.

'He's going back to Australia when his visa runs out' Robbie explained. 'He's asked me to go with him and I've said yes'.

The shock hit Dean's consciousness like he'd never known before. This was it. This was the moment when he had to accept that even his best friend was going to leave him behind. This was a living death he was going through.

'Australia?' he said, trying to make his voice sound light. 'I always wanted to go there. I always thought I would someday. Will you carry on nursing out there?'

'Yes' Robbie confirmed. This was awful. He just didn't know what to say to make it sound different to the reality that life was moving on for him but that life for Dean had stopped. 'Todd has got a job with the flying doctor service in Adelaide which is what he's always wanted to do. I've got one with a local hospital there. His parents are sorting out an apartment in the city for us to move into'.

'It sounds lovely' said Dean who was thrilled for Robbie but heartbroken for himself at the same time. What kind of life could he and Charles have shared? 'But you've kept it all very quiet?'

'I didn't want to say anything about it until it was all sorted'.

'So when do you go?'

'At the end of next month'.

'Oh' said Dean who couldn't hold them back any longer and the tears began to flow down his cheeks. 'Could you wipe my face for me, please? I can't do it myself'.

'I'm sorry, Dean' said Robbie who was crying himself as he performed such an act of tenderness for his best friend.

'Sorry? What are you sorry about?'

'I feel like I'm leaving you when you need me most'.

'Well you can't take me with you'.

'Oh Christ, Dean, you know what I'm fucking saying!'

'Yes, I do, but Robbie, you're my best friend and I love you and I want you to be happy' said Dean. 'It's just the way fate turned out. I met Charles and you met Todd. Those circumstances brought me into this bed and you on a plane to Australia with the man of your dreams'.

'How can you be so fucking strong?'

'Because like I said, I don't have any fucking choice! Just do me one favour'.

'Name it?' said Robbie who was still crying.

'Let this be the last time you come round and see me'.

'What? I'm not leaving for six weeks yet'.

'Respect my wishes, Robbie. I couldn't stand to go through the whole thing of this being your next to last visit and last visit and so fucking on'. He was crying again too now. 'Go off and have a wonderful life with Todd in Australia. He's a good man, he's sexy, he's intelligent, but most of all he worships the ground you walk on. Only think about me in terms of the brilliant nights out we had and the laughs we shared. Not about how things are now. I'll be alright. Mum will take good care of me. Getting complete control of me has been the making of her'.

A couple of hours later Yvonne came into Dean's room and announced the programme for the evening.

'I've marked off what we're going to watch on the telly' said Yvonne. 'And you won't be watching that American drama thing you like on Sky later. It's far too late and I don't think it's suitable. Anyway, I'll get your tea. I'm doing egg and chips'.

'Actually Mum I'm not very hungry' said Dean. 'I don't really want any tea'.

'Dean, I will make you egg and chips and you will eat it just to please me'.

'Well I won't eat it, Mum. You'll feed it to me'.

'Well you know what I mean, son'.

'Do you think they eat egg and chips in Australia?'

'What?'

'Oh nothing' said Dean, a single tear going down his cheek. 'I was just wondering'.

'I shall forbid that Robbie from coming here if he's going to upset you like this'.

'He didn't upset me, Mum, and you won't have to forbid him because he won't be coming again'.

'You see' said Yvonne as if she'd just won the lottery. 'I always said your friends would abandon you just when you needed them'.

'He's not abandoning me, Mum. He's just getting on with his life like I would be doing if things had turned out differently'.

'Well at least you haven't got any of that to worry about now' said Yvonne.

'Oh yes, that is a bonus, not having to worry about what I'm going to do with my life'.

'So, egg and chips in about twenty minutes?'

'Whenever you're ready, Mum. I'm not going anywhere'.

FOUR
MARGARET

Margaret Barton had been through the whole flaming rigmarole so many times she could barely breathe when she recalled the number. When she met Frank all those years ago on that works weekend to Blackpool, Britain had maintained its promise to a world that then overtook Britain and started laying down the shift in economic power that came with the commercial triumph of the United States and the emotional defeat of the old power that was Britain. That's why Frank and his friends had been so determined to protect the jobs in the industries that Britain needed if it was ever going to recover from its fall. That's the bit Margaret understood. That was the kind of principle she saw in that man with whom she fell in love with over a bag of fish and chips along the Golden mile. His black hair was slicked back with brylcreem. His suit was sharp with its narrow lapels and his pencil tie. He swept her off her feet literally. He was the best dancer. They won trophies. They got engaged. She fell pregnant. They got married. They had the kids. It all seemed like a lifetime ago.

'Margaret! This shirt won't do! This shirt won't do at all! Come and look at it, woman! It's got tram lines going all the way down the left sleeve'.

'Will you be taking your jacket off?' Margaret asked as she walked into the bedroom where Frank was getting ready.

'That's not the point, woman! I'll know'.

'This woman has got a name! Use it, damn you!'

Such was the ferocity of their rows these days that they'd gone beyond mere bitterness. She snatched the shirt off him and went down to the utility room where the iron was still hot as it sat on the ironing board. She corrected the crease in the sleeve of his shirt and took it back up to him.

'So you're determined to go through with it, then?'

Frank was doing the buttons up on his shirt before tucking it into his trousers. 'Someone has got to save this country'.

Margaret threw her head back and laughed. 'Oh listen to him! You're no more the saviour of this country than Harry Potter. Our grandson could've done better than that and he's only in reception class. Frank, you're deluding yourself. Passed over for promotion to the Cabinet by both Blair and Brown and now you're packing up and taking your ball home. Pathetic'.

'Have you finished?'

'Finished? I haven't even started. All those years of you and your trade union boys coming round and going behind closed doors to knock a deal together for the workers and there was I, the little woman who brought in the tea and the sandwiches and the beer, the little woman who was seen and not heard'.

'I didn't hear you complaining at the time'.

'That's because you weren't flaming well listening! I've wasted my life on a man who wouldn't know a socialist principle if it leapt up and slapped him across the face'.

'And you say that Blair did?'

'We needed the likes of Blair and Roy Jenkins to show the rest of your kind what real socialism was all about. Your version of socialism only works if you're white, working class, male and straight. You're not interested in real equality. Somebody's race, gender, or sexuality shouldn't matter to you if you're a real socialist'.

'Blair took the white working class down a road they didn't want to go down' Frank insisted. 'We've ended up in a liberal, middle class inspired cess pit of a society that the white working class doesn't recognise as its own anymore'.

'Oh well then the white working class should stop being so flaming conservative! A better deal for the workers as long as women know their place and men don't love other men'.

'It worked before and there's no reason why it can't work again'.

'So you're admitting it! You want to take it all back. You don't want equality for women, you want them to have to rely on the decency of a few decent men rather than be protected by the law. You want gays to have to hide themselves away again or only be accepted if they behave like Larry Grayson. You'd bring back the black and white minstrel show and I bet you'd want to make abortion illegal again'.

'That's a religious conviction'.

'Oh piss off with your religious conviction! You're trying to tell people that if we kick out the foreigners we'll solve all this country's problems? That's simplistic bullshit and you know it. The NHS for one wouldn't be able to function without its foreign workers'.

'You can save your flaming breath, Margaret. The message from my supporters has never been any clearer. I'm joining the British National Party today whether you like it or not'.

'Then I won't be here when you get back'.

'What did you say?'

'If you go through with this ridiculous and dangerous ego trip then don't count on me being here when you get back'.

'You've done well out of this marriage, Margaret. This house on the nice side of town and everything you see around you. Your car, our holidays, the clothes you love spending my money on'.

'Whose money, Frank? You and I both know that an MP's salary couldn't support the lifestyle we lead'.

'Watch your tongue'.

'Well you stand there going on about listening to the working class when you're such a bloody hypocrite!'

'What I've done is for the working class!'.

'What you've done is for yourself! Just like all those bits of skirt you had sex with behind my back. Were you thinking of the working class when you were fucking them? Those two kids out there somewhere that we pay for because you couldn't keep it in your trousers, were they part of the working class struggle too? Do you know what you are, Frank? You're a failure. You're a failure and you're a hypocrite. You preach socialism outside and then act like a petty dictator at home. You've failed me as a husband with all your dalliances. You've failed as a father because neither of your sons want to have anything to do with you. You've failed as a politician because you never got promoted and the only way you can deal with that failure is by turning into the fascist you've always been. Well welcome home, Frank. I'm sure it feels like you've never been away'.

For too many years Frank Barton felt he had doggedly towed the party line on every issue from reforming the NHS to supporting the war in Iraq. But today was about where his political journey had brought him to now. He was so glad to be free. The leader of the Labour party, the general secretary, various neighbouring MP's and councillors had all rung him to try and persuade him not to do what he was planning. But he'd gone too far to put a stop to it now, even if he'd wanted to. There was a cause to fight for. It was his moment in history to change his little piece of the world.

When he got to the hotel near the Reebok stadium in Bolton that had been chosen for him to make his big announcement, he was ushered into a small room at the side of where the press conference was going to be held. Already the newspapers and TV companies were buzzing madly round the whole scene and about thirty-odd journalists had packed the small room. His BNP 'minder' Barry Higgins wanted to know what Frank thought of a journalist from the Northwest Gazette called John Spencer.

'He's trouble' said Barton. 'He thinks he's on some kind of crusade'.

'I understand that he thinks he can damage you?'

'He knows nothing, Barry. He knows nothing'.

'You're sure of that?'

Frank wasn't sure of that at all. He put two and two together and realised that the only person who could've told anyone anything about him of enough significance to cause him any trouble would've been his wife Margaret. Surely she wouldn't be that callous? Surely she didn't hate him that much? Her outburst from that morning made him wonder.

'Quite sure, Barry' Frank lied.

'He's out there' said Barry. 'Waiting with all the other vultures. Are you sure you can handle it?'

'I've been an MP since nineteen seventy-four, Barry. I think I can handle the ladies and gentlemen of the press'.

'Well we've fixed things anyway' said Barry. 'We'll be whisking you away as soon as you've finished your statement'.

Barry led Frank into the press conference flanked by other members of the BNP. He introduced the event and said how delighted he was to be welcoming Frank Barton to his new 'home' in the British National Party. Then he handed over to the 'star' of the show.

'My dear friends' Frank began, looking at the rows of BNP activists that had been brought in to fill up the front rows. 'Today, I have resigned my membership of the Labour party … '

He paused whilst he soaked up his applause.

'… it was an emotional decision but it became necessary for me to escape from the moral bankruptcy of the Labour party. The British National party is now the only legitimate movement I can believe in. We will take over the representation of the working class. We will fight for our right to take our God given country back from the poisonous liberalism of the past decades …'

They loved what they were hearing. A whole wave of approval was going through the activists just like the wind floated purposefully through the air. Someone like Frank who'd turned himself into a modern day Oswald Mosley by crossing from Labour is just the sort of hero they like.

'... my friends, my comrades, the moment is coming for Britain to stand on its own two feet once more and for us to continue that glorious strain in our history that brought us everything that the liberals and the left have destroyed. We will start a campaign to bring back those traditional British values that have been destroyed by so-called progressive politics. Never again will we allow those who've been given the freedom of this country to use it to discredit our brave soldiers ever again ... '

More applause followed which Frank stopped to soak up. He wife Margaret should be sitting out there. But she wasn't.

'... it's been my commitment to the working class of Britain that's driven me and always will be' Frank rolled on. 'Those interests have been let down by the liberal establishment. The chattering classes who took over the Labour party have taken it in a direction that the working class are distinctly uncomfortable with. Now they're looking for somewhere else to place their vote. We need to challenge the established order for a return to Christian values. But just like the Jews are reclaiming land that God gave them three thousand years ago, we, the people of Britain, have to reclaim our land for our principles and our values and for our future. A Britain free from outside control, especially from the unelected bureaucrats in Brussels. A Britain free from the threat of Sharia law. A Britain where everybody speaks English. A Britain which the British are back in control of. We've started, my friends, and we will finish the job ... '

Having signed an exclusive interview deal with the Daily Mail,

Frank was whisked away without taking any questions which caused a furore amongst the members of the press who were there. But before the Mail's chief reporter could take him away for that exclusive interview, Barry Higgins took him back into the side room for what he called a 'debrief'.

'Well played my friend, well bloody played' said Barry with his big arm around Frank. 'You said everything the way we wanted you to say it and it was a perfect delivery. The working classes that I went to work with on the railways all those years ago would've been proud. You'll be the BNP's first MP and we're delighted to welcome you'.

What followed as soon as Frank, flanked by his BNP heavies, came out into the corridor, became an absolute circus. The journalists were clamouring to ask frank if he was going to resign his seat in Bolton Central and force a by-election. They wanted to know how, by just crossing over the floor of the house, his presence could still be deemed as legitimate. They wanted to know where he would be sitting in the House of Commons seeing as no other BNP MP was there. Then John Spencer of the Northern Gazette stepped forward into Frank's line of sight. Frank looked like a rabbit caught in headlights and the more his heavies tried to get him away the more the pack of news hounds tightened their circle around him so that even the hired security guards were struggling to keep order.

John Spencer looked on with a great deal of satisfaction. He'd timed things just right. The normally unflappable Barton looked seriously worried about the torrent of questions that were being thrown at him and he looked like he was ready to kill. But then John left them all to it. He knew the story after all. He had the exclusive.

He followed the barren trail after Frank Barton and caught up with him in the foyer of the hotel. Barton was heading for the car provided by the Daily Mail to take him away for that 'exclusive' interview.

'Hey, Frank!' John called out. 'Fancy giving me an exclusive on what your plans are?'

Frank just glared at John.

'Thought not' said John. 'Just as well I know everything already. Did you hear that, Frank? I know everything. I know it all'.

'You know nothing, Spencer!'.

'You have two daughters-in-law, don't you, Frank?' said John, as he advanced on the main doors in pursuit of his prey. 'I'm talking about Mi Ling Barton, your son Robin's wife? She's Chinese, isn't she, from Hong Kong? Tell us why your son Robin refuses to have anything to do with you, Mr. Barton?'

Frank stopped dead in his tracks. 'That's family business that has nothing to do with you'.

'But your son Robin broke off relations with you just after his wife Mi Ling had been in hospital? Can you not shed some light on that?'

'No, because it's none of your business! Typical gutter press to try and drag the attention onto a politician's family life rather than keep it on the issues. Look, … '

'… she was in hospital for almost a week and your own son hasn't been in contact with you since. What does that tell us, Frank?'

'It tells you nothing!' Barton insisted, his anger almost showing through. 'It tells you nothing'.

'Oh on the contrary, Mr. Barton, it tells me everything. And whilst we're on the subject of the truth, can you tell me how half a million pounds of trade union money found its way into your bank account? I've got copies of your statements. Would it have anything to do with all the back hander's you've taken to make sure their case is presented to ministers? Have a nice day, sir'.

Frank grabbed the lapels of Spencer's jacket and pinned him up against the wall. 'You've never been able to forgive me, have you Spencer? She chose me all those years ago and she dumped you along with all the other trash. It's about time you learned to get over it'.

'Everything comes to those who wait, Frank'.

'What the hell do you mean?'

'You'd best get home to that big fuck off house of yours that was bought with money obtained fraudulently. Champion of the working class? Don't make me fucking laugh'.

When Frank got home Margaret was sitting at the kitchen table with her coat on. It was finally dawning on him just how much she'd hated him all these years.

'Pleased with your hatchet job?'

'No' said Margaret. 'But it was necessary'.

'You look like you're ready to go'.

'Yes, I'm leaving you, Frank. I said I would and I am'.

'Is Spencer waiting for you?'

'As a matter of fact he is, yes' said Margaret as she stood up and put the handle of her bag over her shoulder. 'And he knows the lot. All about the money you took from the hard working men and women who belong to trade unions, and all about the rape of your own daughter-in-law just because she was Chinese. You're finished, Frank. It's all over. I should've done this years ago, perhaps poor Mi Ling would've been spared her ordeal if I had. That's something I'll have to live with. You'll be living with it in prison'.

'She'll never testify against me!'

'Oh but she will, Frank. She's already left a signed affidavit with her solicitor'.

'Why?' he pleaded. 'Why do you want to destroy me?'

'Because you're a bad man, Frank'.

'So what does that make you if you lived for me for nearly forty years?'

'A bloody fool!'

'Margaret, I beg you, I couldn't take going to prison'.

'Save your pleading for someone who gives a shit' said Margaret who'd never felt more sure of herself in her entire married life. 'Goodbye, Frank. Oh and it'll be all over the Bolton Telegraph tonight. I'd expect a few phone calls if I was you and then the long arm of the law. Don't think about running because you won't get far'.

FIVE

SIMON

Just because a man is fifty-one and unmarried doesn't mean to say he's gay. People don't say that about fifty-one year-old unmarried women. They feel sorry for them and say things like 'oh it's a shame she never met the right one' or 'it's a shame he was married because she's never got over him'. But they never say that about fifty-one year old unmarried men. They whisper about them and assume they must be some kind of sexual deviant. Or they imagine some kind of deep seated personality deficiency that stops them from forming normal relationships with women. They think they probably sit in their house late at night downloading child pornography. In other words, women can get away with being unmarried and single at fifty-one and indeed, at any bloody age. But fifty-one year old unmarried men don't get away with it. They're condemned to one unfounded assumption after another.

'Yes, but you are gay, Simon' said his mate Harry who was sitting next to him in the taxi. 'So what's the fucking point of all this?'

'I was comparing myself to Damien, Lucy's new boyfriend. He's fifty and unmarried but nobody whispers about him being gay'.

'That's because he has relationship history' said Harry who'd never quite been able to work out why his mate Simon had been on the receiving end of such bad luck. He was an intelligent man for sure, not a geek or a boring bastard, but someone with a thoughtful eye on the world. But his personal life had always been like a speeding car crashing against a brick wall. 'Damien has been in two long-term relationships with women both of which lasted for years and that's normal for unmarried straight men of his age. They've normally had a couple of long-term serious relationships with women that didn't work out in the end but at least they had them. You haven't had any serious relationships'.

'Don't mince your words'.

'But it's the truth, Simon, and I think the last thing you need at the moment is for me to give you warm words that don't mean shit'.

'I've had sex' said Simon in the way people claim to have eaten suchi. 'I've had more than my fair share of other people's boyfriends and husbands. I've been quite good at being the other woman. The only way I've ever been able to keep anybody is by them calling the shots and me not being able to rely on anything. There's always been someone else ahead of me in the queue for first prize. I was always the bit on the side. I would've loved to have had a crack at feeling what it's like to come first in someone's life'.

'You sound like it's all over, Simon'.

'Well it feels like it is, Harry'.

'You've had some fun though'.

'Oh I've had some fun but could you have got through your life just on fun?'

'Point taken'

'Thank you'.

'Well you did get investigated by the clap clinic that time'

'And even then I was given the all clear' Simon lamented. 'I'm so bloody insignificant I couldn't even catch a sexually transmitted disease. I was the only one in the chain who wasn't infected'.

'I wish you'd been able to find someone, mate' said Harry. 'We all do. We all think you deserve to have someone and we wish we could make it happen'.

'There was Mitch'.

'Yes, but he wasn't gay or even curious' said Harry. 'He couldn't have given you what you needed'.

'You knew what we were like when we were together'.

'Yes but it was a bromance' Harry pointed out. 'Like you and me have always been'.

'I wonder what Mitch is doing now'.

'There's no point in you wondering that, Simon. You'll only make yourself feel worse. You've got to get through today and then move on with your life'.

Simon had heard all this before from his friends. They all went on about how he's got to look on the positive side but it was alright for them. They all had someone to look on the positive side of things with. They all had someone to help them through the bad times. But he didn't and he was lonely. He had plenty of friends. He was swimming in bloody friends even though some of them lately had somewhat disappeared from view. But every time he'd ever wanted to move beyond the limits of friendship with a man and follow through on his desires it was never possible for one reason or another. And the older he got the more difficult and the more painful it became to put on the brave face and bury his disappointment deep down inside where nobody else could see it. Other people seem to be able to find love so easily and yet for him it remained as impossible a dream now as it had been thirty years ago when he first started out on the adult stage of his life's journey. He'd really had enough of it all. He'd been worn down by life. He'd turned into the kind of man who everybody comes to for advice on their relationship but who never has one of his own to talk to them about. In that way he was a bit like a Catholic priest advising married couples. Perhaps he should've gone into the priesthood. At least then he'd have been able to blame his single status on the fact that he was already married to God.

'Anyway' said Simon. 'Next time I'm going to come back as a girl in Australia who marries a big hunky farmer in the outback'.

'Except that it wouldn't work out like that for you, Simon' said Harry. 'You'd come back as some poor girl in Africa who has her switch twitched with a rusty knife when she's too young to resist'.

'So you're telling me there's no hope for me in this life or the next?'.

'Simon, I'm saying you've made some big mistakes and you've also been dealt some pretty cruel blows' said Harry. 'But you've got to concentrate now on getting the best out of the rest of this life instead of fantasizing about what you'd like to happen in the next because there are no guarantees for any of us. We're all just doing the best we can'.

'Easy for you to say when you know what it feels like to be loved'.

'I know, Simon, I know. I'm just trying to … '

'…we're almost there' said Simon who could see the county

court building that appeared to him in the middle distance like a scaffold. He'd wanted to cut Harry off because if he'd sprouted some bullshit about not knowing what's around the next corner he might've hit him.

'I'll pay for this' said Harry. 'You'll be shelling out enough today as it is'.

'Thanks, Harry. Nearly seven hundred quid to go bankrupt. There must be an irony there'.

'And you do know that I'd have you come and stay at mine until you got on your feet again but with me and April only just starting out … well you know'.

'Yeah, I do. I don't want my nose rubbed in gooseberries as well as everything else'.

'Now come on, cheer up. In a year's time, or even less than that, you'll be looking back on this period with a renewed sense of self-belief and optimism'.

'Yes, Harry. And Cheryl Cole can sing'.

'April really likes you, you know'.

Simon wondered why the fuck Harry was telling him that. Did he think that knowing his straight best mate's new girlfriend liked him would somehow help him over the fact that he was about to go bankrupt for a mountain of debt? He genuinely liked April and they got on really well but she'd been gushing to him the other day about how Harry was so attentive and so passionate and never stopped telling her how much he adored her and loved her. Well bully for fucking you, Simon had thought. Nobody had ever told Simon that they loved him, not even his own father. He'd love to know what it felt like.

'That's nice' he said.

'Where will you go when you've finished here?' asked Harry.

'I've absolutely no idea'.

'The world is your oyster'.

Simon laughed at the ridiculous nature of that comment. 'You're forgetting one very important fact, Harry. I have no money'.

'Have you heard from any of your family?'

'Family?' Simon scoffed. 'Now there's a fucking joke. I haven't heard from any member of my family since I told them all I was having to go bankrupt and would be losing my house'.

'Give them time, Simon'.

'I haven't got time to give to them or anybody else, Harry! That's what everybody is consistently failing to grasp about this whole situation. I've lost everything. I have nothing for the future. I'm in the deepest fucking shit imaginable and it doesn't seem like it's getting through to people on any level. You say I've got to give them time when next week I could be trying to sleep in some bloody hostel?'

'They're embarrassed, Simon. They don't know what to say'.

'Well the poor little darlings! When I'm sleeping in a shop doorway I'll forgive them for leaving me there because they're embarrassed. How the fuck do they think it feels for me?'

'That's what people are like. They can't deal with this kind of big stuff'.

'Well I've got to. I've got to deal with it. You say I've got to give my family time? If I'd told them I'd got cancer they'd be rallying round competing to claim the Oscar for best family member in a supporting role. They'd all be fighting to have me stay with them so they could be seen to be looking after me. But go bankrupt and it's not only your material possessions that you lose'.

'I don't know what to say, Simon'.

'I'm terrified, Harry. I'm fucking terrified. I've earned a fortune over the years and I've spent every penny of it and more which is why I've got into this mess. I've spent all my money looking for something I never found. And now here I am. I've fallen off the edge of life, Harry. And I don't know if I'm ever going to be able to get back on my feet'.

'You won't … do anything stupid?'

'I've done a lot of stupid things when it comes to money, Harry'.

'You know what I mean, Simon'.

'Well if I did do away with myself would everybody be standing around at the funeral tearfully regretting that they never offered me a place to live for a while? Because it'll be too fucking late then. But of course that's what people do, isn't it. They spew out their meaningless love for the person after they've committed suicide instead of helping them when they were still alive'.

'What about Eric? I mean, he is helping you?'

'He says he's going to do his best whatever that means'.

'We're here' Harry announced when the taxi pulled up outside the county court building. He then turned to Simon. 'I am sorry about this mate. Really I am'.

'I know you are, Harry'.

'You do believe it though?'

'Yes, Harry, I do believe it'.

Simon did believe it. Harry didn't deserve to be on the receiving end of his resentment. Harry had been as true a friend as he could've been.

Shortly after Simon signed his bankruptcy papers with the court and paid the fee Harry had to go home to meet April. So Simon went into a cafe across the road and ordered a medium sized plain white coffee. He sat in the window looking out at people who were going up and down with shopping bags and mobile phones attached to their ears and although Simon knew they probably all had problems of their own it didn't help his feeling of complete and utter desolation. His life had gone. He used to have an active social life. He used to be invited to parties all over the place. But it had all dried up since people knew of his money troubles. His daily existence felt like somebody had laid the table for breakfast but forgotten to buy any food.

'Do you want topping up?'

Simon looked up. One of the women who worked in the café was standing next to him. She and her colleagues were all middle aged and married and tended to treat their job as an escape from what they saw as the tedium of their lives with their men. He'd overheard them talking that way so many times.

'Oh, yes please' said Simon who'd done a mental calculation in the seconds before answering and decided he could afford another one. 'That would be great'.

'I'll bring it over' she said as she lifted his now empty cup and saucer. 'Two more weeks and then I'm off to the Dom Rep'.

'The Dom Rep?'

'The Dominican Republic' she explained. 'It's a really nice heat there and they speak English. It's not like Egypt where we went for Fred's fiftieth three years ago. It's not a nice heat there and besides, they're always kicking off about something. You'd have thought they'd drop it all in the tourist areas though, wouldn't you?'

Simon wasn't quite sure why this woman was furnishing him with her holiday plans and opinions about Egypt but he couldn't help but respond. 'Well if you're fighting for your freedom and liberty then I don't suppose someone else's holiday plans are exactly top of your list of priorities'.

'Well I don't think it's very considerate of them' she repeated. 'But I'll get you that coffee'.

Simon had spent two years fighting to keep his house and he'd lost. He'd gone from loan to loan, line of credit to line of credit, he'd paid over the odds for work he'd had done on his house because he had the eye for the builder. The rainy day had always seemed light years ahead of him but when he lost his job the rainy day drowned him. It all happened so fast. He couldn't keep up with the payments to all his creditors, including the mortgage company. He'd borrowed on the equity of the house until there was none left and it had gone over into negative. The friendly letters asking if he'd forgotten his repayment date had turned into nasty ones threatening him with all sorts. He became scared to answer the door, scared to pick up the phone when it rang. It had taken less than a year to get to the stage where bankruptcy was his only option according to the Citizens Advice Bureau. Everything he'd worked for would be lost. Everything about his lack of savings haunted him in the still of the night. He'd fucked up. He'd been a fucking idiot with money which in recent years had swept through his hands from what he earned to what he owed like a running tap. He'd lost his job. He'd lost his mother to suicide when he was still a baby. She'd thrown herself out of the bedroom window with him in her arms. She'd died from injuries to her head but he'd survived. She hadn't left a note. He'd then grown up with a father who'd never got over the loss of his wife. Simon sometimes wondered why he'd survived and his mother hadn't. What had life spared him for? Was it really to go through all this shit? Do some people have to take all the pain whilst they watch others take all the joy? That's what it seemed like to him.

'Your coffee' said the waitress as she placed it in front of him. 'Pay when you're going out, love'.

Six months ago he'd called in one of those house clearance people who come and buy the contents of someone's home after they've died. He'd sold them the dishwasher, the cooker, the fridge, and the washing machine. Together they were worth over a grand when he bought them but he'd settled for one hundred and twenty in cash because he'd desperately needed the short term gain in cash flow. He then had no choice but to buy a lot of takeaways which kind of defeats the object when you're short of cash. Going to the supermarket and stocking up on groceries to last a few days is a much cheaper option but he no longer had any means of properly storing anything. It had frustrated him to say the least because he'd always been a reasonably good purchaser of food. He could easily make a chicken last two meals, one hot, one cold, and a sandwich on the third day for his lunch at work. But he didn't know when those days of doing ordinary things like stocking up the fridge would ever come back. He'd never grasped before how much the cost of living for the poor was so much more than it was for the rich because the poor lack basic resources to make things last. And with all those takeaways, including fish and chips for a fiver, it's no wonder the poor suffer such disproportionate levels of ill health. He had to include himself in those numbers now but it was hard after spending years not worrying too much about living a comfortable lifestyle. Whilst there'd been a credit card that wasn't up to the spending limit he could always have just about whatever he wanted. His house had been full of impulse purchases that he would never need. But the purchase of them had made him feel better at the time. And for that he now felt absolutely pathetic.

He'd called the house clearance people back a second time and they'd taken his bed, wardrobe, and chest of drawers from his bedroom. He was so desperate for cash to get through each day that he'd wanted them to take the bed from his spare room but apparently the mattress didn't cover the latest fire regulations so they wouldn't have been able to sell it on. He'd also sold them his books, his CD's, his DVD's and his bookcases. From that night on he'd slept on the mattress that didn't meet the fire regulations. It would never have caught fire though. There was too much moisture in it. He was so stressed out all the time that he was wetting the bed some nights. Fifty years old and wetting the bed. He'd fallen that low.

He'd kept the microwave so he could do some hot meals of his own and he'd switched to powdered milk. Any perishables like low fat spread (well he had to make some effort with the diet somewhere) he kept on the window ledge of the kitchen so they'd keep reasonably chilled if not cold, same for the occasional yoghurt or carton of orange juice. He'd taken a temporary job for minimum wage at a travel agent where they'd used his experience and situation for six weeks to get someone on the cheap to fill a junior post during a peak period. Nobody there had recognised the pattern he was drawing with his behavior or if they did they kept quiet. He'd have a hot meal in a local café at lunchtime and he'd ask them to make him up a sandwich 'for later'. He'd take the sandwich home with a bag of crisps and that would be his evening meal. Slowly but surely, day by day, pieces had been falling off his heart and his soul sank deeper into the unknown. But he kept on the brave face. Even when the mortgage company rang him at work and said they were 'very sorry' but they 'couldn't put any more effort into helping him try to save his property'. He took the call in the corridor and went back into the office where he made everybody a brew, delivered to their desk with the usual smile. The day he'd sent the keys to his house back to the mortgage company he'd left behind everything that had remained after his clear outs and taken only some of his clothes. The suitcase he'd taken them in would become his home.

'Have you ever been to the Dom Rep?' asked the waitress when she came sidling by again.

Will she ever just fuck off? 'No'.

'Oh it's lovely' she went on, ignoring the obvious signs that Simon really didn't want to talk. 'Fred doesn't like it but it's not up to him. He does as he's told. He's paying seven hundred and fifty each all in and the hotel is four star. Not bad is it?'

'Sounds great' said Simon who wouldn't even be able to manage a day trip to Skegness now. 'But you know, I've worked in the travel trade all my life and the trouble with those all inclusive places is that the staff working there get paid peanuts and have to work really long hours. It also means that no money is actually going into the local economy because all the guests like you never go into the local town because you've got everything in the hotel and all the money you've paid goes to the holiday company based here or in Germany or America somewhere. I don't suppose you'll be thinking about any of that when you're sipping your fourth margarita of the day?'

The waitress looked at him as if he was speaking a foreign language. That was the trouble with the upper working class, thought Simon. They have absolutely no solidarity with anybody else who may be struggling to survive. They were selfish. They were the perfect followers of Margaret Thatcher. They want what they want and they don't care what others have to go through in order for them to have it. They go to department stores selling cheap clothes and don't give a shit that someone in a third world sweatshop has had to pay the real price for them by going blind at the age of twelve. Then they blame everything that's wrong with their sad little lives on immigrants and vote for the far-right political descendents of Margaret Thatcher.

'But anyway I thought you said your husband doesn't like it there?'

'Well he doesn't but like I said, he does as he's told'.

'But you're quite happy to let him pay the bill?'

'He doesn't get any choice' she insisted. 'I'm not like my sister Marjorie. Her husband is doing an open university course off his own back and she's devastated. I'd be putting my foot down'.

'About what exactly?'

'Well what's he doing that for at fifty-seven?'

'To stretch himself and show that he can?'

'He should stretch himself and show that he can decorate the dining room at their house before he goes chasing after so-called education. There'll be summer schools and all that. She'll have to go with him to keep an eye on him because we don't let our men stay overnight anywhere on their own. I think he's being very selfish, I really do'.

'And does … forgive me she's so insignificant to me that I've forgotten your sister's name, is it Marjorie?'

'Yes?'

'Well what would happen if she wanted to do an open university course?'

'Well then she'd do it no question'.

'So she doesn't pay her husband the same respect?'

She laughed. 'I can tell you're not married. You've got to be make the men learn from the word go how it's going to be'

'So the secret to a happy marriage as far as you and your mates are concerned is to find a man who's weak enough to let you bully him until death do you part?'

'I wouldn't put it that way, no'.

'Well it sounds that way from where I'm standing. Or does your sister think her husband will get bored with her if he's better educated?'

'Pardon?'

'Well her attitude isn't a very educated one so I'm guessing she's not capable of doing much academically beyond puzzle books?'

'Well as it happens she loves doing puzzle books' the waitress confirmed cheerfully. 'They went to Paris last year and she managed to get through six of them over a weekend'.

'She did puzzle books in Paris?'

'Well she doesn't like the French and she gets bored with all that sight- seeing rubbish. She doesn't see the point and neither do I. When we were in Egypt they kept going on about us going to see some pyramid thing or something but I put a veto on that straight away. Anyway, my sister left most of the so-called sightseeing to my boring brother-in-law. She said they didn't have a decent meal in Paris either'.

Simon was aghast. 'Didn't have a decent meal in Paris? But it's the gastronomical capital of the world? Oh come on, it sounds to me like she was determined not to enjoy herself from the start'.

'Well she does blame the whole experience on leading to her husband wanting to better his education'.

'But I don't understand why you're talking about that as if it's a bad thing'.

'Well I mean, he's doing history of art and French' she emphasized. 'What's the point of doing that when there's a garden to tend and jobs that need doing round the house?'

Simon was so glad he wasn't straight. He hated women like this stroppy nag standing in front of him. He loathed her for her narrowness of view. And he really wasn't in the mood for the pig ignorant bitch so she was going to get it.

'Perhaps he's bored with tending the garden and doing jobs around the house? Perhaps he's sick of doing what he's told by your sister just to avoid upsetting her. Has that ever occurred to you? Have you ever asked yourself what he might want out of this great adventure called life or what he might be thinking?'

'Well what would I do that for?'

'I rest my case. For some reason that's unfathomable to me some men saddle themselves with control freak nags like you and your sister and all your friends here.'

'Now just a minute … '

'… no, you just a minute. You don't want an honest mature relationship. You just want to take a hostage to your insecurities because underneath all that bluster you're just a stupid little girl who's afraid of the big, bad world'.

'I don't know what the hell you're talking about'.

'Well let me explain' said Simon. 'You're useless, mouthy idiots who know fuck all about anything. And I bet you're all useless in bed as well. No imagination and no effort. Your husbands would probably have more fun sticking it into a dead chicken. Send them all to me. I'll give the poor bastards some decent head and I won't expect a new dining room suite in return'.

'How dare you talk to me like that!'

'Well I dare so get over it!'

'I think you'd better drink up and leave. I'd kill you if I was married to you'.

'Oh don't worry, sweetheart. If I was married to you I'd kill myself'.

Simon left the café and then walked through the streets as dusk was falling. He was feeling so wretched and alone. He would never want the kind of relationship, if you can call it that, that those awful women in the coffee shop have got but at least they get to go home to someone to share time and space with. One of his friends who needless to say had always been in a happy, contended relationship was always telling him that the grass isn't always greener and there were always people worse off than him. Well that's true, there were, but conversely there were also people who were far better off than he was.

Simon got himself through his O-levels and A-levels. He'd liked to have gone on to university but he was desperate to get out and get a life where he could earn some money and start broadening his horizons. He'd had to congratulate himself on the grades he'd got. He'd had to go to his grandparents to get any kind of praise and even that meant listening to those on his mother's side get all tearful and say how his mother would've been so proud and how she'd loved him so much. Yes, well he didn't want the pride of a mother from beyond the grave. If she'd thought so much about him she'd have been there for him and nurtured him all the way through.

When the beginning of the end had come it was when the nights had been drawing in. Heading into winter had felt like heading into Hell for him. People were talking about Christmas, about next year's summer holidays, about their son or daughter graduating from university next summer and how proud they were going to be. They were making all these plans with the safe knowledge that they'd have a home in which to stage all these events. As he watched some of the people passing him by, he envied their apparent certainty of destination. They were going home. Even these brain dead control freak waitresses were going to somewhere they could call home. They were going to hang their coats up, switch lights on and go to the toilet. They were going to prepare a meal for themselves and whoever they lived with. They were going to watch the evening news and their favourite TV programmes. He didn't know what home meant anymore and he didn't know how he was ever going to get that feeling back.

'You don't look so great' said Eric.

'Sorry' replied Simon.

'I wish you'd cheer yourself up when you come and see me'.

'I said I'm sorry, Eric' said Simon who knew that Eric liked him to go round and fill his heart with joy but Christ he felt like both of his legs had been broken off. But that wouldn't matter to Eric because it has to be all about him and Simon really didn't have the emotional strength to fight back or even attempt to stand up for myself. His older brother had always been much closer to their father than Simon had been. Eric and their father had always concentrated on the practicalities of life. Simon had always been more of an emotional soul. He supposed he got that from his mother. That's probably why in her absence Eric and their father had grown close and why Simon had grown up not really knowing how or where he fitted into his own family.

'Well come on it's not so bad' said Eric, in his usual optimistic way that avoided mention of the nuclear bomb that had already destroyed Simon's landscape. 'How much are the b and b charging you?'

'It's off season so it's only twenty a night'.

'Well you'll be able to stay there a while with the money I've given you and at least you get a full English out of it in the morning so you're set up for the day. Anyway, eat up your Chinese. Mary will be back by nine and you'll have to be long gone by then. Watch any crumbs falling on the carpet too. I don't want to have to go round with the vacuum cleaner before she gets back and you know what eagle eyes she's got'.

Simon wanted to throw the entire contents of his plate against the fucking wall. But he was rather fond of sizzling chicken in garlic and black bean sauce and to sit and eat a meal on a table in a house had become a novelty to him now. He was getting used to using a small wooden fork to eat his chips with whilst perched on the edge of his bed at the b and b. Afterwards he had to open the window wide to get rid of the smell and then the next morning carefully take out the polystyrene container his supper had been in because the owner of the b and b doesn't like guests bringing their own food in of an evening. She doesn't provide any food herself. She expects everybody to eat out. She lets her husband walk around in bare feet and stinking of beer but her guests mustn't bring in anything that might give off a smell. Most of Simon's fellow guests were contract builders or paper clip salesmen on expenses or people with their own businesses who were too tight to pay for a proper hotel. They didn't seem to care about the awful sight of her husband. They didn't seem to care either about the way she was always made up to the eyeballs and flirty with all the male guests. Perhaps that's how she gets her cock these days. Her husband with his fat belly didn't look like he'd do her any good in the bedroom anymore. She'd been flirty with Simon too until he'd dropped his ficticious boyfriend into the conversation. After that he'd stopped placing a chair against his door at night.

'Don't worry, Eric, I'll use my paper serviette wisely'.

'That's good, son'.

Simon didn't know why the fuck he called him 'son'. He was only seven years younger than Eric. 'I don't suppose Mary knows about you giving me money?'

'Do you think I'd still be alive if she did?'

'Daft question I suppose'.

'Oh don't look like that, Simon. You know how she feels about protecting what she considers to be hers and hers alone and what we'll one day pass on to the kids'.

'Yes I know Eric. There's always somebody more important than me in the lives of those I'm close to. That's the story of my life'.

'Simon, I've got to put my family first'.

'But I'm your brother, Eric' said Simon. 'I'm also part of your family. Doesn't that count for anything?'

'You know it counts for everything as far as I'm concerned but Mary is different'.

'You're right there'.

'Mary has always suffered from being very insecure, Simon, you know that' said Eric. 'And she needs to know that she can count on having all that cash in the bank if she needs it'.

'Oh well excuse me. If I'd known that I'd have been more understanding'.

'Simon, don't be like that'.

'So you're saying that need to be certain that she's got stacks of it in the bank means that you can't help your own brother in his hour of need?'

'Look, I don't want you hating me over this. I'll help you as much as I can but there'll be a limit because I'm going to have to disguise the withdrawals. She went mad when she saw that withdrawal for two hundred from the joint account that I told her I'd given to you'.

'It's not like you can't afford it and I was desperate'.

'But none of that is relevant to Mary, Simon'.

'Even though she's known me all these years and I thought we'd been close'.

'She thinks you've brought your troubles on yourself by being financially reckless' Eric declared. 'That's why she's not willing to help you'.

Eric's words fell on Simon like hard hail stones. Mary was right in some ways. He had been somewhat reckless with his money in the past which that's why he hadn't had the financial clout to get himself through these past couple of years. But all he needed now was help to get his life back in order and he kind of thought that's what family was for.

'So she doesn't care if I'm on the streets?'

Eric hesitated. 'It's not that she doesn't care, it's just that she doesn't want you living here even if it's only for a short time'.

'You've got two spare rooms in this house neither of which she'll let me stay in and I'm only asking to until I get back on my feet' said Simon who was aware that his voice may be taking on a desperate quality and he really didn't want that.

'I know what you're asking, Simon'.

'Oh don't say anymore' said Simon. 'I've heard enough already'.

'Look, we'll put the TV on after' said Eric as he scooped the last of his Cantonese rice. 'Oh and did I tell you by the way that

Mary and I are buying that house we talked about in Spain?'

'No?' Simon replied. More insensitive gloating was sure to follow.

'Oh yes, we're very excited' said Eric. 'What do you think about that?'

'Eric, I'm homeless, I'm living in a b and b. I'm bankrupt'.

'Yes, but what do you think about us buying a house in Spain?'

'I couldn't give a flying fuck!'

'Look, it's not always all about you, you know'.

'Eric, you're asking me what I think about you buying a home in the sun when I face the prospects of living on the streets and you accuse me of being egotistical? I mean, do you want me to shit rainbows for you or something?'

'Well I don't know what the hell I can say anymore'.

'Well I'm glad that's all you've got to worry about. Oh but of course you don't worry, do you? You're like Dad. You just ignore any emotional issue that's staring you in the face. Dad let me grow up thinking that nobody loved me and he did nothing about it'.

'Oh not this again' Eric groaned.

'Yes this again because it happened, Eric! It happened to me and it was real and it broke my fucking heart every single fucking day but you took no notice because you were his mate and you were his pal and neither of you gave a fuck about me!'

'Dad did love you, Simon'.

'Bullshit!'

'Yes he did'.

'Dad blamed me for Mum's death and he resented me because I survived when Mum didn't'.

'He did love you in his own way' Eric insisted.

'Oh the usual clichéd excuse'.

'He just couldn't show it'.

'And that's supposed to be a comfort?'

'Take it how you like' said Eric. 'You're far too emotional. That's always been your trouble'.

'Oh I'm sorry but I didn't think that expecting my father to show me that he loved me was being too emotional but that's the standard line from those who can't show emotion. Eric, my feelings are real and they come from a place of truth that recognises that people get hurt and they need help and doesn't deny them what they feel'.

'Well look, eat up so I can do the pots and have everything cleared away before Mary gets back'.

'And that's all you've got to say? Eric, you and I grew up in two different homes within the same house. There was you and Dad in one and there was me in the other. I've been alone all my life because Dad was a complete emotional illiterate'.

'Simon, I'll give you a lift to the bus stop on the main road but be careful. Someone got mugged and quite badly beaten on that road last Saturday night'.

Simon had to concede defeat. Eric was doing his usual trick of changing the subject when he just wasn't interested. Simon had had a lifetime of it and knew there was no good fighting it. 'You'll have had a few glasses of wine by then, Eric'.

'Oh yes, so I will. I was forgetting. Well will you be able to make your own way to the main road? Watch yourself though. They haven't caught whoever did it yet'.

'By the way, Eric, are you and Mary still going to church every Sunday morning?'

'Oh yes' Eric confirmed. 'Mary especially is well in with the new priest Father Harrison. That's where she is now. She's at a meeting of his inner circle who run the parish'.

As he walked down the street from Eric's house, Simon wondered what whoever this Father Harrison would say if he knew that one of his inner circle was refusing to help out her homeless and broke brother-in-law. He wondered what her beloved Jesus would have to say about it, especially when Jesus knew how much Simon had helped out his brother and sister-in-law in the past when they were starting out and had two kids to bring up without two pennies to rub together. Simon had once got himself into debt so that he could make sure his niece and nephew had food on the table. How quickly the receivers of kindness forget when the boot is on the other foot.

The shopping mall downtown isn't the sort of place to walk around if you haven't got any money. Simon had maintained a tight budgeting regime which meant that after his full English at the b and b he didn't eat again until around four or five. In the meantime he'd spend a lot of time in newsagents reading the magazines he used to buy. He was running out of clean clothes, especially underwear and socks. But a trip to the launderette cost eight quid and so that would have to wait until his dole payment was made.

He'd applied for so many jobs he couldn't remember exactly how many. Most of them hadn't even bothered to reply to his application whilst others said he was over qualified. Some sent the usual bullshit reply of 'we've had so many applications blah, blah, blah' but he was sure that with some of them it was his age that let him down. It's hard for the young to find work but it's also hard for the over 50s too unless they wanted to work in a DIY store and he'd tried there. They weren't hiring for the moment.

He was just coming out of another shop in which he couldn't afford to buy anything when he got the shock of his life.

'Oh my God!' he exclaimed.

Mitchell 'Mitch' Randall was standing there large as life, six foot tall, still with his Ben Cohen build, handsome with a few more lines and a bit less hair but still everything Simon had ever wanted and still with the power to make his heart miss a beat. It was as if he'd just stepped out of his subconscious. He'd been thinking a lot about Mitch recently. He always had done. He was the love of his life.

'Simon!' Mitch exclaimed. He put his arms round him in a bear hug. 'How are you?'

'I'm fine, just fine' said Simon who wondered why his path had to cross with Mitch right at this time when he was feeling such a hopeless failure. 'You look … well you look really well'.

'Thank you' said Mitch. 'I am well. I'm just up here visiting my sister Cheryl for a couple of days. How come you've still got a full head of hair? That's not fair. I'm starting to lose mine a bit as you can see'.

'It doesn't matter' said Simon, smiling. 'Are you still in the RAF?'

'The RAF?' Mitch questioned as if puzzled by the question. 'No. I left the forces years ago. Flying those fighter jets is a young man's game and I didn't want a desk job at the MoD which is where they'd have sent me if I'd stayed'.

'So what are you doing now?'

'I retrained as a commercial pilot and joined Virgin. I'm a Captain now on the Airbus fleet. I do Hong Kong, LA, that sort of thing'.

Simon smiled nervously 'That sort of thing. It seems like a different world to me'.

'But you've travelled'.

'Not much lately'.

'Are you still with the low fares travel agent on St. Peters Street?'

'No' said Simon. 'They made me redundant a year ago. They got rid of all the branch managers and now each of the section leaders takes it in turn to work up as manager'.

'Sign of the times, eh?'

'I haven't been able to find a job since other than a temporary one for a few weeks'.

'I'm really sorry to hear that' said Mitch.

'Is Nicola with you?'

'Nicola?'

'Yeah, your wife Nicola?'

'Simon, Nicola and I split up a long time ago'.

'Oh, I'm sorry to hear that'.

'It wasn't long after I met you when you and our Cheryl were sharing that house'.

'And you came to visit her and stayed for a few days' Simon recalled. 'I remember'.

'Cheryl told me you'd moved away and she'd lost touch with you which is probably why you don't know what's been happening with me'.

'What? Why did she tell you that I'd moved away? Look, Cheryl dropped me when she got married to Adrian years ago. After the third message I left for her wasn't returned I gave up. I haven't seen or heard from her in all that time but I didn't move away. She moved herself away from me if you see what I mean'.

'Well I do but I don't know why she'd do that or why she told me you'd moved away' said Mitch who was as puzzled as Simon was as to why his sister would lie about him. 'Look, you know the pub up by the cathedral? They do good food there. Why don't you join me for lunch?'

'I can't afford to go out for lunch, Mitch'.

'Jesus, are things that bad?'

'Worse'.

'Then let me treat you for old time's sake'.

'I can't let you do that, Mitch'.

'Of course you can' Mitch enthused. 'I want to do it and besides, I'm celebrating'.

'Celebrating?'

'I'm getting married again'.

Oh for God's sake, thought Simon. Did he really have to sit through Mitch telling him how it all fell apart with Nicola but he'd got a new girl now who was making him so happy he was going to marry her?

'Oh' he said. 'Congratulations'.

'Thanks' said Mitch. 'I've got a couple of things to do first so

I'll see you up at the pub in half an hour?'

'Great. See you there'.

'You do want to come to lunch with me, don't you?'

'What? Yeah, yeah of course I do'

'You didn't look too keen?'

'Mitch, I'm just going through a hard time at the moment, that's all'.

'Well then I accept it as my mission to cheer you up' said Mitch. 'After all, I could always put a smile on your face. Remember?'

Simon walked round and round the city centre trying to pluck up the courage to run as fast as he could. Why had Mitch walked back into his life now?

He finally got to the pub a few minutes late. There was a kind of corridor between the restaurant on one side and the bar on the other. He went into the restaurant and Mitch was sitting at a table in the far corner. He was drinking a pint of bitter and reading the Telegraph. There was a time when Simon would've sold his soul to the devil for him. Mitch had been going through difficulties in his marriage to Nicola and they'd decided to spend some time apart which is why he'd come to stay with his sister Cheryl. But Mitch had ended up spending a lot more time with Simon than he did with his sister. Simon and Mitch had slotted in with each other as if they'd been friends for years. So much so that other people were noticing and the whispers had started. Simon kept his true feelings to himself, except when he blurted it all out to Cheryl and told her that he'd fallen madly for her big brother Mitch.

But then one day Simon got up to find that Mitch had gone. The spare room had been left tidy but empty. It was on the day when Simon and Cheryl were throwing a party in their shared rented house. Simon was devastated. He'd so wanted Mitch to be there but he never saw or heard from him again.

'Ah you made it' said Mitch as he looked up and saw Simon. He folded up his newspaper and placed it on the table. 'What can I get you?'

'I'll have a pint too, please' said Simon. 'But look, are you sure this is okay? I really don't have the money to pay my way here'.

'Simon, relax. I earn a bloody good salary and I'm more than okay financially. So please, let me indulge an old friend who looks like he needs some TLC'.

Simon could've just burst into tears at the kindness Mitch was showing him but he managed to hold it inside. Over lunch he relaxed and he and Mitch shared the kind of times they always used to. They talked and talked, laughed a lot, and for Simon it was as if the ten years they'd been apart just disappeared. Every now and then a shiver would go down Simon's spine when he remembered that it was only lunch and they'd soon have to go back to their respective lives.

'So' said Simon. 'Tell me about your new bride?'

'His name is Paul'.

Simon almost choked on the wine they'd changed to for accompanying their food. 'What did you say?'

'Well you knew that Nicola and I were having problems back in the day' said Mitch. 'That's why I was staying with you and our Cheryl that time when the two of you were sharing that house. I was coming to terms with the fact that I was gay, Simon. I always had been but I'd never acknowledged it. Then I met you'.

Simon's mouth had gone dry. 'Sorry?'

'I fell in love with you Simon' Mitch revealed. 'You made everything about me and my life make sense for the first time and I wanted so much to tell you'.

Simon felt a surge of blood rush to his head. 'So why didn't you tell me?'

'I was going to' said Mitch. 'But I asked our Cheryl to sound you out and she came back and told me you weren't interested'.

'She never asked me anything' Simon insisted, tearfully. 'I asked her if you were gay and she told me you were definitely not gay'.

'But why would she do that?'

'How the hell would I know? But your sister deliberately kept us apart and I'm having a really hard time dealing with that. It's just a bit much after everything else just lately, you know, just a bit much'

Mitch felt awful. 'I don't know why she did that' he said. 'But I really wish she hadn't'.

'I'd never had the kind of feelings for any other man that I had for you' said Simon. 'We could've been together all these years if Cheryl hadn't lied to both of us'.

'It took me months to get over not being able to be with you'.

Simon's eyes were full of tears. 'This is just not fair. So Cheryl did know that the reason you were having problems with Nicola was because you were gay but hadn't come to terms with it?'

'She knew it all' Mitch confirmed. 'She knew that I left so suddenly because I'd fallen in love with you but, accordingly to her, you didn't feel the same'.

Simon felt his throat constrict. 'This is really breaking my fucking heart'.

'I had to get away' Mitch confessed. He was almost crying himself now. 'I couldn't be with you anymore if you didn't want me the way I wanted you'.

Simon wanted to scream with frustration at what had been taken away from him. 'But I did, Mitch, I did want you in the same way and I've never stopped wanting you. Jesus fucking Christ! Why was your sister so fucking nasty?'

'I've got no idea' said Mitch who was feeling pretty raw. He loved his intended Paul but Simon was a candle in his heart that would never go out. 'Why didn't you just make a move on me?'

'Because I didn't want to offend you' cried Simon desperately. 'I didn't want to risk the great times we were having. Mitch, I can't believe we could've spent all this time together and been happy. I've been so miserable all these years. Getting drunk on my own and falling into bed. Buying a meal for two deal at the supermarket and eating it all myself. I've never been able to get over you and now it seems I didn't have to'.

'It's come as a bit of a shock to me too'.

'She destroyed everything we could've had'.

'Didn't you ever meet anyone else?'

'No' said Simon. 'I'm not one of those people who gets their broken heart mended, Mitch. Life doesn't do happy endings for me'.

'Oh Christ, Simon, I'm so, so sorry'.

'It isn't your fault' said Simon. 'But it sounds like life put your heart back together again?'

'Paul? Well yeah, we've been together for about eight years now and I have to say we are very happy'.

Simon just couldn't get over this. 'I don't know what to say, Mitch'.

'Simon, I really wish it hadn't turned out this way. I really mean that'.

'Yeah, well it has' said Simon who took a deep breath and knew what he had to do.

'Let me take you home' said Mitch.

'I haven't got a home. I'm living in a b and b. I lost my job, I got into money troubles and had to go bankrupt. If I declare myself homeless they'll put me in a hostel with drug addicts and alcoholics. But don't worry about me when you're tucking into your wedding cake and no doubt jetting off on some romantic honeymoon'.

'I can understand why you feel bitter'.

'Bitter? Oh bitter doesn't even begin to cover it'.

'Simon, if I'd have known how you felt it might've been us getting married'.

'Oh please just don't say anymore! I really can't stand anymore of what might've been'.

'But all this trouble you're in. Is there anything I can do?'

'Like what?'

'I don't know' said Mitch, helplessly. 'Give you some money?'

'I'm not taking your money as some sort of consolation prize, Mitch, and besides, even if your cash got me out of trouble then I'd still be left with a heart that's beyond broken'.

'Simon, I can't end it with Paul' Mitch pleaded. 'Despite how conflicted I feel now about you and me I can't break his heart'.

'But you're happy enough to break mine?' said Simon. 'Whenever the universe needs a heart to break I'm always number one on the list. I suppose it's consistent'.

'We've built a life together, Simon' said Mitch.

'I'm sure you have'.

'Simon, I'm worried about you'.

'Well don't be' said Simon who'd calmed down a little and was trying to be as dignified as he could. 'I'm not your responsibility'. He stood up and made to leave.

'Simon … ?'

'… I'm sorry, Mitch but I've got to go' Simon pleaded. 'Our moment was taken away from us but at least you've had the chance to make it all better. I hope you enjoy your wedding day and I really do hope Paul makes you as happy as I would've done'.

'Simon, please?'

'What is there left to say? You're happy and I'm not but that's just life. Now I really can't stand this any longer so please just let me go'.

Simon had been friends with Mitch's sister Cheryl for several years before they shared a house together. Simon had sold his place but hadn't been able to find another one. Cheryl had split up from her then boyfriend and needed to make a new start. It was an arrangement that they'd intended to last only six months or so but they ended up getting on so well and having so much fun that before they knew it they'd been sharing the house for almost two years. Then Cheryl met Adrian to whom she got married and Simon bought the house that he'd recently been evicted from.

Although they'd grown close during that time Simon was always aware that Cheryl was the kind of person who liked to get one up on even her friends. She always liked to be the one to be envied. Looking back there were several signs he should've read about her. She was little Miss can't do wrong. She was never in the wrong even when she quite clearly was. Most of Simon's other friends had never liked Cheryl. They were nice enough to her face but behind her back they all warned Simon that one day she'd let him down over something. And she had. She'd let him down big time. She'd let him down in just about the most heartbreaking way she could. With one act of deception she'd helped bring him to this state of misery and pain. Well she wasn't going to get away with it. It just wasn't fair.

He vaguely remembered her address even though they hadn't been in contact for years. He spent half of what remained of his weekly budget, such as it was, on the bus fare getting to the part of town where she lived which just happened to be the most exclusive suburb. Houses round there go for at least half a million and that's at the bottom end of the market.

'Oh? Hello?'

'Hello Cheryl' said Simon as calmly as he could. 'It's been a long time'. She looked uncomfortable. 'How've you been?'

'Fine' she answered. Mitch would be back soon and she didn't want the two of them to meet. Mitch had called a few minutes ago and said he was on his way. He'd sounded quite angry with her. She didn't know why.

'It's a shame we lost touch'.

'It sometimes happens. Life moves on'.

'Well I was thinking of you so I thought I'd drop by'.

'Well it's a … it's a good surprise' she said. 'I heard on the grapevine you've been in financial difficulties?'

'To put it mildly' said Simon. 'Look, are you going to ask me in?'

'Oh yeah, sorry, of course, come in and I'll put the kettle on'.

Simon followed Cheryl into her well appointed kitchen. She'd married well. Her husband was a top commercial lawyer with a nationwide reputation. She obviously led a good life. She probably had nothing to worry about. Simon had enjoyed her company once and he'd invested a lot in their friendship.

'I was thinking about when we shared that house together' said Simon as cheerfully as he could considering the anger he felt towards her. The right time would come for him to fire his gun.

'Happy days, eh?'

'Oh we had some good times there alright' Simon agreed. 'Remember that party we had?'

'Do I ever? It was the luckiest night of my life. That was the night I met my Adrian'.

'Oh yes of course it was'.

'It's our tenth anniversary next week' said Cheryl, beaming. 'We're still as happy as that night we met'.

'Well congratulations'.

'Thank you'.

'Your brother Mitch was supposed to have stayed for the party but he suddenly upped and left that morning. Can you remember why?'

'Well it was ten years ago, Simon'.

'Did he and his wife Nicola stay together?'

'Oh yes, they're really happy'.

Simon paused and then said 'How could I ever have called such a blatant and manipulative liar like you a friend of mine?'

'Sorry?'

'Oh I get it all now. Our friendship was based on your need to feel superior. You had to be the happy one whilst I had to stay miserable'.

'Do you normally walk into someone's home after ten years and start insulting them?'

'Only when they turned the luckiest night of their life into the unluckiest night of mine'.

'You really will have to explain'.

'Oh don't be so bloody cute. I stood in the kitchen at the end of that night we had the party with only a bottle of wine for company while you were making out with Adrian in the living room. And now I know that I could've been doing the same with the love of my life but you put a stop to it with your lies. I bumped into your brother Mitch today. He told me the truth. I expect he'll be back soon. I know he's staying with you'.

'Look, Simon, I'll make you that tea but then I really need to get on' said Cheryl avoiding his comments.

'Oh no you don't!' said Simon as he lunged forward and grabbed Cheryl's arm making her turn round and face him. The red mists were almost blinding him as he walloped her across the face with the back of his hand. 'You lying bitch!'

Cheryl tried to compose herself before saying 'Get out of my house'

Simon slapped her across the face again. He'd never been a

violent man but it was all he could think of as he looked at her. 'Why did you do it?'

'I don't have to answer to you' Cheryl sneered, trying not to look scared but feeling terrified. She rubbed the side of her face that he'd now struck twice. She could see the fury in his eyes but she could also see the pitiful hurt and pain. What could she say? She had lied. And to get out of it she'd probably have to lie some more.

'Yes you fucking well do! I could've been happy with your brother. He was everything to me and you knew that but instead you chose to lie to us both and keep us apart. All these years I've spent being lonely when I need not have been. Now I want to know why you did that to me, why you did that to your own brother for God's sake?'

'I had to accept that my big brother was gay even though I didn't like it'.

'Oh so you don't mind people being gay as long as it's not your own brother?'

'Something like that' she admitted. 'I knew that our parents wouldn't be happy about it and they still aren't, not really. But if that wasn't enough he was in love with you. I had to put a stop to it. You weren't suitable for him. You're pathetic and I wasn't going to let my brother be saddled with the likes of you. And yes, I had to be the lucky one whilst you remained the unlucky one. That's how friendship works for me'.

Simon felt a tightening in his chest and his breathing became heavy. 'You're evil'.

'Oh get over it' she snapped. 'Some people were born lucky but you weren't one of them'.

'I was a different person when I was with Mitch. I loved him and I now know that he loved me. I could've known happiness in my life if it wasn't for you'.

'You didn't deserve someone like Mitch. His partner Paul is ten times the man you are. He has his own business, a dealership selling BMW's and they have a wonderful house in south west London on the banks of the river Thames. It took me a long time to accept the way things are but now Mitch and Paul and Adrian and I have some wonderful times together and you see, you just wouldn't have been able to fit into Mitch's world and it would've been cruel of me to let you try. I was really doing you a favour. You'd have been so out of your depth'.

Simon's eyes widened as he leaned into Cheryl forcing her to back up against the unit next to the sink. Their faces were almost touching and Cheryl's face became etched in fear once again. 'I can't believe how callous and smug you are. Well let me tell you, you are nothing. Do you understand me? You are nothing! You are nothing except a piece of lying, cheating, scheming, nasty, viscous, lowlife, self-serving scum!'

Cheryl picked up a knife from on top of the kitchen unit and held it up in front of Simon's face.

'Going to stab me?' Simon goaded. 'Going to kill me? Go on, you may as well. I've been dead all my life and you finished me off the day you destroyed my one and only chance to come alive with Mitch. Thanks to you I've got to think of Mitch being married to Paul and I can't stand that. So go on, make my day and you'll be saving me the job because I've got nothing and nobody to live for now. But I'll know that the consequences of you doing it will mean that in a roundabout way you'll pay for the rest of your life because of what you did to me and your brother'.

'You're crazy'.

'No, I'm not. I just want you to pay for destroying my chance of happiness'.

Simon reached for another knife and got the reaction he wanted. Fearing she needed to defend herself Cheryl stabbed him. He felt the knife pierce his side and he immediately gasped for air. He reached down with his hand and felt that the blade had gone almost all the way in. He saw the shock in Cheryl's eyes and then she started shaking as she watched Simon stumble and try to keep himself upright. But then his legs gave way and he fell to the ground as the shock was replaced by the most agonizing pain. He could feel himself beginning to lose consciousness. Cheryl didn't know what to do. She'd stabbed the stupid little bastard. But he'd driven her to it. He'd goaded her and tormented her and driven her to it.

'Thank you' Simon whispered. 'Enjoy prison'. He tried to smile but it was too late.

The last thing that Simon heard before he left this world was the sound of Cheryl screaming. It made him feel the most incredible sense of peace.

SIX
RUTH

Colin Barnett was knackered when he got home from his business trip to Eastern Europe. The chairman of the firm would be proud of him however. He'd not only managed to exceed his sales target when it came to the industrial machinery, but he'd also managed to secure the ever more lucrative maintenance contracts that would keep the field teams in work for several years to come. Some of those guys loved spending up to five days a week travelling round the former communist countries that were now fully fledged members of the European system. They spent their evenings in the bars of places like Tallinn, Prague, and St. Petersburg, getting drunk on fast flowing, cheap local beer and forgetting they were married when some local bit of skirt made it clear she was ready to wrap her legs round them. Colin couldn't blame them. They probably only got sex at home under sufferance.

'He hates women, you know' said Ruth, Colin's friend and neighbour. She'd picked him up from Manchester airport the previous evening and was now sitting having breakfast with him after bringing in the Saturday morning papers. Colin loved the Guardian, the Independent, and the Times on a Saturday almost as much as he liked his Sunday papers.

'Who?' Colin asked.

'That bastard on the front page'.

Colin lifted up the main section and reminded himself of the eminent surgeon from Germany who'd perfected a revolutionary new way of performing open heart surgery that was going to save the lives of millions from heart disease. He couldn't work out why Ruth had set herself against him.

'How do you make that out?'

'Because it said in yesterday's Daily Mail which is the paper that tells you what you really need to know about a person ... '

'... you mean it loves to pull down anybody who's done any good in the world in that typically British cynical way. You can't just celebrate the good that someone has done in Daily Mail land. Oh no, you have to find where to stick the knife in and twist it'.

'... that he'd recently left his wife of twenty two years for a another woman. There, that rather takes the shine off his so-called achievements, wouldn't you say?'.

'No I wouldn't, not at all'.

'Colin, someone has got to stand up for morality in this increasingly immoral world'.

'Yeah, well it isn't you and it isn't the Daily fucking Mail'.

'Well all I can say is that his copy book is well and truly blotted by his behaviour in his private life'.

'Ruth, you know fuck all about his private life other than what you read about'.

'His poor wife looks heart broken in the picture'.

'So the next time you go and see the doctor are you going to ask him to sign an affidavit to say he's never had an affair before you'll let him treat you?'

'Now you're being ridiculous'.

'I am? You should listen to yourself. You're saying that a man's achievements in medicine are completely wiped out by the fact he's left his wife for another woman, in circumstances that you know nothing about?'.

'Well he can't be that much of a saint if he's prepared to do that' Ruth snarled. 'Typical man. More dick and ego than anything else'.

'You so need a shag'.

'Colin!'

'Well it's true! You're so full of pent up frustrations that they're starting to really twist your mind'.

'I don't need a man' she scoffed. 'I put some shelves up last week. There, that goes to show I don't need a man'.

'No, it just goes to show that you can put some shelves up' Colin countered.

'I don't need sex, Colin'.

'Ruth, you think it's some kind of sin to even fancy somebody! You're like all these married women in this street who probably think that sex means getting that new dining room suite or that holiday in Egypt. Sex is something they use to look down on men as if it's a sin of some kind, some primitive habit that all these naughty little boys have failed to grow out of'.

'Well it is'.

'Don't be soft'.

'Men just don't understand women when it comes to sex'.

'And women just don't understand men. It cuts both ways'.

'I couldn't have this conversation with you if you were straight'.

'Yes, you could' said Colin. 'It's just that you wouldn't allow yourself'.

'I wouldn't want to feel vulnerable talking about it to someone who could take advantage'.

'Hello, hold the front page! Not every straight man who talks to you wants to fuck you'.

'Yes, they do. You can tell'.

'With all due respect, Ruth, only women who don't get any attention think that'.

'Oh, excuse me!'

,'Well it's the truth. Look at that time we were all out together? That bloke in the club asked you to dance and you were so fucking rude to him. You know, I'd hate to be a straight man in today's world. It's almost like they're having to pay for all the sexism of the last generations'.

'I suppose you're going to argue against positive discrimination too?'

'Ruth, they've just promoted a woman to be head of human resources at work. Everybody knows she's fucking useless but she was the only woman on a shortlist of three. I rest my case'.

'Well isn't it time the balance was redressed in industry?'

'Not if it means promoting someone way beyond their capabilities just because of their gender' said Colin. 'That's not equality. That's just replacing jobs for the boys with jobs for the girls'.

'Where do people like you and me fit into today's world, Colin?'

'Well it should be wherever we want to fit in but it doesn't always feel that way' said Colin. 'We're the only single people on this street which feels quite depressing at times'.

'We should get married, you and I'.

Colin sighed. He couldn't think of anything worse than to be married to Ruth. Oh, she was a good neighbour and, most of the time, a good friend, but to be with her all the time? He'd have to have really given up the ghost for that to happen. 'It's an option to be considered for the future if neither of us meets Mr. Right' he said. 'I suppose the absence of sex would make it the perfect marriage'.

'Wouldn't it just'.

'But I haven't given up yet'.

'Did you meet anybody when you were away?'

'You could say that, yes'.

'Colin? You waited till now to tell me'.

'It's complicated'.

'When is it ever not?'

The restaurant in St. Petersburg had been recommended to Colin and he made his way there by a combination of the metro for the two stops from his hotel into the centre of the city and then on foot. It was only a block away from the famous Hermitage museum that Colin would never tire of visiting to gaze again at the superior pieces of historical artwork and he thought the place would be correspondingly expensive. But he'd decided to hang the expense, no matter how much it cost. He'd worked hard for his money and he was bloody well going to treat himself.

A tall, slim and typically Russian young twenty-something girl who had one of those smiles that suggested that she and her fellow countrymen were only just getting used to the idea, showed him to his table. She was in a one piece pink dress in what looked to Colin like a silk type of material and it was so short that she must have to purposely keep her legs together as she walked and then stood. The dress was sleeveless with shoulder straps that gave something for her straight auburn hair to rest on, and a top line just below her neck. Her soft features were in contrast to the set nature of her face. If she allowed her face to relax a bit more she would be quite beautiful. She was a little reminiscent of the old Soviet days with just a touch more make-up and a lot more style.

The moment when Colin's heart lurched however was when the waiter came to take his order. His name was Mikhail and he was tall and thick set. He had short dark brown eyes that was combed forward but exposing his entire forehead. His eyebrows were thick and very Russian, almost meeting in the middle above his nose. He had dark brown eyes, a wide smile and a cheekiness that Colin immediately warmed to. He wasn't fat but he was imposing with his straight unyielding shoulders, big arms, legs, and hands. He could probably dominate a small room with his presence. He spoke good English but it was what he wasn't saying that was interesting Colin. Those eyes and that smile were flirting. They were laughing as if the rest of the restaurant just wasn't there. It was one of those moments when two souls had been hurtling through the universe and had now finally found the one with whom they were meant to entwine. Colin thanked his lucky stars and hoped that he wasn't just getting away on an infatuation.

'So how old are you? Mikhail?'

Mikhail winked at him. 'Old enough not to have to tell you'.

'Oh come on, don't be shy'.

'Think of a number between twenty-two and twenty-four and you might get it right'.

'Twenty-three?'

'No, I was lying. I'm twenty-five'.

Colin watched Mikhail walk over to the service desk to punch his order into the machine and breathed in deeply. That young man was a little dreamboat sailing down Colin's tunnel to the sea. Or at least he was in Colin's dreams. Following each course Colin looked forward to Mikhail coming back to his table and engaging him in further conversation. It turned out that the restaurant belonged to Mikhail's father and that Mikhail had just finished university in Moscow and was learning the ropes before taking charge of a restaurant his father was planning to open in New York.

'A lot of people got very rich very quickly after the fall of the Soviet Union' said Colin.

'Russian people adapt very quickly to the changing situations' Mikhail explained. 'We've had to throughout history but today is a good time to be Russian'.

'With a strong man at the top?'

'We are a large country with many different groups. We need a strong leader to manage all of that. Democracy can't work here in the same way as it works in countries like Britain. That's what you in the west don't seem to understand'.

'Oh I understand' said Colin. 'I do business with the system here all the time. But I do accept that many people in my country probably wouldn't get it'.

'You understand my country?'

'I think I do, yes'.

'Then you'll understand why ... '

'... why what, Mikhail?'.

'Oh it doesn't matter '.

'Yes, it does' said Colin, desperate to sort out whatever knot had been tied in an otherwise harmonious evening. 'Did I say something wrong?'

'No, it's... I'll bring you your coffee'.

'That was the first of our awkward moments' Colin explained to Ruth. 'It was as if he wanted to say something but couldn't'.

'What do you think he wanted to say?'

'I found out the next night'.

'You went back there again?'

'Sure did' said Colin. 'I couldn't just leave it like that'.

'God, your bloody credit card bill'.

'I couldn't give a flying fuck about that, Ruth! I had to talk to Mikhail and try and get him to explain what he'd meant. Thankfully, he was on duty'.

'So you've come back?' said Mikhail without looking up at Colin. He just stood there with his pad and pen waiting for Colin to order another dinner that would cost him close to a hundred pounds.

'I needed to know what you meant when you started to say something last night and then stopped'.

'I thought you said you understood my country?'

'I do ... '

'... well then you'll understand that some things are better left alone. Now, the seabass is very good tonight'.

'Mikhail, I'm thirty-eight years old and I know when someone is trying to deny something about themselves'.

'We serve it with a selection of vegetables in a garlic sauce and I can recommend a recently imported Sauvignon Blanc to go with it'.

'Mikhail ... '

'... look you don't understand what you're risking for either me or yourself' said Mikhail, firmly but quietly so that nobody else would be able to hear. 'Why don't you take your English ways back to where they belong when you go home? Now, an appetiser for you?'

'Mikhail, we both knew as soon as we saw each other'.

'What I know is that you haven't completed your order'.

Colin finally made up his mind on an appetiser and ordered a large scotch on ice to start things off with. He felt terrible. How come love can make you so blind and so selfish? He should never have come here. It was pathetic to pursue the chance with this young Russian man from a different world. That's the trouble with people from the west. They always think their ways are supreme and that they have a right to practice them wherever they go. They never think of the consequences for those they're touching with their desire. He glanced around, certain that he was set for another heartache and beating himself up for being so fucking naive. The restaurant was so elegant. All the tables had fresh white linen cloths and soft black leather chairs that didn't have a single mark or scratch on them. There were two enormous chandeliers hanging from the ceiling at each end and the place was busy. It looked like Mikhail's father had a full house. Colin wondered what he was like. Would he be a frightening, imposing figure that Mikhail had every reason to be scared of? Or would he be a simple man in business to make money and who would love his son no matter what he turned out to be? Was it Mikhail who was more worried about himself than about anybody else? Was that the problem?

'And was it?' Ruth wanted to know.

'No' said Colin. 'I actually met his father that night. He came into the restaurant to say hello to all the clientele. Mikhail actually introduced me and explained that this was my second visit in a row'.

'What was his father like?'

'Quite a soft, gentle, unassuming type' Colin recalled. 'A tall man with grey hair and wearing a burgundy coloured leather bomber jacket. He sat at my table and talked with me for a minute or so, thanked me for my custom, blah de blah de blah. But he seemed okay'.

'I'll bet he's an absolute tyrant at home and what you saw was just an act put on for the customers' said Ruth.

'Oh trust you to bring his character down just because he's a man'.

'But men are so duplicitous' Ruth insisted.

'And women aren't?'

'Only if they're driven to it by men'.

'Oh for fuck's sake, look, are you going to listen to the rest of the story without coming out with all this anti male bullshit?'

'I speak the truth'.

'As you see it from your own very narrow, very twisted perspective' Colin insisted. 'You know what a merry dance my Mum has led my Dad all these years and yet, more fool him, he keeps on taking her back because he loves her'.

'Well you're probably too close to see how much your Dad drives her to it and has made her so dependent on him that she can never really leave'.

'How can you even begin to defend my Mum making a fool of my Dad the way she does? She flirts with other men in front of him for God's sake! She rubs his bloody nose in it'

'Like I said, a woman's behaviour can always be explained and there's usually a man behind it somewhere'.

'Christ, Ruth, you really need to open your bloody eyes!'

'Look, I know enough about men to know that they're always responsible for a woman's bad behaviour'.

'That's absolute crap!'

'No, it isn't'.

'So my Mum's affairs with other men are all my Dad's fault?'

'I think they probably are deep down, yes'.

Colin was close to blowing his top. How fucking dare Ruth condemn his father when it was his mother who'd done wrong. His mother needed more attention than any one man could give her and as far as Colin was concerned, his father was either mad or a saint for taking her back as many times as he had.

'Well alright then' said Ruth. 'Tell me the rest about lover boy Mikhail and we'll see who's right about men'.

Colin watched Mikhail and his father together. They were obviously close. It made Colin think of his own father and how close he was to him. But his father would never stand in the way of his relationship and he was convinced that Mikhail's father wouldn't stand in the way of his son's happiness either, despite the difference between British and Russian families. So what did Mikhail mean? Why couldn't he just take Mikhail out for a drink somewhere?

'Look, I'm really sorry about this' said Mikhail after he'd sidled up to Colin's table once his father had moved onto the other side of the restaurant.

'You don't have to be sorry' said Colin.

'I have to go dancing tonight'.

'Are you a good dancer?'

Mikhail flashed Colin that cheeky grin that Colin had come to love so much. 'Of course'.

Colin didn't know why but he just wanted the ground to open up and swallow him and take him as far away from this situation as possible. He then followed Mikhail's eyes to a young woman who'd just walked into the restaurant. She was dressed in an elegant camel coloured coat and her black hair and dark looks came from what Colin later found were her parents who'd moved to St. Petersburg from the former Central Asian Soviet satellite republic of Kazakhstan. 'Who's the girl?'

'Her name is Anastasia' said Mikhail. 'We're engaged to be married'.

'Oh my God!' gasped Ruth. 'The deceitful son of a bitch. What did you do?'

'I left the restaurant'.

'But where did you go? Back to the hotel?'

'Eventually' Colin revealed. 'I wanted some air first'.

It wasn't the first time that Colin had fallen for someone whose sexuality was dubious. He seemed to have met a lot like that in his time and he didn't know why. They just seemed to find him. Not for any romantic purposes usually. Colin often felt like he was the one they came out to but not the one they came out for. Bus this time was different. This time he really did believe that he'd made the young man with the big expressive eyes think again about his impending nuptials. But typical of Colin's luck for it to happen in a faraway land that was now open but not for every type of happiness. Why couldn't it have happened in somewhere like Barnsley where the only barrier between them and their future happiness would be the M62?

He wandered down to one of the many canal sides in this great historical city that until only recently was known as Leningrad. He wondered what Lenin would've made of the way things turned out for his revolution. He suspected he wouldn't have liked it at all. They'd exchanged the oppression of the Tsars with labour camps for those who wouldn't accept the party line, appearances and executions for the liberation of justice, royal corruption for party corruption, a royal elite for a party elite. Then, decades later, perestroika to cleanse the system and make it alright for people to have aspirations. The kind of democracy based on materialism that looked like anything the masses of the West would be happy with. Everyone obsessed with brands like Nike, McDonalds, and Dolce and Gabbana. They weren't interested in goods made by the people for the people. Even the dishonesty of that had been abandoned. A lot of people were getting rich, many more were staying poor, and there wasn't much in the middle. Colin was no revolutionary but he did think that the whole concept of democracy needed something of an overhaul because he didn't see that in any country all the people were benefitting from it.

He bought himself a packet of cigarettes from a small shop that was still open and lit one up. He started smoking it whilst leaning forward on the railing that stopped people from falling over the edge into the canal. This was not the first time he'd been in this kind of emotionally reflective mood. Nor was it the first time he'd felt a sharply chilly wind blow on such a warm and balmy summer's evening. It would be so good to sit down with a lover and talk about stuff with someone who really knew him and what he was on about. One of the first things he'll ask God if he gets up there is why some people find their soul mate whilst others carry the burden of loneliness like the weight of a thousand stones in their heart. He had a nice house, a bloody good job, he wasn't short of cash, he had some great friends but they were all, with the exception of his neighbour Ruth, in a couple of one form or another. He was so tired of doing everything alone. And now he'd made a fool of himself once more with a man who he'd have to hope would be there for him in the next life. That's how he consoled himself at times like this. Otherwise, what would be the point of life delivering him into the heart of someone he couldn't have?
Surely if it meant anything it was that Mikhail and all the others like him were glimpses into some future life? Or perhaps even reminders of the glories of past journeys on earth? These were theories that lasted until he could lay his hands on some alcohol. It was all very well thinking about past lives and future lives. He'd like a bit of benevolence from the universe in this one.

He looked up and saw a half decent looking bar on the corner of the street. He planned to get a little hammered and then take a taxi back to his hotel. He threw his now smoked cigarette butt into the canal and was about to walk off when he felt a tap on his shoulder. He turned round and it was Mikhail. He'd changed. He was now in a hooded grey jacket and blue jeans. His hands were in his pockets.

'Where's Anastasia?' asked Colin.

'She's gone home' said Mikhail.

'I thought you were going dancing?'

'I said I was tired. She understood. She always does'.

'She sounds very understanding. When's the big day?'

'The what?'

'The wedding?'

'Oh, it's not until next year'.

'I've got time to save up for a new suit then'.

'What?'

'Nothing, it doesn't matter. It was just a figure of speech'.

'Sometimes I don't know what you mean because of my English' Mikhail explained. 'I want to understand but I don't'.

'What is it you want to understand, Mikhail?'

'Myself' answered Mikhail. 'And what that means to you'.

They went back to Colin's hotel where they made love once, twice, and again in the morning. Colin held Mikhail in his arms and Mikhail held on like he would fall if he let go. When Colin finally woke up the space in the bed beside him was empty but then he heard noises coming from the bathroom which reassured him that Mikhail hadn't just upped and done a runner. He got out of bed and walked round to where he could lean against the open bathroom doorway and watch the naked Mikhail splashing some water on his face.

'Dobrau utro' said Colin.

Mikhail turned and smiled at him. 'Dobrau utro'.

Colin stepped forward and wrapped his arms round Mikhail. His body was firm, his nipples large and he had a small patch of hair in the middle of his chest. Colin loved the bones of him. He rested his chin on Mikhail's shoulder and they looked at each other in the mirror.

'You can't tell me that was your first time?' said Colin.

'No' Mikhail answered. 'Of course I've been with men before'.

'I thought so'.

'But not like that'.

'Like what?'

'Oh I don't know ... you know better than me what I'm trying to say'.

'What are we going to do, Mikhail?'

'There's nothing we can do' said Mikhail, his face slipping from the gaze of Colin's eyes. 'I have to marry Anastasia'.

'Why do you have to marry her?'

'Because her father is investing in my father's business and if I break off the engagement he won't make good on that investment and the deal my father has to open the restaurant in New York will fall through. I can't do that to him'.

'One business deal measured against a whole lifetime?'

'To someone from the West, yes' said Mikhail. 'But to businessmen like me and my father it means the old days are finally gone. It's much bigger than one love affair'.

'But how will you feel, Mikhail? How will you feel when you look at Anastasia knowing that you don't love her? How will you feel when you have children inside a loveless marriage?'

'I do love Anastasia'.

'You can't' said Colin. 'Not after last night'.

'Colin, I will never forget last night but I said to you before that you didn't understand the ways of my country. And you don't'.

Colin accepted defeat and though he wished to God he could turn the clock back and have last night all over again, he knew that the inevitable was about to happen and his happiness had been a momentary snatch from the jaws of solitude. He'd save his crying for later.

'Want to step in the shower with me?' he asked.

'I thought you'd never ask'.

'You know some English sayings then?'

'I saw someone say it in a film' Mikhail replied. 'Someone big and handsome, just like you'.

One week later

It wasn't the first time that Colin had received strange phone calls. The last time, just like this one, they'd come through at all hours of the day and night and the caller had been there at the other end but hadn't said anything. It had driven Colin mad, especially when he'd received them at times like three in the morning. It had gone on for weeks until Colin had asked the telecoms company to put a trace on his line. It turned out that the calls had come from some stupid girl in his office who'd had a crush on him and thought she might be able to tip him over into the ways of men and women. How she was going to do that when she didn't even say anything during these calls remained a mystery to Colin but shortly after she'd been discovered she left the company and Colin has never heard from her since.

It would seem a fairly wild coincidence that after his brief encounter with Mikhail in St. Petersburg during which he gave Mikhail all his contact numbers, that the calls would be coming from anybody else. But he didn't know what to do. That first and last morning Mikhail had left his hotel room and Colin had watched him from his window disappearing into the crowds on the city streets. He'd flown home that afternoon looking round all the time at the airport in case Mikhail decided to turn up. He checked his mobile for messages but none came. He really thought that had been the end of it all. A burning heartache that would eventually, with time, become a delightful memory that would warm his consciousness during the coming cold of winter. He'd never forget Mikhail. But he'd one day come to terms with the fact that he couldn't be with him. He'd had a lot of practice at doing that.

But another strange thing had happened this time. The calls had stopped as suddenly as they'd started just after his return from Russia. For three or four days they'd gone on and then nothing. As he drove home from work he realised that the calls had stopped the night his neighbour Ruth had been round waiting for a local builder who was due to come round and quite Colin for an extension at the back of his house.

He pulled onto his drive and looked over to see if Ruth's car was there. It was so he went straight round. She poured him a glass of wine from the bottle she was consuming and they sat down in her lounge.

'Ruth, are you sure there were no calls when you were sitting in my place on Wednesday night?'

She hesitated then said 'No. Why?'

'It's just that the strange calls I was getting stopped that night'.

'So what's that got to do with me?'

'Well nothing' said Colin. 'I was just wondering if you'd remembered any calls coming through, that's all. Sometimes you don't remember until a few days later'.

'I told him I was your wife'.

'What did you say?'

'It was your stupid Russian lover who'd taken all those calls to pluck up the guts to speak to you and I told him I was your wife!'

'What the fuck did you do that for?'

'To save you from making the biggest mistake of your life!'

'How fucking dare you!'

'Colin, I'm your best friend and I was protecting you'.

'You were interfering in things that don't concern you' said Colin who was furious. 'God, what must he think of me?'

'Well he'll forget you now and you can go back to living your life and getting on with it in the same way as before'.

'But I hate the way I live my life! Don't you understand? I'm not like you. I've got the guts to admit that I need a man in my life instead of covering it up like you do with all your anger and resentment'.

'Oh, so that's what I do, is it?'

'You know you do! It's as clear as day what you long for and yet the lady doth protest way too much'.

'But what would I do if you ended up living in bloody Russia?'

Colin looked at her with a mixture of rage and pity. 'Whatever you need to do, Ruth'. He stood up and made for the front door.

'Where are you going?'

'To pack a case. I've still got some time left on my Russian visa. I'm going to fly out there as soon as I can get a flight'.

'But what about work?'

'I'll take some time off! Christ, Ruth! You know, there's something pretty sad about a straight woman who attaches herself to a gay man. I intend to get a life, Ruth. So should you'.

Less than twenty four hours later as he walked into Mikhail's father's restaurant in St. Petersburg his memory of his row with Ruth was fading fast. He was sorry it had happened. They'd been good friends for a long time but he had grown tired of her bitterness and her neurotic anti-man attitude. He'd sort it out with her when he got back. In the meantime he had other matters to sort out.

As soon as Mikhail saw him he came straight over to his table.

'Does your wife know you're here?' Mikhail wanted to know with more attitude than Colin thought he deserved.

'I don't have a wife, Mikhail'.

'But the woman on the phone ... '

'... the woman on the phone is my friend who thought she was doing the right thing by putting you off. Anyway, how's Anastasia?'

'She knows there's something wrong with me' Mikhail admitted. 'She can tell how much my mood has changed and last night she accused me of not loving her anymore'.

'And do you?'

'No' said Mikhail as he played with the menu in his hands.

'Come away with me, Mikhail'.

'As if it were that easy'.

'Well alright, I'll move over here'.

'Like that's easy too! You westerners are too romantic'.

'Mikhail, I want to be with you. Don't you feel the same?'

'You know I feel the same'.

'Then we can make it happen' Colin insisted. 'West or east, north or south, Russia or fucking anywhere, I don't care as long as we're together'.

'You've come all this way to tell me that?'

'Well I wanted to know why you didn't say anything when you called?'

'Because I was scared' Mikhail admitted. 'I was going to see if I could come over and see you for a few days'.

'And then Ruth stuck her bloody oar in'.

'Her what? Her oar?'

'It really doesn't matter' said Colin. 'It's just another one of those English expressions. If you'd only spoken to me when you first called you could've been in my house right now'.

'It isn't as easy as you seem to believe, Colin'.

'Maybe not' said Colin. 'But it's worth a try?'

'Look, have your meal and then we'll talk' said Mikhail. 'We've got a full house in tonight and I need to get back to work. But I promise we'll talk later'.

Mikhail hadn't been kidding. The restaurant filled up over the next half hour and as Colin waited for his main course his head turned, like all the other patrons, when he heard a car screech up outside and two masked men came bursting in through the door.

Mikhail knew exactly who the men were. His father owed money to the wrong people in St,Petersburg and they'd threatened to come after Mikhail if his father didn't pay up. He didn't believe they would actually do it. He thought they were bluffing, just like so many of the idle threats that are made. But this was no bluff. People started screaming and everyone got down under the tables. But Colin couldn't do that. He saw that the men had pointed their guns directly at Mikhail and he leapt into the space between them. His body twisted and turned with each bullet and then he came to rest on the floor. The assailants then ran out and jumped back into the car that had brought them there.

Mikhail knelt down and lifted Colin's head in his hand. He was crying. 'Colin, I'm sorry, I'm so, so sorry'. Colin tried to speak but he couldn't. Blood was pouring out of his mouth and the light that had brought him into this life was fading fast. 'I'll never forget you, Colin. I promise I will never, ever forget you'.

Colin tried to squeeze Mikhail's hand and then he was gone.

SEVEN
JESSICA

Susan Bailey was thirty-six years old. She didn't make anything of herself. She didn't use make-up and the clothes she wore made her look like a woman twice her age. Nobody ever bought her anything for Christmas or her birthday and she didn't have a circle of friends to be with. She existed as Susan Bailey, spinster, living in the semi-detached house she'd grown up in on an anonymous road in Cheadle, one of the more bland of South Manchester suburbs and therefore one of the most sought after for those who think they needed to live in the 'right' area. It was a place for people who'd searched and found the kind of family life that would sustain them for the rest of their lives. It wasn't the sort of place that Susan Bailey could find much in the way of inspiration now that her mother had died.

Susan had been engaged once. Phil was a mechanic at the local garage and when she was with him she'd become a different person. He'd brought out everything in her that her family had suppressed. He didn't earn much and in her parents eyes would never amount to much but he loved her and she adored him. He didn't live in Cheadle either, which was another reason why her parents had disliked him. He came from Failsworth, a not so salubrious part of the city, full of back-to-back terraced housing and council funded dwellings. At least Phil's parents had owned their own home but that wasn't enough for Susan's family. Phil still came from the 'wrong' area so he wasn't suitable for their daughter. They did everything they could to make him feel unwelcome when he came round to the house but Susan had soldiered on, determined that this time she would get her way.

But then Susan's father became sick. A combination of emphasima and angina meant that he had to have a bed made up downstairs. Then her mother was struck down with parkinsons' disease and another room downstairs had to be turned into a bedroom. It was all taken for granted. There was no discussion. No agreement was made. Susan had to give up work to look after her parents and that was that. Her older sister Jessica was married with a daughter called Emma and couldn't possibly help Susan when she had her own family to take care of and a career. She was a buyer for one of the country's biggest female clothing labels and was forever telling Susan how proud their parents were that she'd married 'so well' to company director Jonathan and had done 'so well' in her chosen career too, not to mention dear Emma and the gorgeous detached house in Hale where every bedroom was en-suite. Susan got sick of hearing it but never said much. Instead of rubbing Susan's nose in it whenever she came round on her weekly half-hour visits, Susan wished Jessica would do something practical in the house that would allow Susan to sit down and take it easy for a short while. But Jessica couldn't do that or else she'd ruin her perfectly manicured nails. Their parents never asked her to do anything. They were too enthralled with her tales of the Cheshire set life she led and would go back to being as grumpy as hell with Susan once Jessica had gone and taken the sunshine with her. Susan had sacrificed her life for them but nothing she ever did was right. They never expressed any gratitude or thanks. Jessica was the golden girl and always had been. Nobody ever cared about Susan's feelings. They were dismissed. She had to brake off her engagement to Phil. He'd begged her not to but there was no way she could ever get married whilst she had her parents to look after and whilst they expected her to be there for them. A few months after Susan had broken it off with Phil he met someone else and eventually married her. The day of their wedding was the saddest day of Susan's life. Secretly she cried her heart out all day. She'd lost him forever and there was nobody she could turn to. She still sees him out and about. He's got three little kids now and a life that Susan should've been leading with him. The garage where he works is only a mile or so away and if he sees her when he's passing he gives her a wave which initially makes her day and then destroys it when she thinks of what could've been. He doesn't wave if his wife Donna is with him. On those occasions he just looks and then looks away again.

She suddenly thought about Phil as she sat in the office of family lawyer Martin Robotham waiting to be called in. She'd love it if he walked through the door right now. She'd probably never stop loving him.

'I see you've dressed suitably for the occasion' said Jessica who was sat beside Susan and was dressed all in black from her wide-rimmed hat to her polished high heels. Susan was in an ordinary skirt and blouse with a light grey jacket. She didn't have much else and couldn't afford to buy anything either.

'I don't think there's a dress code for the reading of a will'

Susan snapped.

'There's no need to be like that, Susan' said Jessica in her high handed reproachful way. 'I was only saying'.

'No you weren't, you were having a go just like you always do'.

'I didn't realise you were so sensitive about stepping out of your comfort zones'.

'You don't realise much where I'm concerned. You never have'.

'Susan, can't we try and get on? We're all we've got left'.

'You've got Jonathan and Emma'.

'But you're my sister' Jessica entreated. 'We need to be there for each other now'.

'Do you mean that?'

'Of course I do' Jessica insisted. 'Why wouldn't I?'

'Because you've never taken any interest in whatever I've done before, not even when we were little. You didn't even choose me as a bridesmaid at your wedding'.

Jessica placed her hand on Susan's. 'I know it's going to be hard for you to accept that I'm being genuine but let's put all that behind us now, shall we? Start again? I know we've left it pretty late but surely we can try?'

Susan wasn't sure. Jessica turning into a proper sister was a bit hard to take but Susan was feeling desperately lonely and she thought that perhaps some bridges could be built.

'Where's Jonathan?' Susan asked.

'He's in the States on business' Jessica revealed. 'He's about to conclude a deal that's going to make the company an awful lot of money'.

'Good for him' said Susan, quietly.

'Yes, he's flying back from San Francisco first class on Friday' Jessica revealed.

'Isn't that very expensive?'

'Well once you've tasted first class you can't possibly go back to flying in economy'

'I wouldn't know' said Susan. 'The express bus into Manchester is as far as I get'.

'Yes, well that's your reality' said Jessica. 'Whereas my reality is something quite different'.

'And that's what you put it down to? My life is beyond compare to yours and it's all down to a difference in reality?'

'I thought we were starting again?'

Susan took a deep breath. 'We are' she said. 'We are'.

They were called in to see Martin Robotham and immediately Jessica open her arms and gushed 'Martin! So wonderful to see you!'

Martin and Jessica exchanged air kisses and he shook Susan's hand. Jessica took over the whole situation and Susan let her. She was so at ease dealing with people whereas Susan didn't have much of a clue. She felt like she'd been living under a rock for so long. It was as if she had to start learning how to live again. Maybe Jessica's overtures meant that she would be willing to help her. She needed someone. It may as well be her sister.

But then her moment of hope was crushed. She could hear Martin Robotham speaking the words but she didn't believe them. It couldn't be. Her mother couldn't have been that cruel.

'... the family home at 37 Bathgate Avenue, Cheadle is left entirely to Jessica to do with as she pleases. Her father and I have many fond memories of our darling daughter in that home and it's only right that she should have it. She can keep it or sell it. Current market value puts it at around four hundred and fifty thousand pounds. All of my jewellery is left for my dear granddaughter Emma whose been a credit to us since the day she was born ... '

'She goes on' Robotham continued. He hadn't looked at Susan throughout the reading. 'To detail various investments and money in two accounts all of which total one hundred and twenty thousand pounds. All of this is also left to Jessica'.

'Then ... well what's left for me?' asked Susan, feebly.

Robotham cleared his throat. 'Nothing I'm afraid'.

'Nothing?' Susan repeated.

'Other than the wish that you're able to start your life again and make a success of it and to understand that the will has been written in this way because your sister Jessica has a daughter and her husband has a thriving business. She needs the money more than you do'.

'But I've got nothing!' cried Susan. She was distraught. 'My sister has got a house and a family and a job. I gave up my life to take care of my parents and this is how they thank me?'

'I will be selling the house, Martin' Jessica announced, ignoring her sister's quite obvious distress. 'It will be a useful sum to put into Jonathan's business. I'm sure many of your other clients have told you how difficult it still is for businesses to get credit in the current climate'.

'But that's my home!' Susan protested.

'Was your home, Susan, was your home. I won't expect you to move out until it's sold so you can't say I'm being unfair'.

'But where am I going to go? I haven't got any money!'

'You can get help' said Jessica. 'God knows people like Jonathan and I pay enough tax so that people like you can be accommadated appropriately'.

'But where do you expect me to go? Some council flee pit?'

'You'll need to get a job, Susan, so you can earn some money which will enable you to make some choices'.

'Jessica, why are being like this? I'm begging you!'

'You've always said I was selfish, Susan. Well I'm just proving your point for you'.

Susan out her head in her hands and wept. She was utterly devastated by what had happened. She couldn't believe her parents could've done this to her but what was even more heart breaking was Jessica's attitude. She really didn't care. She'd got everything and she really didn't care that her own sister was now homeless and destitute.

'Susan?' said Robotham. 'Let's see if we can work something out'.

Susan lifted her head. 'What?'

'Jessica?' said Robotham. 'This is a time when as a family you should pull together'.

'My mother's will is quite clear, Martin' said Jessica. 'She left everything to me'.

'But your sister really does have nothing'.

'And that's my problem because?'

'She's your sister, Jessica!'

'Yes, and it's about time she learned to stand on her own two feet'.

'You rotten bitch!' Susan cried. 'All those years I looked after them and you came round for half an hour once a week to talk about yourself and your wonderful life. You even admitted to passing the end of the street countless times but you never called in. You never once asked me how I was doing. You never once offered to help. All that talk before about starting again? You were just softening me up in case the will went in my favour'.

'Every good strategist needs to make contingency plans' said Jessica. 'That's why I'm in the position I am in life and you're where you are'.

Susan shook her head. 'The way you talk. It's so cold'.

'Well look, now that it's all over and done with there's nothing to keep me here' Jessica announced as she stood up. 'I've got plans to make. You know, Susan, everybody has a purpose in life and you know what yours has been? To show me that parents who adore their first child should never have a second one because they just won't be able to love it as much. That's why I never had anymore children after my darling Emma. I wouldn't have wanted them to end up like you'.

And with that she swept out of the room leaving her broken hearted sister crying her eyes out on Robotham's shoulder.

The next few days proved to be a really testing time for Susan. The morning after the reading of the will her sister Jessica assigned an estate agent and Susan's home went up for sale. Miraculously, given the state of the housing market, it sold for the full asking price of 495,000 within the week. Susan had to gather the shattered pieces of her life and move herself on to somewhere else.

She had about a hundred pounds in her bank account and that

was all. She had no savings. She hadn't earned a wage for several years and she'd received no regular income from her parents or the state whilst she cared for her Mum and Dad. The solicitor Martin Robotham had again appealed to Jessica to release some funds for Susan to help her sister get on her feet but again Jessica had refused. Robotham did find her a flat, a small one bedroom conversion in an old mansion block at the back of Stockport station on the road that eventually led to her old home in Cheadle. The flat, which was owned by a lawyer friend of Robotham's, was furnished but she still needed a few essentials like bed linen, a kettle, a TV. Robotham bought them all for her and a week's supply of groceries. His kindness broke her heart again but this time in a good way. It gave her a little confidence that she would find people who would help her. The area that the flat was in wasn't the best but it was okay and once she got used to the sound of the trains going in and out of the station she'd be alright. She needed housing benefit to be able to pay the rent and this was, thankfully, paid to her in full.

At the Stockport job centre she was assigned a caseworker called Nathan. He was softly spoken and kind, he had powder blue eyes and a big wedding ring on his finger. He was about the same age as Susan but their lives had been so different. He'd travelled after graduating from university and had gone into the civil service because he'd wanted to 'do something useful'. He was proud of his wife and his little daughter and Susan had a crush on him from the start. They clicked and she looked forward to their fortnightly meetings like a lovestruck teenager looked forward to seeing her man. It was pathetic but it helped her through.

The only job she'd ever had was as an office admin assistant for a local firm but she'd resigned from that back in 2002 when her parents first became ill. Nathan said that the best thing to do was to update her skills so he arranged for her to do some courses in IT and finding her way around the modern world of computers. He sympathised with her plight. He thought it was awful the way she'd been treated by her family. She'd broken down during one of their meetings. He'd been so good about it. The touch of his arm round her shoulder had meant everything. She was the sort who had to be grateful for small mercies.

'Susan!'

Susan couldn't believe it. She'd opened the door to her flat and it was Phil's voice that she could hear booming down the corridor. She turned round and there he was. He was a bit more chunk than hunk these days but other than that his late thirties really suited him. His hair was greyer than it used to be but he was still pretty fit. This was the attraction of a lifetime.

'I was just going for a walk' said Susan, rather more weakly than she'd intended. She'd been on the jobseekers allowance for a couple of months now and despite her meetings with Nathan, she was finding the whole process to be pretty hard going. The jobcentre itself was such a depressing place. She couldn't identify with any of the people there. She had to go out for walks to stop herself from emotionally crashing.

'I was in the area dropping a car off'.

'It's good to see you' said Susan. She'd always liked the look of him in his overalls, dirty oil stains on dark blue cotton. Underneath, he was wearing a red t-shirt with a white collar and the beginnings of his chest hair were clearly visible.

'What are you doing round here?' Phil asked.

'I live here'.

'Since when?'

'Since my Mum died and I was left out of the will'.

'Shit! I had no idea'.

'Can you stay for a coffee or tea?'

'I'm due a lunch break' said Phil. 'So, yeah. Get the kettle on'.

'It really is good to see you, Phil' said Susan. 'You don't know how much'.

'Sounds like we've got a lot of catching up to do?'

'We have' said Susan. 'But it's not a feel good story'.

'I didn't think so' said Phil. 'Just start at the beginning'

It all started off with Phil coming round for coffee and sometimes a bite of something for lunch. Susan began to spend her weekends dreaming about what she and Phil would be getting up to if they were together and by the time their re-kindled friendship progressed to sex, Susan was on cloud nine.

'Thank you' she said as she lay in Phil's arms on that first afternoon.

'What for?'

'For giving me my life back'.

Their affair lasted for several weeks, all the way through Susan starting work in the office of the local bus company, making sure that if someone needed the number 79, they knew where to get it in the labyrinth of Stockport's Mersey Square bus station. But she was happy. Phil's wife had found out about their affair and kicked him out but he'd moved in with Susan. She took care of him like her life depended on it. He woke up each morning and there was a mug of tea there, just the way he liked it, and she cooked meals for him in the evening that were invested with so much love. She'd got him back and she wasn't going to let him go again. The joy she felt about being with Phil made her forget all the shit that her sister and her parents had put her through. It was finally her time to be happy.

But Phil wasn't altogether happy. He knew he'd made the right decision to leave Donna for Susan. He loved Susan in a way he'd never loved Donna but he missed his three kids.

Donna made it clear that she was going to use the children as a weapon against Phil. She wouldn't agree to any visiting order and she told Phil that if he went ahead with a divorce then she'd take the kids away somewhere and he'd never see them again.

It was New Year's Eve when Susan finished work early and went down to the supermarket to buy the rest of the things she needed for her dinner with Phil that night. They were going to eat at home and then join their friends at the pub to see the new year in. She had a spring in her step. They'd had a fantastically happy Christmas and she'd never looked forward to a New Year's Eve quite so much.

When she got home she went into the kitchen and put all the food away. Phil was going to pick up the wine. Then she noticed the note on the table. It was clearly in Phil's handwriting. He said he was sorry but though he loved her, he couldn't bear to be without his kids so he was going back to Donna. He said he hoped she'd understand.

She let the note slip from her fingers and threw up all over the kitchen floor.

Three months later

It was just after ten on a Sunday morning when the buzzer started blaring out in Susan's flat. It was unusual for the buzzer to go off on any morning because she never had any visitors but she thoughtlessly went to answer it.

'Yes?'

'It's me, Susan'.

'Who?'

'Your sister Jessica'.

'Oh' she said and then pressed the button to open the front door downstairs. She threw a big baggy cardigan over the long t-shirt she'd been wearing in bed and went into the kitchen, stopping on the way to open the door for Jessica. She heard Jessica come in and close the door behind her.

'It'll have to be black if you want tea or coffee' said Susan without turning round and looking at her sister. 'I'm right out of milk'.

'Is the coffee instant?'

Susan could've slapper her. 'Of course it's bloody instant. Funnily enough I've never had the money to buy one of those fancy coffee machines'.

'Then I'll have tea'.

'So sorry to disappoint'.

'I heard Phil moved in with you for a while?'

'Yes' said Susan who was picking at the wrapping around a box of tea bags. 'He went back to his wife because of the children'.

'That must've been hard for you' said Jessica. 'I'm sorry'.

'Jessica, what the hell do you want?'

'I'm dying, Susan'.

It was then that Susan noticed the felt hat that was covering her sister's head and the lines on a previously flawless face. 'What of?'

'Leukemia' said Jessica. 'Do you think I could sit down?'

Susan pulled back one of the chairs at the kitchen table and Jessica sat down. Susan sat in the other chair.

'Jonathan drove me here. He's outside in the car. He thought we should have this conversation in private'.

'Can they do anything?'

'Yes. That's why I'm here'.

'I don't understand?'

'I need a bone marrow transplant, Susan, and the best match would be you'.

'That's what you've come here for? To ask me to save your life?'

'In a nutshell, yes'.

'Then the answer is no' said Susan who felt powerful for the first time in her life.

'Susan? I'm dying!'

'It happens to us all eventually'.

'How can you be so callous?'

'As if you don't know? You've hated me all my life! You let me give up everything to take care of our parents and then you scooped up all the cash once they'd gone and wouldn't even give me the price of the bus fare home from the solicitors! And now you walk in here expecting me to come to your aid? You really think the world revolves around you, don't you?'

Jessica had tears in her eyes. She hadn't been expecting such an outright refusal from Susan. It had come as quite a shock.

'Susan, you may as well be signing my death warrant by refusing to do this'.

'Oh and if it was an execution I'd be on the front row to watch you burn and scream'

Jessica stood up and steadied herself. 'I suppose I'd better go. I haven't got the strength to argue with you'.

'Tell Jonathan not to bother inviting me to the funeral' said Susan. 'I'll be celebrating that day'.

Jessica was crying. 'I never knew you hated me so much'.

'Because you never asked me!. Because you and Mum and Dad always acted as if my feelings didn't matter. Yes, I've carried it for a long time and now I'm in a position to finally deny you something and it feels oh so good'.

'But I'm dying!'

'And I couldn't care less! You sent me into this arse end of hell with your selfishness and your greed. Just think about that when St. Peter comes knocking'.

'You're looking at a dying woman! Your sister!'

'You may have been my sister according to biological fact but you never were my sister. What was it you said at the lawyer's office? That my purpose in life had been to show you that parents can find it impossible to love a second child as much as they adore the first. After you've said something like that, don't try and pull the sister card on me'.

'No wonder Phil went back to his wife'.

'Oh sticks and stones! But you see, they can't hurt me because

I'm not ill and I'm going to be alive long after you're dead and forgotten about'.

'You'll pay for this one day. God doesn't pay debts with money but he'll find a way'.

'Oh, found Jesus in your dying days, have you? Well you can tell him that I think forgiveness is an overrated concept and only meant for those who mean it. I've been paying the price of being your sister since the day I was born'.

Jessica turned the handle on the door and then Susan's voice stopped her.

'Oh and Jessica? I'm fine, thanks for asking. I'm in a dead end job that barely pays the bills and I can't afford a social life. But don't worry about me. You never have done before'.

Jessica was weeping as she went down the stairs and out to where Jonathan was waiting in the car. She looked up but Susan wasn't in her window. She'd never see her again.

EIGHT
ROSIE

Roy Carter went downstairs and into the dining room. Rosie, the Filipino housemaid, was preparing breakfast. She knew he liked his food piping hot and so didn't put the light under it until he was sat down at the table. He wouldn't stand for scrambled eggs that had gone even slightly hard. They had to be runny. His bacon needed to be soft, not crispy, his sausages cooked through but not burnt on the outside. He'd earned his right to click his fingers and get whatever he wanted. That's what people with money did. That's what he did.

His wife Denise only had fruit and coffee for breakfast and was already on page 7 of that day's Daily Mail when he kissed her on the cheek.

'Morning, babe' she breathed.

'Morning' said Roy.

'You okay today, babe?'.

'Oh yea, sound' said Roy. 'So how's my hot girl this morning?'

'Patiently waiting' said Denise.

'What for?'

'To see if I come on!' she snapped. 'Don't you remember anything that isn't all about you, Roy?'

Roy had momentarily forgotten that Denise was desperate to be pregnant. They'd been trying for years without success and it was starting to affect her. She was a fit bird who worshipped her figure and Roy wasn't sure whether she'd really take to having a baby. She wouldn't like what it would do to her shape but the clock was ticking, they were both forty and Denise was becoming obsessive. Roy wasn't fussed either way. He already had a child that Denise didn't know about.

'Sorry, babe' said Roy. 'That was thoughtless of me'.

Denise felt hurt by Roy's apparent indifference to what she so wanted and did the only thing she could in the circumstances. She took it out on Rosie.

'Rosie! I want a mango! Prepare one now and bring it me!'

Rosie trembled as she brought a plate with slices of the golden flesh of mango for madam. She knew what would happen is she upset madam. Last month she'd dropped a mug and madam had beaten her and docked her two month's wages. The master left her alone. He acted almost as if she wasn't there but the madam had taken her passport, her mobile phone. She'd given her a uniform and locked away the rest of her clothes. She'd been working there for a year and she'd only just been given a mattress for the tiny room she slept in just off the kitchen. She went back into the kitchen and plated up the master's breakfast. Rosie herself would eat whatever was left and if there was nothing left then she wouldn't eat. She took the breakfast out and placed it in front of the master. He didn't look at her or say anything. He just started eating. She'd also brought the madam a glass of freshly squeezed orange juice with two cubes of ice as madam had requested.

'Rosie!' Denise called out, holding up the glass in disgust. 'This isn't cold enough. Put some more ice in it'.

Rosie took the glass of orange juice away and put two more cubes of ice in it. She then brought it back to the table and gave it to madam. Denise took one sip and pulled a face. 'Rosie! This is far too cold. Just forget it you idiot'.

'What have you got on today, babe?' asked Roy.

'A manicure at eleven then lunch with the girls in Wilmslow' Denise replied. Then she sighed. 'But I'm behind with my magazine reading and it's really starting to get to me. There's a stack of them on the table in the lounge that I've got to somehow find the time to get through. I just pray to God that the girls don't start talking about the latest fashions at the charity lunch because I won't have the faintest idea what the hell they're talking about. You see, they look upon me as some sort of big sister, you know, some sort of role model. I'm quite proud of that but it is a responsibility. Anyway, what are you up to?'

Roy sipped his coffee. 'Just a little discipline problem to sort out'.

'Show them who's boss'.

'Yeah, you could put it like that'.

Roy had set up a piece of theatre that nobody would ever pay money to go and see. The audience about to witness the show in the big warehouse he owned were frail and tired and several days into a life of terror. They huddled together in absolute fear. They were all young girls who'd been recruited by Roy's agents in their home countries on the fringes of Eastern Europe to fill vacancies in England for the jobs of cleaners in offices, schools, and hotels.

They'd been assured they'd have enough cash to be able to send some home each week and if they didn't settle down in England then they'd be free to go back.

They all should've known when they'd handed over their money to the agent for finding them a job and he'd told them that there'd been a change in the transportation arrangements that they were in for it. But they'd trusted. They'd latched on to a glimmer of hope that would take them away from the miserable lives they were destined for at home. They didn't see any wrong to hope. It was a natural thing to do in their circumstances. Some of the countries next to them had already joined the EU and had food on the table and goods in the shops. They'd thought that by going to a country like Britain they'd be able to get on the ladder before their country was deemed fit enough by Brussels to apply to join.

A plane ride of two or three hours had been replaced by a squat for four days in crates hidden behind legitimate cargo in the back of a container lorry. A bottle of water and a sandwich were thrown at them once a day and by the time they'd arrived in England they could barely stand up because their legs had been folded for all that time and they'd had to squint to deal with the daylight. They'd been slapped, beaten, raped, injected with heroin, their passports confiscated, and they'd been told that if they made any trouble their families back home would suffer. There was no way out. The only release would come with death and how they longed to see the faces of their families again. They hadn't known that when they waved goodbye to them with their hearts full of excitement about the cleaning jobs they were going to in England that they were actually on their way to a living hell.

Roy stepped forward and spoke to them as if he was some kind of preacher.

'Now I'm a fair man, ladies' he began, his hands held out expansively. 'You do right by me and I'll do right by you. I've already proved that by the work I've given you since you've been here. You're all turning out to be so good at it and earning me lots and lots of money so I'm grateful. Truly, I'm grateful for all your efforts'.

He turned and looked at the half dozen of his cronies who were stood around watching him. He exchanged knowing smiles with them all. He'd be sinking a few beers with them later. But first there was a lesson to be taught.

'You all look so scared, ladies' he went on. 'There's really no need. None of you are in trouble. You can all breathe without fear. But I have come to show you what can happen if you betray me'. He clicked his fingers and stepped back as the large black curtain behind him fell to the ground.

The girls gasped with terror at what they saw. A naked man who they recognised as one of those who'd escorted them to England was stretched out between two trucks that were facing in opposite directions. His arms were bound to one and his feet to the other. His body was covered in blood and even though he was gagged he was trying to say something and was struggling to break free even though it was clearly hopeless. They all began to cry.

'Save your tears, ladies!' Roy commanded. 'This man is a traitor. He's been selling secrets about my organisation to the highest bidder. Well this is where greed gets you. If any of you are thinking about crossing me then I strongly advise you to think again'.

Roy gave the nod and the engines of the two trucks roared and moved forward. There was a moment of resistance as the human body tried to struggle against the inevitable and then the man's limbs were torn from him in an explosion of blood, bone, and torn flesh. The girls screamed. They were absolutely horrified at what they'd witnessed. Then they were rounded up and taken back to their places of work. They had clients to see.

Denise was sitting with her feet up on one of the three white leather sofas in her cavernous lounge with its large windows that overlook the vast Cheshire plain. She was surrounded by a stack of magazines that she was finally slowly but surely leafing through. There was so much to catch up on it was almost overwhelming. She fiddled with a strand of her recently extended hair and inwardly groaned when Rosie came into the room.

'Excuse me, madam?'

'Yes, what is it?' Denise asked without looking up.

'I wonder, madam, if I could have next Sunday off?'

Denise carried on reading about the wedding plans of a premiership footballer who lived just a couple of houses along the private drive from them. Denise and her husband Roy had received their invite to the ceremony quite a while ago but the details had only just been released to the press.

'Madam?'

Denise screwed up her face. 'What is it, Rosie? Can't you see I'm busy?'

'I would like to have next Sunday off'.

'Well you can't'

'Why not?'

'Because I say so and don't question me'.

'But madam I have checked in the diary and you have no engagements at home that day'.

'Well that might change'.

'Madam, I have been asked to do the reading at Mass by Father O' Donnell'.

Denise laughed. 'He asked you? Is he trying to get into your knickers or something?'

Rosie was outraged. She'd grown very close to Father O' Donnell and the circle of friends she'd made at the local Catholic Church and wouldn't have his name tarnished by the low thinking of this English tart. She wondered why English people turn everything innocent into being something about sex. When madam went out she was dressed in such a way that every man would have sexual thoughts about her. Rosie felt honoured that she'd been asked to read at church but her boss would never be able to understand something like that. It would be completely beyond her.

'May I ask you not to speak about Father O' Donnell in that way, madam'.

'May I ask you to remember who the fuck you're talking to, lady! So why is he asking you to do the reading? Nobody will be able to understand you'.

That was a joke, thought Rosie. Her English was better than madams any day.

'Please don't insult me like that, madam'.

'I will insult you any way I like, Rosie, because I can'.

'My friends at church say my English is impeccable'.

'Impeccable? What the hell does that mean? We don't use

words like that in England, Rosie. You must be getting confused with your own Fillipino language'.

Rosie was at her wit's end. This was important to her. Her friends at church were like a family. They'd embraced her and made her feel welcome in a strange land and she really wanted to do this reading.

'Madam, please'.

'Rosie, when I say no I mean no'.

'Then I want my passport back'.

'I beg your pardon?'

'You don't have a right to keep my passport and I want it back!'

'You'll get it back when we're ready to terminate your employment and not before!'

'You don't have a right to keep it! It is my passport'

Denise put down the magazine she'd been reading and walked over to where Rosie was standing. She looked at her for a moment or two and then said 'Ask me that about your passport again'.

Rosie was frightened but she had to stand up for herself.

'I want my passport back, please'.

Denise punched Rosie deep into her stomach, winding her and causing her to fall to the floor, doubled up with agony. Denise then kicked her in her lower back and Rosie screamed out in pain once again. She yanked Rosie's head up by grabbing a handful of her hair. Rosie was gasping with a mixture of fear and agony. Denise knew exactly what she was doing. She'd done it many times before.

'You don't get a say in anything' snarled Denise, leering over her and pulling ever more tightly on her hair. 'You ungrateful little bitch!'

As madam pounded Rosie's head against the floor, all Rosie could think of was her mother, father, her four sisters and two brothers, all waiting back in Manila for the money she sent them.

She also thought about the secret notes she was making about her employers business, all the comings and goings and the names of their associates. One day they'd learn she wasn't so daft. One day they'd learn that she could speak better English than they gave her credit for and it would cost them.

A few days later, Rosie was cutting the madam's toenails and washing her feet. Denise had slapped her when she'd dropped the set of nail clippers onto the top of Denise's foot. It had hardly made any impact. Rosie had only dropped it from a couple of centimetres above, but the slap had carried enough force to knock Rosie off her balance and onto the floor. Denise had then raised a clenched fist at her maid until the look of fear in Rosie's eyes had been enough to quell her mounting anger. Then after Rosie had finished, Denise got herself dressed and said she'd be out until the early evening and Rosie would have to have dinner prepared for eight o'clock.

Rosie never felt safe. Her madam was so temperamental and could strike out with more viciousness than any of the snakes back home in the Philippines. Her sister worked in Paris for a group of American diplomats. They treated her well. They were polite and courteous. Her sister had begged her to join her there but she couldn't go anywhere without her passport and the Carter's had that. She was trapped.

She was so tired and hungry. She thought about going down to the church to see father O' Donnell and her friends there but she hadn't enough money for the bus fare and she didn't think she could walk the couple of miles there and back. She was too exhausted. She had no energy. Last week Father O'Donnell had made her something to eat and had remarked on how enthusiastically she had cleaned her plate. He'd questioned her about how worn out she looked and how pale she was. He'd wanted to drive her back to the house but she couldn't have let him do that. Madam wouldn't have liked it.

She thought about eating that food in Father O'Donnell's kitchen. She thought about the kindness shown to her by him and his housekeeper.

She didn't want to exploit their kindness by asking them for more food.

Roy was always grateful that Denise came quickly during sex. It spurred him on to his own climax and the task was over with. It's not that he didn't find her attractive anymore. She still turned him on but sex for Denise was all about trying to make a baby these days and he didn't like having to perform to order.

Once they'd finished Denise twisted herself round so that her legs were halfway up the wall and her waist was aligned with Roy's head. Her face was looking up at him and she propped herself up on her elbows.

'Babe, what are you doing?' Roy asked.

'Somebody told me that if I lie like this straight after sex it gives the sperm more of a chance to find my eggs' said Denise.

'Oh, right' said Roy who then lit up a cigarette.

'You know I'll try anything, babe'.

'I know, babe' said Roy who placed his free hand on her breasts and began caressing them. Her nipples were hard to the palms of his hands. 'Remember when we used to be at it like rabbits every minute of the day?'

'Yeah, but life moves on, doesn't it. Back then all we wanted was each other. Now we want the two of us to become three'.

Roy wondered whether he did want that or not. He moved his hand away from her breasts.

'Do you want a boy or a girl, babe?' Denise asked.

'I don't know' said Roy. He already had a son. He never saw him. He'd never seen him. He just sent his mother money every month.

Denise was once again riled by her husband's apparent indifference. 'You don't seem as keen on having this baby as I am, Roy'.

Oh Christ, thought Roy. He knew what that tone of voice meant and that reproachful look. And he wasn't in the mood.

'Denise, I've just fucked you … '

'… fucked me! I'm your wife! You don't fuck me, you make love to me!'

'Well what's the difference when all you want me from me is to fertilise you?'

'Babe, how can you say that?' said Denise as she started to cry.

Roy got out of bed and began to put his clothes back on. Denise shifted back into a normal position.

'Where are you going?'

'Out'.

'It's past midnight'.

'You're forgetting who I am, babe' said Roy. 'I've got places to go whatever time I want'. He picked up his mobile and pressed the button for Tommy's number. 'Tommy? Bring the car round, I want to go into town'.

'You're really going to leave me like this?' Denise whimpered.

'Babe, I love you loads, you know that' said Roy, snapping his phone shut. 'But you're doing my head in with this baby thing. I just need a bit of space, that's all. I'll be back before you've woken up in the morning. Try and calm down and get some sleep'.

'I am calm you selfish bastard!'

Roy didn't look back as he slammed the door shut and headed outside to meet Jake. He couldn't stand Denise when she got like this. Everything was about getting pregnant and whilst he didn't begrudge her that dream of motherhood, he did begin to wonder if it was all she was living for. He'd built the dream for them. This house in the part of Cheshire where the smell of cash came up when the air was sniffed, the social circles they now moved in, the clothes she was able to buy, the cars, the holidays on exclusive Caribbean islands. Wasn't all that enough?

'Why did you get married, Tommy?' Roy asked as Tommy drove them down the M56 motorway past Manchester airport and on towards the city.

'The test was positive, boss' Tommy answered.

'Fair enough' said Roy. 'You did the right thing. Would you have got married then if she hadn't been pregnant?'

'No, boss' said Tommy. 'But that's how it works. She decides she wants to get married so she makes sure it happens. Nobody ever has sympathy for a man who doesn't want to marry his girlfriend when she's pregnant. It's just not how things work'.

'A baby is supposed to change everything'.

'Something like that, boss, yeah' said Tommy.

'And does it change everything?'

'No' said Tommy. 'It just means you've got something else to pay out for. So is it the Pinewood club we're going to, boss?'

'Please, Tommy'.

'To sit with all the bent coppers who've gone there for the late night drinking?'

Roy smiled. 'Well I only go there for the beer, Tommy'.

'You own it, boss'.

'Yeah, there is that too. Oh and Tommy, be ready to bring a couple of them back to my place later. Rosie might have some work to do'.

'Hello, Rosie?' said Father O'Donnell. The poor girl looked terrified as she stood there not quite knowing what to do. He spoke gently. 'Are you going to let me in?'

Rosie stepped back to let him pass. She flinched every time she thought he was going to touch her. Jim O'Donnell had seen that many times and he knew exactly what it was all about. She'd been attacked.

'Rosie, do you need to talk about anything?'

She looked at him for several seconds before falling to the floor in tears. She wrapped her arms tightly around herself.

Jim O'Donnell crouched down beside her. 'Somebody's hurt you, haven't they, Rosie?'

'You won't send me back to the Philippines?'

'No, of course not if you don't want to go' said Jim.

'My mother needs my money'.

'Don't worry about that' said Jim. 'Just tell me what happened, Rosie. You can trust me'.

'They hurt me' she wailed.

'Who did?' Jim asked.

'Mr. and Mrs. Carter'.

'What did they do?' Jim wanted to know.

'Mrs. Carter beat me' she said. She pulled her blouse out of her skirt and showed him the bruises she'd received at the hand of her mistress.

'Jesus Christ' O'Donnell exclaimed. Rosie's torso was covered in bruises. 'She did this to you?'

Rosie nodded her head. Then her face screwed up in pain and anguish as she tearfully revealed. 'And Mr. Carter. He made me dirty. He and his friends took away my gift to my husband. I begged them to stop. Nobody will want to marry me now. My life is over. I may as well be dead'.

Jim had dealt with several rape victims in his time as a priest and he stayed back whilst Rosie explained everything that had happened when Roy Carter had brought his friends round. Jim was disgusted but also relieved that he finally had something to nail on Roy Carter, a man he'd known was motivated by evil for a long time. But he'd never had enough evidence to get him. Until now that is.

'Rosie' said Jim. 'We have to call the police'.

Rosie was hysterical. 'No! They have kept my passport. If I go to the police they will never let me have it back'.

'Rosie, they can't keep your passport. It's against the law'.

'I have no right to law'.

'Yes, you have' said Jim who then drew Rosie close and she let him hug her. 'Come on now, Rosie. It's over, it's all over. I'm going to help you'.

'You can't! They will never let me go'.

'Rosie, they can't keep you a prisoner' said Jim. 'This is not the dark ages. You're not a slave, you're an employee and you've got rights'.

'I have no rights!' she cried. 'You don't understand'.

'Oh Rosie' said Jim as he held her close. 'Now, where are they now?'

'They've gone to Barcelona to celebrate madam's birthday' said Rosie. 'They won't be back until tomorrow night'.

'Good, now I want you to pack your things in a bag. Then we're going to go to the police so that you can make a statement'.

'I cannot, I cannot!'

'You can, Rosie. I know it isn't going to be easy but you can because I will be there to help you'.

'I am so hungry' she sobbed.

'Then we'll take you to get something to eat too' said Paul. 'I'm so sorry, Rosie. I'm so sorry for what they've done to you but they can't hurt you anymore. I'll make sure of that. Now go and pack that bag and we can be out of here'.

'You can help me?'

'Yes, I can help you'.

'You are sure?'

'I'm certain, Rosie' said Jim. 'But you have to trust me'.

'But will I get another job? I have to send money home'.

'Rosie, I will do whatever I can to make sure you're able to send money home but they cannot get away with doing these awful things to you and that's what we'll have to deal with first'.

Jim helped Rosie to her feet and she led him to the small room off the kitchen where she slept. There wasn't even a proper bed. Just a mattress on the floor.

'They make you sleep in here?' Jim exclaimed. 'This is where you live?'

Rosie seemed embarrassed at her surroundings. Jim shook his head. They were treating her as a slave. It was a bloody disgrace.

'Come on, Rosie' said Paul. 'Let me get you out of here, my dear, dear child. When did you last eat?'

'Yesterday morning' said Rosie. 'I am only allowed to eat what is left over and if madam is upset with me then she throws the leftovers away in front of me'.

'You mean you don't get proper meals?'

'No' said Rosie. 'Father, I am so hungry'.

'Then the first thing we'll do is to stop and get you something to eat. Okay?'

'Okay' said Rosie, wiping her face with her hand.

Jim kept his mounting anger under control as he led Rosie out to his car. He wanted to stay outwardly calm for her so that she'd have confidence in him. Rosie had come thousands of miles to a supposedly civilised country only to be treated like a slave. She probably wasn't the only one either. It made him feel ashamed to be British. He smiled as Rosie got into his car and fastened her seat belt. The poor thing still looked absolutely terrified.

The medical report showed that Rosie Lorenzo had sustained

numerous injuries to her torso, leaving it covered in bruises.

'She's been used as a punch bag' said the doctor. 'Whoever did this was very careful not to leave any obvious signs of their handiwork on the exposed parts of her body like her arms, face, and legs'.

'And how long have these attacks been taking place in your opinion, doctor?' asked detective sergeant John Blackburn of Greater Manchester police.

'Hard to say' said Doctor Latif, consultant at the local casualty unit. 'Some of the bruises are older than others certainly. How long has she been employed by the Carter family?'

'Just under three months' said Jim O'Donnell.

'Then that's how long the abuse has been going on' said Doctor Latif. 'This kind of thing doesn't just happen one morning. This young girl would've suffered right from day one just like many others in her situation. There's a refuge in Stockport for girls like Rosie and they see people who work in some of the big houses across Cheshire and South Manchester. Their stories of physical and sexual abuse are all similar. Nouveau riche British families who've come from nothing and think that now they've made it they have some right to treat their servants like dirt they've just scraped off their shoes'.

'But why don't they ever come to us?' DS Blackburn wanted to know.

'Because like Rosie, their employers take their passports and threaten them if they make any official complaints. This is slavery in the modern world, detective'.

'And going on right under our noses' said Jim.

'It's truly sickening' said Blackburn.

'So is something else' said Doctor Latif. 'Only a few weeks gone but she is definitely pregnant'.

'What's your connection to Rosie Lorenzo, Father O'Donnell?' asked DS Blackburn in the corridor outside the ward where Rosie was being treated.

'She's a member of my congregation' Jim answered. 'But we hadn't heard from her for several days so I decided to go and see if she was okay. My congregation is drawn mainly from the poorer areas of South Manchester but our church has also become the local place of worship for many of the Fillipino workers from the more well heeled parts and stretching out into Cheshire. That's how we got to know Rosie but detective, there are other forces at work here'.

'How do you mean?'

'Roy Carter and his wife Denise each come from two of the most problem families on the Wythenshawe estate. Now they have a multi-million pound house with a swimming pool and acres of some of the most expensive ground in the area. He made his money from a debt collection business he started in the nineties which made so much out of people's misery and suffering. But since then, he's diversified. It's very well known that he runs rackets of young girls that he traffics from Eastern Europe and forces into prostitution. I've been warned off, detective. Carter's gang have smashed my car up, broken the windows of the presbytery, paid me late night visits when the menace behind their call was very clearly spelt out. But I don't fear Carter, detective. I fear for the young lives that he's destroying with his greed and his connections'.

'Connections?'

'Detective Blackburn, I have files and files detailing Carter's work. I can give you dates, people, addresses across this city where girls are being forced into prostitution. Now you tell me why your colleagues also have all this information and yet nobody moves to close Carter down?'

Father O'Donnell arranged for Sally Williams to meet with detective John Blackburn in the presbytery of his church to talk about her son Andrew.

'Before I start, I want you to assure me that Roy Carter is safely behind bars for the rape of that poor Filipino girl'.

'You read about that in the papers?' John asked.

'Yes' said Sally.

'Well he's been remanded in custody pending further questioning' said John. 'Why? Do you have some more information for us about that case?'

'Not about that one, no' said Sally. 'I'm here to talk to you about Roy Carter's other activities'.

'How do you know about them?'

'Because I was involved with Roy when he set it all up' said Sally as she broke down and cried.

John poured her a glass of water from the jug that Father O'Donnell had left out on the table.

'Thank you' said Sally.

'Just take your time, Sally' said John.

'I'm sorry about this' said Sally as she wiped her eyes.

'It's okay' said John.

'We were in our teens but already Roy was showing he was

going to break away and get somewhere' Sally recalled. 'But somehow I managed to get close to Roy. I don't know how it happened but before we knew it we were an item. It seems ridiculous to say under the circumstances but I fell in love with him'.

'It happens in those kind of situations, Sally' said John. 'But go on'.

'I lost count of how many men Roy forced me to go with' said Sally.

'He made you go with other men?'

'His interest, shall we say, in prostitution started early' said Sally.

'And how old were you when all this was happening?' John asked.

'Fifteen' said Sally. 'But then all the trafficking started from Eastern Europe. He'd already made a packet from the debt collection business and from pimping me out. But I was the experiment. I was used to test his methods. But then I got pregnant'.

'And what happened?'

'Well, it was Roy's because at that time I'd gone back to being just his girlfriend. But he'd made it clear that he didn't want to have children and he ditched me. Not long after that he took up with Denise. My son Andrew and I have been well taken care of financially but he threatened me that if I ever told anyone what I know then he would kill our son'.

'Then you're showing a great amount of courage here today, Sally'.

'Father O'Donnell has been a great friend and a tremendous support to us. I knew that the truth would have to come out one day and I'm sorry that poor Rosie had to be raped before Roy could be brought to justice'.

'Sally, will you put all of this into an official statement?'

'Yes' said Sally. 'But I should watch your back if I was you'.

'Me? Why?'

'Well why do you think that Roy has got away with it for so long? Because he has very helpful friends who are all your colleagues'.

The operation to close down all of his businesses seemed to have caught Roy Carter by surprise but that didn't alter his cool demeanour as he sat waiting to be interviewed by John Blackburn and a uniformed colleague sat beside him. John thought that Carter looked like nothing could ever touch him. No doubt that is what he thought and there'd been no sign of the protection that everyone had talked about.

'Your wife has been charged with some very serious offences, Mr. Carter' said John.

'I put my faith in good old British justice, detective' said Carter.

John could've been sick. 'Mr. Carter, what kind of man lets his wife take the rap for the unlawful things he's done?'

'You tell me, detective, if you know of such a man'.

'I'm looking at him' said John. 'Every bit of your business empire is in her name'.

'Oh I'd be careful about throwing out your nasty little accusations, detective' said John, a snide grin on his face. 'Especially with my brief being present'.

'Your wife claims to have had no idea that all of your businesses were in her name, Mr. Carter' said John.

'Detective, I'm a very busy man and I don't have time for this crap' said Carter. He stood up and began to button up his jacket.

'You're not going anywhere, Mr. Carter' said John.

'Oh yes I am'.

'Sit down, Mr. Carter'.

'Oh no, I'm out of here'.

'I said sit down, Mr. Carter!'

Roy looked at his brief and then sat back down. ',You've got nothing on me at all and never will have'.

'You seem very sure of that, Mr. Carter'.

'That's because I've done nothing wrong'.

'Where were you on the night of Wednesday, March 19th, Mr. Carter?' John asked.

'That was nearly two weeks ago, detective'.

'Well let me jog your memory for you' said John. 'You brought several friends back to your house for a party. Your housemaid, Rosie Lorenzo alleges that she was the victim of a serious sexual assault that night'.

Carter shrugged. 'I may have brought some friends back but I don't know about any assault'.

'It was rape, Mr. Carter. Rosie alleges that she was raped in your house that night'.

'She can allege what the hell she pleases' said Carter.

'So you have no idea who could've assaulted her?'

'No idea at all, detective' said Carter.

'Mr. Carter, when your wife realised how much trouble you'd dropped her in she became very co-operative with us. We told her about Rosie Lorenzo's allegations and she told us how, on your instructions, she'd made Miss Lorenzo dress up as a schoolgirl that night and then left when you and your friends arrived'.

'She beats that girl black and blue'.

'Yes, she's admitted all of that' said John. 'Just like she's admitted that you and her have been trying for a baby without success for some time now and that when you went for tests they found that the problem was with her'.

'That's very personal' snarled Carter.

'Well you see, Mr. Carter' said John. 'She's given us a list of the men who were at your house that night. All we need to do is take DNA samples and compare them with the sample we've taken from Rosie Lorenzo. When we get a match we've got our rapist and you won't be able to claim infertility problems if it does turn out to be you'. He shuffled a notepad across the table at Carter. 'So why don't you write down the names of all your friends who were there that night and we'll compare it with the list your wife has given us'.

'My wife would never co-operate with you'.

'Oh that's where you're wrong, Mr. Carter' said John. 'She's falling over herself to co-operate as a means of helping her case'.

'You can't prove … '

'… oh but we can, Mr. Carter' said John. 'DNA is a truly wonderful science. All it would take is a swab or two so stop wasting time and, whilst you're thinking about that, why don't you tell us where it is you take the girls that you traffic from Eastern Europe?'

It was the first time Carter had looked uncomfortable and the narrowing of his eyes gave everything away to John. Then Carter spoke in measured tones. 'I have absolutely no idea what you're talking about'.

'Oh but we think you do, Mr. Carter'.

Carter was seething with anger. This should never have got this far. He looked at his brief who was sitting beside him like some deaf fucking mute. He needed to get out of there and start looking for whoever the bastard was who'd grassed him up.

'Mr. Carter, we have all your crew in custody' said John. 'All we have to do is lean on them and wait for one of them to squeak. Oh but of course, one of them already has, otherwise you wouldn't be here at all. Doesn't that bother you, Mr. Carter? You're stuck in here and someone who worked for you may be singing like a canary in one of the other interview rooms. Doesn't the sense of absolute betrayal get to you? Does it bother you to know that we know who ordered Ian Bottomley to be torn from limb to limb in a grotesque piece of theatre?'

'I have absolutely no comment to make' said Carter. 'No comment at all'.

DS John Blackburn walked into the church and thought about blessing himself with some of the holy water that was in a type of bowl nailed to the wall at face height. But then he thought better of it. The only times he'd been in a church were when he got married, when his two kids were baptised, and for his father's funeral. He'd been divorced for three years now and the church held no promise for him anymore. He just wanted to speak with Father O'Donnell. He was probably the only person he could trust given the circumstances.

'I've got a mate who was in the Derbyshire force' said John as he sat side by side with Father O'Donnell on a pew. 'He blew the whistle on a network of police corruption that led to six officers being sacked'.

'What happened to him?'

'He was ostracised by his colleagues and ended up being moved to the Nottinghamshire force'.

'So what are you saying, John?'

'That this network of police corruption I'm about to expose will probably destroy my career' said John. 'I know how it works, father. No matter how worthy the sting proves to be I won't be forgiven by some for having instigated the whole thing'.

'You will be fulfilling your duty as a police officer, John' said Jim. 'Nobody should be above the law'.

'Well that's the talk but when it comes to fellow police officers, that's not the walk'.

'Then you have to think about Rosie Lorenzo, Sally Williams and her son Andrew, all those girls who've been brought thousands of miles from their homes only to be abused by evil, twisted men. Pitch all of that against your other concerns and see what you come up with'.

'Ooh, you're tough'.

'You're an honest, honourable man, John Blackburn. You know what to do. And you know how to deal with the consequences. Now I think that's what you came here for, isn't it?'

'I'm not a church goer' John admitted. 'I'm not even a Catholic'.

'Well hold the front page before the Vatican finds out!'

John laughed. 'You've got such a strong moral centre' said John. 'That's why I needed to talk to you'.

'Yes, well, it hasn't always done me any favours' said Jim. 'I'm a priest in my early fifties and by now I should be out in some suburban or even seaside parish somewhere where nothing much goes on. But you see, I'm a big mouth. I challenged the church's teachings on a few things and it got me into hot water with the bishop'.

'What sort of things?'

'Oh, nothing trivial, just the big three of contraception, divorce, and homosexuality. Then I challenged the sainthood of Mother Teresa. I wanted to try and understand why she'd spent a lifetime getting the poor to get down on their knees and thank God for having nothing instead of challenging all the reasons why they were poor in the first place. So you see, I know how it feels to stick your neck out and get your head chopped off. But some of us are chosen by Him upstairs to fulfil that sort of task'.

'You make sense, I'll give you that'.

'So tell me, what happened to your friend who was moved from the Derbyshire force to the Nottinghamshire force? Did the move solve his problem?'

'Not really' said John. 'Word gets round. Eventually he resigned and took a job as a security consultant with a firm over in Nottingham. It's not exactly police work on the cutting edge but he wears a nice suit, drives a nice car, does some travelling around the place advising companies. He earns good money too'.

'And does he regret what he did?'

'Not for one minute'.

'And is he happy?'

'Yes, he says he is'.

'Then you could always ring him and ask if there any vacancies where he works' Jim suggested. 'Just in case the same thing happens to you'.

'Thanks, father'.

'What for?'

'For telling me what I already knew'.

'Sometimes you just need someone to spell it out to you and give you courage'.

'You've been a great help'.

'I've always got time for a good looking man'.

'Pardon?'

'Well I did say that homosexuality was one of the issues I had with the church' said Jim. 'And I do find you good looking'.

John blushed and then smiled. 'Thanks, father. I'm flattered. But I'm straight'.

'I know and don't get too flattered or else it'll become a sin' said Jim. He winked at John. 'I'm here anytime you need to talk and I won't tell anyone you're not a Catholic if you don't. Him upstairs will know of course but I hear he's lost the bishop's phone number'.

Roy Carter would be going down for a very long time and Denise Carter had been charged with causing grievous bodily harm to Rosie Lorenzo. She'd co-operated fully with the enquiry and dropped her husband right in it from a very great height in return for the possibility of a lighter sentence. The trafficking operation of girls from Eastern Europe would be the hardest to fully complete but with the co-operation of forces from other European countries, and EU wide arrest warrants, they would get everything they needed to nail

Carter once and for all.

John Blackburn wasn't cold shouldered out of the Greater Manchester force. Instead he was promoted to Detective Inspector and given a commendation from the chief constable for exposing corruption and all the activities associated with the Pinewood club that was once owned by Roy Carter but which had now been confiscated by the state as evidence of 'proceeds of crime'.

John Blackburn was told that it was a job well done and his professional kudos was at an all time high.

A month later

'Hey!'

Father Jim O'Donnell turned from walking up the aisle of the church to see his favourite unexpected visitor. 'Detective Inspector John Blackburn. To what do I owe this honour twice in one week and it's only Thursday?'

'Well you see father, it's like this ... '

'... John, I've taken a vow of celibacy and besides, I didn't think you were like that?'

John smiled. 'I'm not. But you've been good counsel to me and in the absence of my own father who's no longer with us, I like to come and talk to you. Just as a friend'.

Jim O'Donnell was delighted. 'Then I'm grateful for having even that much of you. Come on into the presbytery and I'll make us a brew. I'm expecting Rosie any minute. She'll be glad to see you too'.

'Don't you ever get lonely, Jim?'

'That was a bit out of the blue'.

'I was just wondering' said John. 'You've got this big church and all these parishioners with their problems and whatnot'.

'And nobody to go home to at night'.

'Yeah' said John. 'I haven't at the moment but I don't want it to be that way forever'. It had been eighteen months since his divorce from Debbie and he missed sharing his life with someone. He wasn't very good at being on his own. That's why he'd thrown himself into his work. It was classic male emotional avoidance behaviour. He missed sex. He shouldn't be pleasuring himself in the shower at his age. Debbie seemed happy enough living her new life with her multi-millionaire property developer in Alderley Edge and with the half of John's salary that he has to give her every month. That's why whoever he met would have to be on at least the same financial footing as him because he couldn't keep anyone. He was one of those forgotten victims of divorce. The man who has to give up so much to a woman who's left him for a much richer man and has relatively little chance of starting again financially.

'John? You look like you've gone and left me?'

'What? Oh sorry Jim, I did go miles away for a second. No, I do want to settle down again with another lady. I hope there's another big romance left in me'.

'I'm certain there is and she'll be one lucky broad, John' said Jim.

John smiled. 'But you're biased'.

'Oh don't be such a tease, John' said Jim, enjoying the banter.

'Well alright then, back to you'.

'Well yes, of course I get lonely. I am only human after all. It's okay having a lot of friends but it doesn't make up for not having that someone special. But we all have our cross to bear of some kind, John. And look, if I hadn't gone into the priesthood there's no guarantee I would've met the love of my life. I could be sat in some stupid flat somewhere with nobody to take care of and only a stack of TV soaps to fill the gap in my life. I'm always grateful for even the smallest mercy, John'.

'It's called having faith I suppose'.

'Yes, I suppose it is. Now, what's the latest on the case?'

'The trial is still set for next month' said John as he fell into step with Jim on the way to the presbytery. 'Denise Carter is still keeping low out on bail'.

'There must be something very satisfying about charging someone about whom you have no doubt about their guilt?'

'Yes' said John. 'In the case of Roy Carter, it's very satisfying'.

They both heard the screeching of tyres, a piercing scream and then a sudden thump before a crash. They looked at each other wondering what the hell was going on before running out and standing at the top of the dozen steps that led to the door of the church.

'Oh dear God, no!' Jim exclaimed. 'Rosie!'

Rosie was lying in the middle of the road with blood pouring out of her head. Denise Carter had been driving the car that had sent Rosie flying into the air and then crashed it into the church notice board just to the side of the building. John Blackburn called for back-up and an ambulance and then ran over and dragged Denise out of her car. She was sobbing but it didn't inspire any sympathy from John.

'Right' he said as he held her up against the side of the car. 'You can add attempted murder to your list of charges, Mrs. Carter!'

'You don't understand! She could give him a baby and I couldn't! She's destroyed my life!'

'Yeah, yeah, yeah, tell it to the judge or somebody else who might be interested'.

John put Denise in handcuffs and then put her in the back of his car. He then went over to where Jim O'Donnell was holding Rosie's hand and trying to comfort her. Jim looked up and shook his head.

'Tell my mother I'm sorry' Rosie whispered.

'No, Rosie' said Jim. 'We're the ones who should be sorry'.

Jim O'Donnell then proceeded to read the last rites to Rosie and her unborn child that she'd planned to have adopted.

NINE
HELEN

'Let me make myself very clear' said Helen as she sat beside Linda Hamilton on the sofa in Linda's apartment which was ten floors up in one of the new blocks in Salford Quays. 'I want my ex husband dead. Your part in it is to set up the honey trap according to my clear instructions. Now if you're not up to that then I'll just get somebody else and don't think that if I did that you could get away with blackmailing me. Try that and believe me, you'd end up being very sorry indeed'.

'Okay, okay' said Linda. She'd never met anyone quite like Helen. She was so fucking ruthless. She could imagine she really would sell her own Grandma. 'I get it and I am up to it, Helen. That's why you hired me in the first place, remember? Because I've done it before for women like you and none of them have complained'.

'Women like me?'

'Women who can't do anything as normal as divorcing their husband' Linda explained. 'That's not enough for women like you'.

'Well I'm glad we understand each other because I don't take kindly to being let down'.

'You won't be' said Linda who felt a chill go through her from the look Helen was giving her. 'Look, I promise you alright. I just wanted to know why, that's all. On all the previous occasions I've worked it out as soon as I've clapped eyes on the creeps. But Mark seems like a decent enough bloke to me'.

'Oh he is' said Helen. 'A very decent bloke. But that's not the point'.

'So what is?'

Helen dragged on her cigarette and then said. 'Mark has become an inconvenience to the life I'm starting with my new partner, Dominic, who's a very powerful man and has no patience with all this joint custody and weekend visits stuff. Either we're a family, him, me and my daughters, or we're not. With Mark out of the way we would be that family with no interruptions, no distractions'.

'But your daughters would lose their natural father'.

'They'll get over it' said Helen. 'Besides, he tried to go for full custody of them after we divorced so I owe him nothing'.

'Yeah, but even so, murder is a little extreme'.

Helen took a thick white envelope out of her handbag and gave it to Linda. 'Now will that shut you up for a minute or two because all this bleeding heart crap is starting to get on my nerves'.

'Thanks' said Linda.

'It's all there as we agreed' said Helen. 'A third when you first agreed to the deal, another third now, and the remaining third on completion. I take it you have slept with him?'

Linda gave Helen a look that was more surprise at the directness of the question than anything else.

'Oh I don't think there's any room for you to get all prudish on me now. You're pushing forty, love, and soon all you'll look is sad when you dress yourself up like a dog's dinner and do the bars. You've got to get it while you still can'.

'You're such an inspiration to me, Helen' said Linda, sarcastically.

'So the answer is yes?'

'Oh, yes, half a dozen times if you must know!' said Linda. And it had all been very nice. Mark was a good lover, a man who really knew the geography of a woman's body and knew how to give it to her slowly but surely, urging her on whilst he made her gasp and moan.

'And from the look in your eyes I can see that you've fallen a little bit in love with him?'

'That's none of your business'.

Helen grabbed hold of Linda's wrist and twisted it until Linda's face was contorted in pain. 'Now listen to me, young lady, with my divorce settlement from Mark and the millions that Dominic is worth, I'm set up for life. Whereas you're just a month's rent away from going back to being poor white trash and dreaming the impossible dream. Okay?'

'Yes!' Linda splurted out. 'Now let go of my wrist'.

'So don't back out on me over some stupid notion of love!'

'I won't, now please, let go of my wrist!'

'Good' said Helen as she released Linda from her agony and stood up. 'Now the next time I see you will be at the house in Nice. I've made all the arrangements and you'll be quite safe as long as you do as you're told. If you don't then it won't just be Mark's body that's sent back to the UK. Do I make myself clear?'

'Crystal'.

'Alright. Don't get up, I'll see myself out'.

'Will Mark's death really make you happy?'

'Yes' said Helen without hesitation. 'It will because it will help me get exactly what I want and in the end, that's the most important thing'.

'I'd hate to get on the wrong side of you'.

'Then don't' said Helen. 'Or you'll live to regret it'.

The arrivals hall at Nice airport was pretty crowded. Flights had just come in from Zurich, London Heathrow, Amsterdam, Munich, and the one that Linda and Mark had flown in on from Manchester. Linda didn't know why some people get so fucking pretentious when they were placed in the environment of air travel. They seem to feel they've got to bang their chests at the slightest problem. An announcement was made to say that the baggage from the Manchester flight would be delayed by about ten minutes due to congestion in the baggage delivery area. So what, thought Linda. Anybody could see it was busy. But people were getting up in arms at the airline staff, telling them they'd never fly with the airline again and all that shit. All because of ten fucking minutes. Get over yourselves!

But Linda was forgetting herself. She was getting carried away by the reality of being in the south of France. It was a place she'd only ever dreamed about going to before. But now she was here, treading in the footsteps of all those celebrities who come down here for the Cannes film festival and to spend their summers at the houses they kept here. Some others were like the ones they'd been on the plane from Manchester with. All Cheshire set affected grandness just like Helen, the woman she'd come here to do a job for.

'This is the life, eh?' said Mark as they drove along the motorway with Nice airport behind them, the Mediterranean to their left and the mountains of the Cote D'Azur to their right. He'd hired a soft top and with the top down and the wind blowing through her hair, Linda could quite easily forget the fact that she'd already been paid twenty thousand pounds for her part in arranging to kill the man beside her and that once he was dead there was another ten thousand to come.

'It's wonderful, darling' said Linda who was making the most of the time she had left with this handsome man with the grey flecks in his otherwise black hair.

Mark reached over and gently held her hand. 'This is only the beginning. We're going to have everything, you and me. I never thought I'd ever be this happy again after all the shit I went through with Helen. I thought I was doomed. Then you came along and I'm looking forward to the future again'.

Linda managed a smile. This was going to break her heart. 'I'm happy too'.

After about forty minutes of heading west towards Marseilles they turned right off the motorway and headed for the mountain village of Fayence. The house they were staying in had a tennis court at lower level and then the drive swept up to the swimming pool in front of the house itself which was on two levels. The Mediterranean was around seven kilometers away and the view was spectacular. The sun was shining high in the sky. It was all perfect and for Linda that couldn't have made it any worse.

'Are you alright, darling?' Mark asked. 'You look like you're faraway'.

Linda fingered her long blond hair behind her ears. 'How could I not be alright with all this? And I haven't even been in the house yet'.

'A bit overwhelming?'

'Just a bit, considering where I grew up'.

'Well that's a long, long way behind you' said Mark. 'You're with me now and you'll need to get used to it. Helen may have thought she'd cleaned me out financially in the divorce settlement but when you own an insurance company then believe me, you're never going to be poor. And it'll be great when we come here with the girls. I'm so pleased you got on with them so well when you met'.

'They're lovely children' said Linda. 'It isn't hard to get on with them'.

'And they love you' said Mark. 'You're cool in so many ways their mother isn't'.

'We're probably more alike than you think, Helen and I'.

'Why do you say that?'

'Well you probably subconsciously looked for similar characteristics'.

'Linda, you are nothing like Helen' Mark insisted. 'She was always so intense and nothing was ever good enough. She'd have arrived at this place and found fault with it straight away. She always answered every positive comment with a negative one'.

'It worked for you all those years'.

'You try to see things differently when children come along'.

'And what about Dominic? He's a multi-millionaire. He must

see something good in her?'

'Yes, well I hear there's trouble in Shangri-la'.

'Really?'

'The relationship is on the rocks apparently' said Mark. 'He's tried to pull the plug a couple of times but she's begged him and he's taken her back'.

'How do you know all this?'

'I've known Dominic for years' Mark revealed. 'We've been friends in the Manchester business community for a long time and recently we became personal friends. We meet up regularly now and talk about this and that. He's a good bloke'.

'I didn't realise'.

'Well why would you? Come on, lets get the bags out the car and go inside'. He leaned forward and took her in his arms. 'I want to check out the bedroom'.

'Didn't you get enough of that last night? And first thing this morning? We almost missed the flight because of it'.

'Well … live each day as if it's your last is what I say! We could all be dead tomorrow!'

Linda was terrified as she listened to Mark telling her about the couple who owned the house they were staying in. If Mark was in cahoots with Dominic then who knows what the two of them had managed to find out?

'Bill used to fly jumbo jets around the world for British Airways' Mark explained as they walked around the house with its high ceilings, big windows, and tiled floors. 'Mary was one of his stewardesses. They got together after they were both with other people but they made it in the end. They're off travelling in South East Asia somewhere at the moment. They like to do the whole remote thing. Last time they emailed me they were in Laos about to cross the border into Cambodia'.

Linda had never heard of either place. She was driving herself crazy with putting two and two together over Mark, and Helen's new boyfriend Dominic. Helen had never mentioned that they were friends. Perhaps she didn't know. But why wouldn't she know? This wasn't going to end well. She had the most excruciating feeling that it was all going to go very horribly wrong.

'That was a lovely meal, darling' said Mark as he put his knife and fork down and refilled their glasses. They were sitting just outside the front door on white chairs at a white table.

'I've never been shopping in a French supermarket before' said Linda who was rather enjoying the Bordeaux they'd bought. She'd opened a second bottle and that was already half way down. 'I didn't know what to expect'.

'Well you did marvellously' said Mark. 'I'm proud of you'.

'Not as well as Helen would've done'.

'Linda, you excel Helen in so many ways' said Mark. 'She's insane, you know?'

'Insane?'

'Oh she's been committed twice' Mark revealed. 'Over a period of years she's had electric shock treatment and the lot. Chronic manic depression is what they call it. You have to feel sorry for her'.

'Do you?' Linda questioned as she filled up her glass again.

'You're knocking it back a bit, darling?'

'Sorry? Should I slow down?'

'Linda, have you got something on your mind?'

Linda paused looking at him. 'You know, don't you?'

Mark sat back in his chair and crossed his legs over. He brought his hands together and rested his fingers under his chin. 'Of course I know'.

'How did you know?'

'Dominic became suspicious of Helen's behavior and had her followed. She's a fairly transparent villain which makes her pretty useless'.

'And what exactly do you know?'

'I know that you've been paid to lure me here and that she's arranged to have me killed'.

Linda broke down and cried. Mark shifted his chair along and put his arm round her. 'Hey, hey, don't get upset'.

'But how can you be so calm? How could you bring me here, make love to me, treat me better than I've ever known before and all the time you knew?'

'It's alright' Mark reassured. 'You fell in love with me and that's changed things for you. I know you wouldn't have gone through with it'.

'But how can you ever trust me again?'

'I can' said Mark. 'I don't need any other proof than the way you're falling apart now. And in any case, you wouldn't have got the chance to go through with it'.

'I don't understand'.

'You don't have to, Linda, darling' said Mark. 'And you don't have to worry'.

'Why not?'

'Because I've changed the rules of the game and let's just say that Helen has got a little surprise coming. But like I said, you don't have to worry about anything'.

Linda woke with a start and immediately reached for the gun on the bedside table.

'I wouldn't if I were you'

The voice of warning came out of the darkness and almost freaked Linda out. She switched on the light and there was Helen, standing at the foot of the bed pointing a gun at her.

'How did you get in here?' Linda demanded as she pulled the bed clothes up over her naked body. Where was Mark? He'd been sleeping beside her.

'Oh, how nice it is to be made to feel welcome' said Helen, sarcastically. 'I have a key, remember? Now I want answers. Why hasn't it been done?'

'How do you know it hasn't?'

Helen laughed at the girl's stupidity. 'Because I know that the people I hired were called off but not by me, you stupid bitch! Do you think I was born yesterday? You have gone soft on me, haven't you? You've fallen in love and you couldn't do it. I knew it was wrong to trust you. You're going to pay for that now'.

'You really think she'd be that clever, Helen' said Mark as he appeared at the door dressed only in a pair of boxer shorts. He was holding a gun and it was pointing at Helen's back. 'Don't turn around. I don't think I could stomach the look of pleading in your eyes before I kill you'.

Helen turned round and stared him out. 'Then go ahead and do it if you've got the guts'.

'Defiant to the last' said Mark. 'That's impressive but it's about the only thing about you that is these days'.

'You won't kill me, Mark' said Helen, defiantly. 'Not in cold blood'.

'It wouldn't be in cold blood' said Mark. 'You're an intruder. And besides, once I've told the French police all about your mental history, they'll believe me when I tell them that you came here because you'd found out about my affair with Linda and it had finally pushed you over the edge. Your poor little head couldn't take it'.

'You're a callous bastard' said Helen, coldly although she was beginning to feel desperate. She'd never known Mark sound so determined.

'Oh come on, darling! You've no cause to sound so bloody righteous. Let's not forget that you're here because you arranged to have me killed and all because you think of me now as an inconvenience to be got rid of just like that'.

'But how did you know?'

'Dominic worked it out a while ago and he was so fed up with you and your antics and your petty little grievances that he decided to tell me. You've got no future with him, Helen. Right now he's probably packing all your stuff together and throwing it out'.

Helen couldn't help but feel tears come to her eyes. 'But what will happen to my beautiful, beautiful girls?'

'They'll be a lot better off once you're dead. I'll find a proper, sane woman to help me bring them up'.

'Mark?' Linda said, quietly, her voice trembling with fear. 'Isn't that going to be me?'

'You?' Mark exclaimed. 'You really think I'd want to spend the rest of my life with a gold digger like you? Not only a gold digger but someone I could never turn my back on in case she was plotting something against me?'

'But Mark … '

'… oh, the sex? I was fucking you. That's all. I was using you to get my end away but quite frankly, I've had more fun pleasuring myself in the shower'.

Linda burst into tears. 'You don't mean that'.

'Oh will somebody shut this pathetic creature up!' Helen demanded.

'Yes, that's what I've got you here to do, Helen' said Mark who'd worked it all out very carefully. Pretty soon he'd be free of them both.

Linda screamed. 'Mark, you can't mean that!'

'Okay, this has gone far enough' said Helen, trying to sound determined. 'You found out everything, Mark, and you used the information to call my bluff. But you're not like me. You've never been like me. You're only responding to what I've done to you'.

'Don't try appealing to my better side, Helen' said Mark. 'You destroyed it'.

'So if I do as you ask?' asked Helen. 'If I kill Miss Barbie doll here?'

'Then I may just let you live and see our daughters again'.

'How can I trust anything you say?'

Mark laughed. 'Trust went out of our window years ago,

darling! You'll just have to make a judgment but in the end if you don't kill her, then I'll kill you and that will destroy any hope you've got twisting around your poor little broken heart'.

The next few seconds went by as if they hadn't happened at all. Linda reached for the gun on the bedside table and managed to fire it before Helen fired her gun in return. Linda died instantly but Helen dropped to the floor before managing to drag herself towards the door, howling in agony and appealing to Mark to help her. But Mark kept stepping back further and further away from her, watching her die with a mounting degree of satisfaction, and knowing that his gun had not been fired at all so with careful explanation to the police he really could say that his jealous, mentally unstable wife shot his lover in the split second after his lover had shot her. It had worked out just how he'd planned it. He'd told Linda to lunge at Helen and she'd done so. The things people will do for love. The sad, pathetic cow.

And then Helen laid out as dramatically in death as she'd been in life.

The world would be better off without both of them.

TEN
CHARDONNAY

Alex and his wife Dawn went out for a drink with his friend and colleague from work Barry and his new girlfriend Christine. Dawn hadn't wanted to come out although, as usual, she was dressed up to the nines in a short skirt that made all the men in the pub avert their eyes when she crossed her legs and a top that exposed a more than fulsome chest. But she thought she was above socialising with the men, like Barry, who worked for Alex in his hardware store in Bolton. She was always accusing Alex of being over familiar with his employees and that he should do more to keep his distance and make sure they knew who was boss.

They'd been in the pub barely half an hour when Dawn went to the toilet and when she came back she said she wanted to go home.

'Why?' Alex asked, surprised at the request.

'I just want to, Alex' said Dawn who hadn't sat down again. 'We've shown our face with these people and that should be enough'.

Alex was mightily embarrassed at the way Dawn was talking about Barry and Christine as if they weren't there. He'd seen it all before but he kept hoping she'd change and start acting like a decent human being. Barry and Christine's faces were a mixture of bewilderment and sheer, bloody anger at Dawn's arrogance.

'But we've only just got here, Dawn' said Alex, quietly.

Dawn bit her bottom lip. 'Alex, why are you being like this?'

'Like what?'

'So disrespectful to me'.

'Dawn, I don't understand why you suddenly want to go home. Did somebody say something that upset you?'

'No'.

'Well are you feeling ill or something?'

'No!'

'Then what is it?'

'There doesn't have to be anything, Alex' said Dawn, crying. 'If I say I want to go home you should just come without questioning it'.

'Dawn, sit down and finish your wine. Please'.

Dawn then picked up Alex's pint and poured it over his head.

'There! Will you come with me now?' she squealed before running out of the bar and down the corridor leading to the car park.

Barry and Christine looked at each other and didn't know what to say. They felt so embarrassed for Alex. It seemed that Dawn was more highly strung than the Halle orchestra.

'I'd better go after her' said Alex who was mortified. He knew he'd now be in for a long night. 'Make sure she's alright. I'm ... I'm sorry'.

'It's okay, mate' said Barry. 'I'll see you at work tomorrow'.

'It was nice to meet you, Alex' said Christine.

Alex stood up and let some of the beer drip off him. Then he smiled at Christine and left the same way as Dawn a few seconds earlier.

'What was that all about?' Christine asked. 'Is the cow always like that?'

'I can tell you a few stories' said Barry. 'You know she won't let him bring newspapers into the house in case there's a picture of a good-looking girl in them. If they're watching telly of an evening and a good-looking girl comes on she'll ask him if he fancies her and when he says no she tells him he's a liar. So then they have a row and the telly gets switched off and then he has to pander to her as if he's done something wrong. It wouldn't just drive me crazy. I'd end up killing her'.

'Me too' said Christine. 'Well anyway, come on and let's go and get a curry. I'm hungry'.

'Okay' said Barry as he began to drink up the remains of his pint. 'But don't be eyeing up the waiter now'.

The pub landlady came over and started to wipe up the mess of beer left by Dawn's temper tantrum.

'Jesus, he's got his work cut out for him there, hasn't he?' she said.

'Looks like it' said Christine. 'I wouldn't like to be in his shoes'.

There was silence in the car as Alex drove them home.

'You stink of bloody beer' Dawn snarled. 'As soon as we get home get in the shower straight away! Got it? I don't want out Chardonnay smelling you like that. I said, have you got it?'

'Yes' said Alex who was raging inside but knew it was no point trying to reason with her when she was like this. 'I've got it'.

Dawn slapped his shoulder. 'And don't fucking answer me back in that tone! If you want someone to blame for what happened, look in the mirror because it was all your fault!'

Dawn paused for a few seconds and then said 'What did I just say to you?'

'You said it was all my fault'.

'And do you believe that?'

'Yes. Yes, of course I do'.

'Then say it like you fucking mean it! Say it like you truly believe it was all your fault and that I did nothing to cause the scene in the pub'.

'It was all my fault, Dawn' said Alex. 'Everything that happened tonight was all my fault'.

'I'm not convinced you mean it'.

'Ah for crying out loud, Dawn, why does it always have to be like this?'

'Because you're not man enough to admit it when you're in the wrong! That's what you are. Weak, spineless, feeble'.

When they got home Dawn paid the baby sitter and Alex went up to have a shower. When he came out, Dawn was waiting for him. She thumped him in the face so hard it drew blood. He stepped back. Even thought she'd done it a hundred times before it still had the power to shock.

'You made me do that' she hissed. 'You shouldn't have humiliated me in the pub with your little scene and you should've been man enough to admit that. And don't look at me like that, Alex. Because you know there's plenty more where that came from'.

'Dawn, ...'

'Enjoy it, did you?'

'What?'

'Making a fool of me in front of Barry and his new tart!'

'Dawn, I didn't mean to do that, I ... '

With that he earned himself a second punch to the face then a knee in his groin that made him buckle at the knees and fall to the floor. She carried on kicking him for how long, he didn't know, but when she'd finished she marched out of their bedroom and spent the night in the spare room.

The next morning Dawn was as bright and breezy as if last night she and Alex had won the pub quiz.

'Morning, gorgeous' she greeted. 'I've done you the lot. Bacon, sausages, beans, tomatoes, mushrooms, fried bread. Sit yourself down and I'll pour you a cup of tea'.

Alex was still in the pyjama bottoms and t-shirt he wore for bed. He flinched when he sat down at the kitchen table. She'd laid into him good and proper last night. And now she was acting as if everything was perfectly normal. He couldn't stomach the food that she laid out in front of him but if he refused it would only mean more trouble. He couldn't think of how it had all started. She'd always had a temper and she'd always been moody. It was only after they'd married that the scales had started to fall from her eyes and she'd started using him as a punch-bag. Sometimes she was sorry afterwards. Other times like now it was as if last night had never happened.

She was rambling on about something or nothing. He wasn't listening to a word. He was just aware of her voice as he forked pieces of sausage and runny egg yolk into his mouth. It was when she said 'estate agents' that his senses filled with dread.

'What did you say?' he asked.

'Are you saying you weren't listening to me?'

'I'm saying that I didn't hear that last bit'.

'Did you hear the bit about it being a good idea if we sold up and moved away? Made a fresh start somewhere else?'

'A good idea to who?'

'I've decided' said Dawn. 'You can sell the business and start another one somewhere else'.

'That business has been in my family for four generations'.

'And is that more important than what I want? It had better not be, Alex. I'm warning you. It had better bloody not be!'

Their daughter Chardonnay came running into the room and went straight to her father.

'Daddy!'

'Hey, princess!' Alex greeted his little four-year old as she ran up to him. He had to hold his breath as she jumped onto his lap but it was all worth it when she gave him a kiss. But then her mother's reproachful tones killed the momentarily loss of tension from the room.

'Chardonnay, what have I told you about being a mither?'

'She's not being a mither, Dawn, she's saying hello to her Daddy'.

'Are you really sitting there and disagreeing with me in front of her?'

'Dawn, I'm just saying that I don't mind'.

'Yes, well I do and you should back me up. Come on Chardonnay, get down off your Daddy's lap because he's trying to eat his breakfast that Mummy cooked for him'.

'I don't want to' said Chardonnay who then buried her head in Alex's chest.

'Don't you dare disobey me you evil child!' Dawn raged.

'And don't call her that!'

'I'll call my daughter what the hell I fucking well want!'

'And don't swear in front of her!'

The scene that followed broke both Alex and Chardonnay's hearts. Dawn literally tore a sobbing and screaming Chardonnay away from her father and held her so tight she could barely breathe as she took her upstairs. Alex felt useless. He was that little girls' father and yet he couldn't protect her from the violence of her own mother. He followed them upstairs. Thankfully Dawn wasn't slapping Chardonnay like she so often does.

'It's okay' snarled Dawn with a look of sheer contempt for her husband. 'I haven't touched her but if I had it would be her own fault for pushing me beyond my limits'.

'Listen to her crying her little heart out. How can you stand there and say it's all her fault?'

'Because I can and because you know what will happen if you try and cross me on this'.

'But there was no need for it, Dawn! No need for it at all! All she was doing was sitting on my knee'.

Dawn slid down the wall and burst into tears.

'I don't know what comes over me, Alex' Dawn pleaded. 'I love you so much and I get so jealous'.

'Even of your own daughter?'

Dawn nodded her head. 'I can't help it'.

'Dawn, we can't carry on like this'.

'Everybody loves you. Everybody sees you as Mr. Nice guy and a saint for putting up with a bitch like me. Everybody hates me'.

Alex squatted down next to his wife. 'No they don't'.

'Yes, they do!' Dawn insisted. 'You're a liar!'

'Well I don't know what to do'.

'I really hurt you last night, didn't I'.

'I'll survive'.

'You wouldn't have to if I could get myself under control' said Dawn. 'That fresh start I was talking about? Why don't we move out to the coast? We've always liked Blackpool and we've always been happy there. What do you say? It would be really fun for Chardonnay and perhaps I could relax a bit more there and maybe get some help? I know it's not right the way I behave. The three of us moving out to the seaside might be just what we need'.

Three months later

He wasn't one for browsing. Unless it was a book shop he wasn't really that interested. So the girls left him in Waterstones' and picked him up an hour later after he'd bought another half a dozen books for his already bulging bookshelves. Then they decided to go for a pizza.

'It feels good to relax for a bit' said Joe as he looked at the menu. He was with his friends Lauren and Mandy. Joe was a paramedic on the local ambulances, Lauren was also a nurse but at the same casualty unit at the Blackpool Victoria hospital where Mandy was a consultant. They'd all been friends for years.

'It must be hard for your Mum after your Dad died' said Lauren.

'It is but she's doing okay' said Joe. 'You know what my Mum is like? She copes and gets on with it although I can tell how much of a struggle it is for her to keep putting on that brave face'.

'It'll ease in time' said Mandy.

'Oh, I know, but she misses him. They've been together since they were both eighteen and that was forty years ago. She's lost, bless her. And what with me doing the shifts I do, our Tony in Canada, and our Pam down in Birmingham, it isn't like she's always got one of us on hand'.

'She's got good friends around her though' said Mandy.

'Oh yeah, and I thank my lucky stars for that. She's close to all my Aunts and Uncles too which helps. She's never off the bloody phone at the moment'.

'You needed to take a break, Joe' said Lauren. 'It was wearing you out'.

'It's what you do though, isn't it' said Joe. 'He was my Dad and everyone who says that time is the great healer is a liar. I miss him more each day'.

They ordered drinks whilst they made up their minds and Joe was careful to place his mobile down on the table so he could answer it sharply if his Mum called. Joe went for a meat pizza, Mandy ordered a seafood one and Lauren opted for one with goat's cheese and spinach. Each of them had a gin and tonic and they ordered a bottle of Rioja to go with their pizzas. Joe did manage to relax and laugh a lot with his two 'sisters' but then he heard a voice in the background that at first he couldn't place. He turned round and when he saw who it was he blushed.

'What?' Lauren asked.

'You see that guy sitting a couple of tables back with fair hair and wearing a light blue polo shirt?'

'Yes?' said Lauren. 'He's got a little girl with him and let me say'.

'Yes, me too' Mandy agreed. 'I wouldn't mind finding him on top of my pizza'.

'Yes, with extra parmesan' said Lauren as the two girls eyed up what they both considered was a rather lovely gift for their eyes.

'Who is it?' Mandy asked.

'It's that plumber I told you about' said Joe 'The one who moved in next door last week. The hunky one I was getting all worked up over'.

'And you were right' said Mandy. 'He's a bit of alright'.

'Yeah, well' said Joe. 'I'd better forget all about that. He's clearly straight'.

'So is spaghetti until it gets into hot water, darling' said Lauren. 'And we all know what a big kettle switch you've got, Joe'.

Joe feigned offence. 'I've had my moments'.

'Moments?' Mandy teased. 'Sleeping with men who are supposed to be straight is called moments, is it?'

'Well I'm still single at thirty-six and the moments are getting fewer and further between. Anyway, can I remind you pair of lust crazy poodles that you're both happily married?'

'It doesn't mean to say we're dead to the charms of other men' said Mandy. 'How come whenever I call out a plumber he never looks like that?'.

'Well he's only been one for five minutes' said Joe. 'He and his wife and daughter moved over from Manchester. He had a hardware store which he sold but he couldn't find any suitable business here to invest his money in. So he's retrained as a plumber and set up on his own'.

'What's she like?' Lauren asked. 'The wife?'

'All over gushing one minute and cold as ice the next' said Joe. 'A bit of a strange one if you ask me'.

'Some women don't know they're born' said Mandy.

'Er, excuse me, neither of your two husbands are exactly ugly'.

'Well that's what I mean' said Mandy. 'We women sometimes don't know when we're born'.

'He's just paid and he's coming this way' said Lauren.

'Don't talk to me' said Joe. 'I'm not here'.

'Hiya' said Alex.

Joe could've died. 'Hello' he said. He went hot. 'Have you just finished?'

'Yeah' said Alex. 'I recognised you sitting there but I didn't want to intrude'.

'Oh you wouldn't be' said Joe. 'These are my friends Mandy and Lauren'.

Alex exchanged greetings with the girls.

'And who's this gorgeous little one?' Mandy asked as she looked at the pretty little girl with long, sandy brown hair, and blue eyes just like Joe's.

'This is my daughter' said Alex, proudly.

'And what's your name, precious?' asked Joe.

'Chardonnay Barnes'.

A look flashed between Joe, Mandy, and Lauren. Chardonnay?

'Chardonnay?' said Joe. 'That's a pretty name for a pretty girl like you'.

'Are you having a nice day with your Daddy?' Lauren asked.

'Yes' said Chardonnay. 'I like being with Daddy'.

'Dawn is at work' Alex explained. 'She's doing some agency nursing at Blackpool Victoria until she finds a permanent post'.

'Blackpool Victoria?' Mandy questioned. 'But we all work there'.

'Of course you do' said Alex, snapping his fingers as he recalled the conversation. 'Joe told me. Well she's in the gynaecological ward at the moment. It's suiting her for the time being'.

'Well we'll have to look out for her' said Lauren. 'What's her surname?'

'Well for work she uses her maiden name of Fraser, Dawn Fraser. Her married name is Barnes'.

'Are you Daddy's girl, Chardonnay?' Joe asked.

Chardonnay wrapped her arm round her father's leg and pressed her cheek into it.

'I think you are' said Joe. 'I think you love Daddy very much'.

Alex picked Chardonnay up but the pain in his ribs almost gave the game away. 'Who's always going to be the only man in your life?'

'Daddy!'

'You're in for an expensive time' said Lauren.

'She's worth it' said Alex who then kissed his daughter. 'Aren't you, princess?

'Has Chardonnay started school yet?' asked Lauren.

'Yeah, she started last September' said Alex. 'We've got her into a good one here too now which is a relief. Well look, we'd best be off. It's been nice to see you again, Joe, I'll in for that beer sometime'.

'If the light is on you're welcome'.

Alex smiled at his new neighbour. 'You're on'.

Joe liked the way Alex looked in his chinos and light brown corduroy jacket. His face was covered in a kind of thick stubble that made him look like someone off the front page of GQ and very desirable. Joe had always liked stubble on men. He thought it was horny. He watched Alex leave the restaurant with his daughter in his arms and he longed for him. He then looked up and saw that Mandy was staring knowingly at him.

'What?' Joe asked.

'Joe, his eyes were all over you' said Mandy.

'Oh fuck off'.

'It's true' said Mandy. 'He got all embarrassed when you looked straight at him. And what colour will this light be that you'll have on for him? A red one?'

'He's just another straight man who gets off on a gay man fancying him' Joe insisted. 'That's if he realised that I do fancy him'.

'And if he does then why is he encouraging you by saying he'll be round for that beer? I'd say he was hoping for more'.

'Oh rubbish! I'm not listening!'

'Come on, Lauren, back me up' said Mandy.

'He might not be completely straight' said Lauren.

'Lauren, I'm not a holiday resort that welcomes tourists' Joe protested.

'You don't know anything about his life, Joe' said Mandy. 'You're making a lot of assumptions to protect yourself and your feelings, which I can understand, but you don't actually know anything about him for sure'.

'He likes you' said Mandy.

'He does not' said Joe. 'He's just being friendly. Now eat your pizza and stop giving me indigestion'.

'What are you thinking about, Lauren?' asked Mandy. 'You look like you're miles away'.

'The penny has just dropped' said Lauren. 'I've got a mate on gynae and he told me about this new agency nurse called Dawn who caused all sorts of trouble on her first day. Wouldn't be told what to do, kept on bursting into tears, virtually told everybody that they were incompetent and that, as always, she was saving the day for them. If she wants a permanent post, I don't think she'll be getting one at Blackpool Victoria on that little performance'.

Dawn came home in a foul mood and threw her things down on the living room sofa. She'd been doing a late shift and Alex had put Chardonnay to bed and was now watching an episode of Inspector Lewis on the TV.

'What's the matter?' Alex asked, gingerly.

'Your faggot friend next door, that's what's the matter!'

'I beg your pardon'.

'There was a permanent job going at the hospital but they've decided to give it to someone who they've never known before instead of me who's been working there now for three fucking weeks!'

'Well by faggot, I presume you mean Joe?'

'Well how many other faggot friends have you got, eh? Got

yourself a little fan club, have you? Do you all get together and dance to Kylie whilst you slag me off?'

'Dawn, I really don't know what you're talking about'.

Dawn picked up the TV remote control and switched it off.

'Thanks, i was watching that' said Alex.

'Listen to me! That Joe hasn't liked me since the word go and who else could've stuck the knife into me getting a permanent job at a hospital where he knows all the people who do nurse recruitment?'

'Dawn, Joe wouldn't do anything like that'.

'Then how do you explain it then?'

'Well I can't explain it'.

'Right, well shut your stupid, fucking useless mouth then and I'll deal with this'.

'What do you mean, you'll ...'

'... swapped techniques, have you? Compared the way I give it to you to the way he does?'

'Dawn, there is nothing going on between me and Joe!' Alex insisted. 'For crying out loud, I'm straight!'

'Yeah, well you're always round there and they say six pints of lager is all that does it'.

'I go round there because he's a mate' said Alex. 'I don't go round there for any other reason'.

'So you say'.

'Yes, I say!'

Dawn screwed up her face in anger and then she slapped Alex sharply across his face. His head swung round to the side and he placed his hand on his cheek. That one was one of her hardest. She must be really angry this time or she'd been eating all her breakfast cereal. He had to at least try and make a joke to himself at these times. It was the only way he could get through it. As long as Chardonnay didn't wake up and the whole scene frighten her. That had happened too many times in her short life as it was.

'If you ever talk to me like that again, I will kill you' said Dawn. 'and anyway, why should I suffer? This is all your fault'.

'I thought it would be'.

'And don't answer me back! If it hadn't been for you moving us over to this place in the shadow of the fucking Pleasure Beach. You've got a lot to answer for'.

'You wanted to move. You chose Blackpool and you chose the house'.

'If you dare to contradict me I'll break your bloody face next time, alright?'

'I don't know what to say anymore, Dawn' said Alex, shaking his head. 'I really don't know what to say'.

'Well let me just make things crystal clear for you, shall I? If you go anywhere near that viscous little faggot next door, there will be consequences. I absolutely forbid you from having anything to do with him'.

'He won't have had anything to do with you not getting the job, Dawn, now think about it and be reasonable for God's sake'.

'I'm sorry, did I not spell it out the first time?' She slapped him again only this time he fell back against the sofa. He curled himself into a ball and wrapped his arms round his body as she rained the punches down on him until she had no strength left in her body.

Chardonnay was sitting on the upstairs landing and knew from the sounds she could hear what was happening to her poor Daddy.

Then it all went quiet again and she heard her Mummy say 'You made me do that. Do you hear me? You made me do it'.

A few days later Joe came home from work and parked his car on the drive he shared with Alex and Dawn. Alex pulled up a second or two behind and Joe was glad to have seen him. He'd been acting very strange lately.

'Alex?' he said after they'd both got out of their cars. He put aside the momentary fantasy of a working man like Alex coming home to dinner with him. Alex was in a dark blue overall with a white t-shirt underneath and big, thick black boots. He looked a bit dirty but Joe liked that. He also looked tired but not because he'd done a hard day's work. The moment was awkward to say the least. 'Alex? Look, what's wrong? Have I done something to offend you or something?'

'No'.

'Then what's with the sudden silent treatment? If I haven't done anything then what's it all about?'

'Why is it any business of yours?'

'Because it's me you're suddenly ignoring and I thought we were friends?'

Alex took his keys out of his pocket and went to unlock his back door.

'Alex, what the fuck is going on? We're two grown men for God's sake'.

Alex didn't know what to do. He so needed his friend but if Dawn found out it would only mean trouble.

'Where's Dawn?' Joe persisted. He was still in his paramedics uniform.

'Late shift' Alex answered. 'Chardonnay is having her tea at one of her little mates'.

'She's got a good little social life'.

'She needs it' said Alex. 'She needs to get away from here'.

'Alex, will you come inside with me and talk?'

'Dawn has forbidden me from having anything more to do with you' said Alex who still hadn't looked Joe properly in the face. 'She thinks it was you who put in a bad word for her when she didn't get that permanent job a couple of weeks back'.

'That's totally not true, Alex'.

'I know that, Joe. But you don't understand how it is'.

'Then come in and tell me'.

'I feel ashamed'.

'If you're going to tell me what I think you're going to tell me then it isn't you who should feel ashamed, Alex'.

Alex looked up at him.

'Alex, I've got eyes and I've got ears. I've also got nearly fifteen years experience as a medic. So come on. Once you tell someone you'll be halfway to sorting it out'.

Alex laughed. 'Sorting it out? It'll never be that'.

'It has to be, Alex. For your own sake and for the sake of Chardonnay'.

Alex looked into Joe's eyes and knew that if he went into Joe's house now then things would never be the same again but he didn't care anymore. He followed Joe in through the door that led straight into Joe's kitchen. He sat down at the table, put his head in his hands and cried for what seemed like a very long time. Joe was beside him, holding him like a child, helping him to release every pent up emotion that he'd carried around for so long.

Then they were kissing. Alex responded slowly at first to Joe's tenderness but before long he knew he needed more of this feeling. Joe led him by the hand upstairs. Then they were naked and suddenly Alex began to shake. He was nervous. A kiss was one thing but now he was exposed as the weak man Dawn was always accusing him of being.

'Oh my God' said Joe as he gently ran his fingers over some of Alex's bruises. 'Did she do all this to you?'

Alex folded his arms without looking up and said 'Yes'.

'Come on' said Joe. 'I can make you feel better'.

Alex knew that he wanted this. He laid himself down on Joe's bed and let the sensation of two men together seep into every pore of his body. He hadn't really known what to expect. He'd thought it might be cold. He'd thought it might feel almost like some out of body experience where things were being done to him but he wasn't feeling any of it. He didn't know if he'd be able to let go enough to feel everything that had come to mind since Joe had started to mean more to him than just a friend. That in itself had come as something of a shock. But now, as the late afternoon sun shone through the windows, Joe's experienced hands warmed every one of those fears away. Making love with Dawn these past few years had been an exercise in avoiding the truth. Now, with Joe, he'd found a much deeper truth and one that he'd never thought about before.

'Thank you' said Alex as he lay there in Joe's arms. As part of the act of love making, Joe had kissed every bruise, every scratch, every red mark, even the tooth marks on Alex's shoulder that provided further evidence of Dawn's monstrous temper. Alex had almost felt like crying again a couple of times. For so long he hadn't known what sensuality could do for him.

'How are you feeling?'

'Like we've spent the last few weeks knowing this was going to happen but that we were just waiting for the right moment'.

Joe kissed Alex's head. 'You've no regrets then?'

'No' said Alex. 'And you?'

'Absolutely not' said Joe.

'You're not going to ignore me now you've finally had your wicked way with me then?'

'Fat chance of that' said Joe. 'The truth is I don't want to let you go now'.

'I come with an enormous amount of baggage'.

'Yes' said Joe. 'I can't bear the thought of her hitting you like this again, Alex, when I'm not there to protect you'.

'It's not as easy as that though'.

'I know' said Joe who was running his fingers through Alex's chest rug. The hairs in the middle of his chest were so long he could curl them round his fingers. He liked that. 'But you and Chardonnay have got to get out of there before something really serious happens. We're going to have to work something out and fast'.

'I knew this was going to happen between us' said Alex. 'I don't know who the hell I was kidding. Even though I'd never been with a bloke before, something about you made me realise that I wanted to. Perhaps I always have, and you brought it out'.

'I sometimes didn't let myself think that it might happen' Joe admitted. 'But it was getting frustrating. It's all very well having straight mates and I've got plenty of them. But when you've got a straight mate for whom you've got feelings there comes a point when you don't want to have yet another conversation with the elephant in the room. You want to just get down to it and start talking intimately, dirty even. You want to tell that man that it's great having a drink down the pub with him but you actually fancy the fucking pants off him'.

Alex laughed. 'Is that what you thought about me?'

'Thought? That's what I think about you, Alex'.

'Are you saying this could turn into something special?'

'Yes' said Joe. 'That's exactly what I'm saying. And if you let me help you break away from Dawn I'll make it my life's work to take care of you and Chardonnay'.

'And to think I might not have met you if we hadn't moved'.

'Well I'm bloody glad you did'.

'You're not the only one'.

Dawn sat in front of the interview panel and she could've shit herself. Ever since her step sister had spent a whole fucking lifetime constantly undermining her and Dawn's own mother had gone along with it, she'd never liked to be in the spotlight and yet, perversely, she'd also craved attention at the same time. But as soon as she'd got it she'd ripped it to shreds with a temper that even she could be afraid of at times. She was desperate. She always had been. She was insecure. She had been since her Daddy died and her mother had taken up with a bloke who had his own daughter and had made it clear that he hadn't wanted to take on another man's child. Yet her mother had always took his side and had never even tried to protect her from the constant barrage of negative comments that her step-father and step-sister had stabbed her with time and time again. And now she had to contend with the fact that her husband had left her. He hadn't left her for another woman, oh no, it couldn't be anything as plain and straightforward as that. He'd left her for another man and she didn't think she'd ever be able to get over the shame of it all. She'd known from the word go that Joe was a treacherous little bastard. Well he'd pay. They both would. Nobody humiliates Dawn and gets away with it. Refusing to let Alex see Chardonnay was only the beginning.

'I've been agency nursing for several months now' said Dawn. She reached into her handbag and took out a paper tissue. 'I really need this job to provide stability for myself and my daughter now that my husband has left me'. She wiped away the beginnings of tears that were falling down her cheeks. 'He's left me for another man and it's been horrible. I need this job because I've got to have a regular wage coming in'.

The interview panel weren't used to people crying at interviews. The two women and one man were all nursing staff and were looking to fill a position in the cardiac unit, but they'd never experienced this sort of thing before.

'Isn't your husband ... providing?' asked the older of the two women interviewers, Hazel, with her tweed two-piece and polished black court shoes.

'But how can I rely on what he gives me?' Dawn pleaded. 'He could be off on some other flight of fancy next week. I don't know him anymore but sooner or later he'll be begging me to take him back and I can tell you now that I won't'.

'Would you like to pause the interview for a while, Mrs. Barnes?' Hazel asked.

'And that's another thing, I'm keeping his name, oh yes, I'm keeping that for the sake of our daughter who cries her heart out every night longing for her Daddy'.

'Well if that's the case then why don't you let me see her, Dawn?' asked Alex as he walked in the room. 'I've made constant requests through friends, family, solicitors, and the courts. You've found a way to stop me seeing her at every turn so if anybody is to blame for Chardonnay not seeing her Daddy, it's you'.

'What the hell are you doing here?' Dawn demanded.

'This is most irregular' Hazel protested.

'I know and I apologise' said Alex. 'But I'm a father who's desperate to see his daughter and I've tried everything else. I knew she'd come here and tell you a pack of lies. It's true I've left her another man. I've fallen in love for the first time in my life and it feels wonderful. It feels so much better to be treated like a human being instead of a punch bag'.

'A punch bag?' Hazel questioned.

'Are you going to let him interfere like this?' Dawn protested angrily.

The three members of the interview panel were taken aback by the sudden ferocity of Dawn's anger.

'Well I think it might be useful to our considerations, yes' said the younger of the two women on the panel, Deborah, in her high neck, sleeveless red dress and short blond hair. 'Despite the unusual nature of it. Please go on, Mr. Barnes'.

Alex produced a large manila envelope from the briefcase he

was carrying and put a series of six photographs on the desk in front of the panel. They were all of himself showing the various bruises and injuries Dawn had inflicted on him. Joe had taken them shortly after they'd started seeing each other.

'Have you shown these to the courts, Mr. Barnes?' asked Hazel.

'Oh yes' said Alex. 'But it's like this. A man can beat his wife and lose access to his children. A woman can beat her husband and she's able to ignore the judgements of the court with regard to access and if the man dares to protest then he becomes the one in the wrong. Now I'm still waiting for someone to talk me through that with regard to where I'm going to find justice. Pulling a stunt like this is all I had left to get somebody to see things from my perspective. I'm a father who loves his daughter more than life itself. But I'm prevented from seeing her because of the lies her mother has told about me being the abuser in the family'.

'Is this true, Mrs. Barnes?' Deborah asked. She used to work on the unit that dealt with domestic violence and what she was hearing appalled her because of all the genuine cases of abuse that are out there.

'He made me do it all!'

'Pardon?' Deborah questioned.

'This bastard here knew what buttons to push and he pushed them!'

The man on the panel, Colin, in his light grey suit then spoke up. 'I've heard that excuse from so many weak, pathetic men, Mrs. Barnes, and you disgust me equally as much as they do'.

'Absolutely' Deborah agreed.

'But you don't understand anything about me or my life!'

'I understand that many people grow up in difficult circumstances but who don't use that as an excuse to turn violent against their partners' said Hazel.

'I'm just a man, you see' said Alex. 'I'm not what you'd call greatly educated. I took over my father's hardware shop and then I re-trained as a plumber. I'm a working man. I'm not supposed to hit women and I'm not supposed to hit them back when they hit me. And yet I thought we were supposed to have equality in this country? Well if we do then isn't it supposed to cut both ways?'

'But he's left me for a fucking queer!'

'Yes, and I'm having the time of my fucking life!'

It took the combined strength of the three members of the interview panel, plus two men from the office just outside, to get Dawn off Alex. She'd literally gone for his throat and if they hadn't managed to get her off him in time he'd have been strangled. As it was it took him a few moments to get his breath back. Dawn was restrained by hospital security staff.

'We'll make a joint statement on your behalf for the court, Mr. Barnes' said Hazel.

Alex's voice was croaky. 'Thank you'.

'There's a refuge for male victims of domestic violence' Hazel went on. 'They're over in Preston which isn't far away as you know. I'll give you their contact details and perhaps they might be able to help you'.

A year later

Alex, Joe, and Chardonnay had sold their respective houses and moved to one they'd chosen together on the North Shore of Blackpool near Bispham. It was a block away from the cliff top beach which Chardonnay loved going to and they'd got her into a good school nearby.

Alex had taken so much to the refuge and the people who worked there that he was now a part-time volunteer talking to men who were in a similar situation to the one he'd been in. He couldn't believe that it was still such a taboo for men to admit that they were victims as well as women, and for society, particularly other women, to accept that men were victims too.

It was Chardonnay's fifth birthday coming up and they were planning a big party. Alex had never seen his little girl looking as relaxed and happy as she did now. After the incident at the hospital interview, Dawn completely turned the other way and gave Alex sole custody of Chardonnay. It pleased him and Joe no end because it meant that they wouldn't have to have anything to do with Dawn but they also worried about her growing up without knowing her Mum, despite everything. But they had lots of female friends who gave her all the feminine influencing she needed. She seemed to rather like having two daddies. She apparently boasted about it at school. Alex was relieved that she was now growing up in a house of love as opposed to a house of violence, tension, and intimidation. He never heard from Dawn. He kept her informed of Chardonnay's progress but that was always through her mother and he never heard anything from Dawn herself.

It was a Saturday morning and Alex was playing with Chardonnay in the living room and watching Dora the Explorer on a DVD. Joe was on early shift and when he got back they were planning to go on the beach with a picnic. It was a beautiful day and the sky was a crystal clear blue.

All of a sudden, Alex was aware of a presence behind him. He turned round and Dawn was standing there with a kitchen knife in her hand.

'You shouldn't have left the back door open, sweetheart' said Dawn. 'Very careless of you. Anybody could just walk straight in'.

Alex reached for Chardonnay but Dawn was too quick and lashed the top of his arm with the knife. Alex gasped with pain but then he told a distraught, crying Chardonnay not to worry and that everything was going to be alright. Chardonnay clung to her Daddy as if her life depended on it.

'Why did you leave me for him?' Dawn yelled.

'Because I love him'.

'Were you gay when you married me?'

'No' said Alex. The knife had gone quite deep into his shoulder but he was as okay as he thought he should be. 'He found me. He found a need in my soul and he answered it. I wouldn't expect you to understand'.

'You talk a load of shit' she sneered.

'It's the truth'.

'Is it fuck the truth! You married me knowing you were gay and I want to hear you admit it'.

'Then you'll have a long wait' said Alex as he held the top of his arm as tightly as he could. 'And don't use language like that in front of Chardonnay'.

Dawn waved the knife in the air. 'I don't think you're in a position to tell me what to do'.

'For God's sake, Dawn! Can't you see how you're upsetting Chardonnay? What do you hope to prove by being here?'

'That I'm Chardonnay's mother and that I'm here to claim that right'.

'You gave it up. You gave her up. She's happy now with me and Joe. If you were anything of a mother you'd see that and leave her alone!'

That was enough for Dawn to see red. 'Oh you need teaching a flaming lesson!'

Dawn stabbed Alex in the chest and this time he collapsed onto the floor. She panicked. Seeing the terrified look in her daughter's eyes, she ran outside, got into her car and sped off.

Chardonnay lifted up the phone next to the sofa and pressed the button that said 'Joe's number'.

'Hello?'

'Joe, please come home'.

'Princess? What's wrong, darling?'

'Mummy hurt Daddy with a knife'.

'What?'

'She's gone now. There's a lot of blood everywhere. Please come and save Daddy, Joe. He won't wake up. Please come home, Joe. Please come home and save my Daddy. I don't want him to go to Jesus'.

ELEVEN
JULIA

When she got to the address she'd been given she was rather surprised. It wasn't anything like she'd expected. It was on what they call a development of semi detached modern houses on the 'border' between Sale and Altrincham, and knowing how the postcode snobbery worked round here, she thought it highly probable that they all considered themselves to be residents of the nice, leafy Cheshire town of Altrincham, rather than be thought of as part of the greater Manchester conurbation. The difference in house price between Sale and Altrincham would be enough to make up for the stretching of the truth over boundaries.

The house itself, number five, Milton Crescent, was in a small cul-de-sac of twelve properties. Everything looked very nice. There were pretty net curtains at the windows but they were pulled back sufficiently for anyone passing to see inside the living room. It all looked spotless, clean and tidy, a testament to middle class living. It wasn't like Julia's own house, or the one she was about to be thrown out of by the council, and which was a tip of great proportions, especially since her mother had died. They'd lived in the same council house in Fallowfield, just south of the city centre, for as long as Julia could remember and when she was little the toilet had been outside. Gradually over the years the council had made improvements, brought the toilet inside and upstairs, fitted a shower, central heating, double glazing. They'd even fitted a kitchen which was what had finished her mother off. She hadn't been able to cope with the 'upheaval' even though it was making the house a better place to live and not costing her a single penny piece. When the shower was fitted all her mother did was moan about how she liked 'a good soak in the bath' and she didn't 'hold' with this modern tendency for showering. She didn't see the point somehow. When Julia had pointed out on many occasions that a daily shower was all about personal hygiene her mother had just had a go at her for smelling in the first place. Julia had given up explaining any further. Then when her mother had started buying her 'personal stuff' from the local hardware shop, Julia gave up altogether. It was as if her mother was determined to 'de-feminise' herself in some way. She never wore make up and she never wore a skirt or a dress. It was always trousers, or 'slacks' as her mother called them and they were always in the darkest most miserable colours. She never thought that her mother could be a lesbian underneath it all. She just seemed determined to make a negative statement about herself every time she went out and she wanted to give herself a reason for never getting any attention from men. In her later years, Julia didn't think her mother wouldn't have known what to do with any male attention.

Julia on the other hand had never gone short on male attention. When she was younger she'd decided she had a choice to go down one of two paths. Either she could be a slut who'd sleep with almost anything and regret nothing, or she'd find the boy-next-door type and live happily ever after in a place like Milton Crescent and raise some kids. She'd started off with the former. In her teenage years and going into her early twenties she'd slept with so many men she really didn't know how many. When she and the girls went on their annual holidays to Spain or Greece, they all had score cards and Julia would always end up in front. She wanted the excitement and the challenge, the attention and the sex, oh yes, she liked her sex alright. But now she'd settled down with the latter. She was going out with Liam, a six foot tall boy-next-door who kept in shape by running and going to the gym and was great in bed. He loved her too and that's what mattered the most. They worked together at Manchester airport and he'd asked her to marry him and she'd said yes. They hadn't made any definite plans yet though. They were still having a good time.

Julia sat in her car and smoked another cigarette. Because of the nerves and the tension she had thought about coming on the bus but it would've meant getting two buses and that would've brought back too many memories from her childhood. When she and her mother used to go and visit her Aunts and Uncles when Julia was little, they had to take two, sometimes three buses to cross the city and see them for Sunday tea. Her mother used to complain bitterly that they all had cars on the drive and it wouldn't have hurt them to come at least half way and meet them. But all of those visits fizzled out when Julia was about ten or eleven. That's when she and her mother began what she called 'the wilderness years' as far as the family were concerned. None of them ever came round or even rang. Her mother had the odd friend here and there but she never went out much. She grew skinless and defensive to the point where she just couldn't take a joke or the mildest form of banter. It got on Julia's nerves. She spent so much time treading on fucking egg shells around her.

Her Mum did have her moments though. For a few years she was seeing a much older married man called Charlie who she met on the bus one day going into town. He bought her a washing machine, a second hand three piece suite, he paid for her and Julia to have little holidays in north Wales, and he gave her cash to supplement the meagre income she got from working at the local bread factory. He said he was giving Julia's Mum the money now that he wouldn't be able to give her in his Will when he died, for obvious reasons to do with his wife and family. Julia didn't think they ever had sex. Lots of cuddles and affection but nothing more.

Charlie was well into his seventies and probably couldn't manage it anyway. But he was a good man and when he died, sure enough, there was nothing in his Will for Julia's Mum who'd been his mistress for, by then, almost three years. That's when Julia's mother began her problems with money. She hadn't admitted how much she'd relied on Charlie to keep the household going. The slide accelerated over the following few months until her mother had no choice but to declare personal bankruptcy.

It was just another nail in the coffin that Julia's mother probably never recovered from. It was embarrassing sometimes when Julia's friends from school came round. Her mother could barely afford to give them a glass of orange juice. But she had good friends who stood by Julia during all the dark times. She was lucky in that respect. They'd all gone to the funeral. They'd all been round to see her mother after she'd been diagnosed with the heart condition that eventually killed her. At the funeral Julia used her friends to shield herself from her so-called family. All those Aunts and Uncles who all promised to stay in touch with her and make sure she was okay. It had now been three months since her mother's funeral and Julia hadn't heard a Dickie bird from any of the hypocritical wankers. It was all very well making a show of sorrow and grief at somebody's funeral. It was whether you were there for them when they were alive that counts.

She checked her hair for the umpteenth time and freshened up her make up. She'd put on her best dress in burgundy and was wearing a black Chanel type jacket over it. It was the outfit she'd worn to Liam's brother's wedding last year and everybody had complimented her on it. She wanted to look her best for her Dad. This was the first time they were seeing each other.

There was a driveway between the two sets of semis and it was down this side of the house that the front door was located. The door of number five was painted in a burgundy red and, true to what was looking like the form, two rather neat looking plant pots with things growing out of them that Julia didn't recognise, were either side of the door. Julia rang the bell. She'd thought about this moment for years. What was she going to say to her father? This was a man she'd never known, a man she'd never ever seen. All she'd ever had was a name, Geoff Coleman, and through some very basic investigating, she'd managed to find his address. She'd thought about trying to get in touch with him many times but she hadn't wanted to embarrass her mother when she was alive. What if she and her father had hit it off and that had led to her mother feeling left out? Her death had made it all so much easier to contemplate somehow.

Julia waited for a response. She was nervous. The palms of her hands had turned sweaty and a trickle of perspiration was making its way down her spine.

'What do you want?'

The voice that came from the other side of the still closed door was accompanied by the shadow of a man whom Julia could see through the frosted glass.

'It's ... it's Julia?'

'I don't know anything about any Julia'.

'I'm Rita's daughter? Look, I wrote and asked if I could see you and you told me to come round at this time'.

'Well I've changed my mind. There's no good that can come from raking up a past that should be left there'.

'But I'm your daughter!'

'No, you're not. You're nothing to me. Never have been and never will be'.

'You can't say that!'

'Look, you've got by without me all this time so you can carry on. You're obviously good at it'.

'I haven't had any choice!'

'I've got a daughter and she's all the children I've got as far as I'm concerned'.

Julia thought she could actually feel her heart breaking. How could he be so cruel?

'You can't do this to me!'

'Look, just clear off! I want nothing to do with you. Live your life and be happy but I don't want to be a part of it'.

'But why not?' she pleaded.

'Because I never wanted you! I wasn't in love with your mother.

She was in love with me but I never returned it. Then when she told me she was pregnant I couldn't bare the thought of being tied down to her and a kid. So I legged it. And I've not regretted a single moment'.

'But you've missed out on so much. I'm getting married in a couple of years and you'll have grandchildren!'

'They'll be nothing to do with me'.

'But who's going to give me away at my wedding?'

'Look, this isn't very dignified. Just clear off and forget you ever came here because that's what I'm going to do'.

'You bastard!'

'Yes, that's it, get it all out of your system and the go!'

Julia was shaking as she got back into her car. She sat there for ten minutes crying her heart out, hoping that her father might change his mind and come out to her.

But he didn't.

She turned the key in the ignition and drove off.

A year later.

Julia was now senior customer service agent for the ground handling company at Manchester airport for whom she'd now worked for eight years. She loved her job. She loved working with people and she was popular amongst the rest of the staff. It was also where she'd met Liam, now her fiancé, and in six months time, her husband. Liam worked in a department called 'dispatch' where they liased with the pilots of the aircraft to sort out how much fuel they'd need, where the baggage was going to be distributed in the various holds, how much cargo they were carrying and what it was, and if the cabin crew needed any extra supplies if the passenger load went up. They also supervised the customer service agents like Julia when it came to boarding the passengers on time and making sure the flight left on schedule. Julia had once thought about going for the same job but had decided against it. It was interesting enough but the 'dispatchers' could be under a lot of pressure if the flights were running late or if anything went wrong. Sometimes, when Liam had finished his shift, he'd go round to Julia's flat and she would turn out the lights, light some candles, and massage all the stress out of his shoulders and back. They both liked that and they also both liked where it usually led!

But one of Julia's duties as the 'senior' customer service agent was to interview candidates for the role of customer service agent. Their contract was usually for the summer months initially with a view to making it more permanent once the winter came. Each candidate had to go through a group exercise to show who was assertive without being arrogant and who wasn't, a basic geography test, a general knowledge test, and if they got through all that, and some really didn't know that Berlin was in Germany, they had a one to one interview with Julia.

They were conducting the interviews at a hotel near the airport. She'd already seen nine candidates and approved seven of them. Then the tenth one came along. Her name, Tina Coleman, didn't strike any chords with Julia initially. But then when she read the address on the application form of 5, Milton Crescent, Altrincham, and looked at Tina as she walked into the room for the interview, she realised that this was her half sister. She tried to hide her shock. She didn't want to automatically dislike the girl. But this was her half sister and she didn't know whether or not to laugh or cry. This was the girl who'd grown up with her father whilst Julia had grown up with her mother and her ever increasing lapse out of normality. This was the daughter who her father spoke of so glowingly when she went to try and see him last year. She seemed nice enough. It looked like she used to bite her nails but she'd obviously used that clear nail polish that stops people doing that and now, although still relatively small, they were growing.

She had a good figure and, unlike some, she'd actually dressed up for the interview. Some of the other candidates hadn't bothered and had turned up in track suits or outfits that they'd clearly thrown together at the last minute. Some had moaned about having to do shift work. What did they expect when they were being interviewed to do check-in and passenger boarding at one of Britain's main airports? What rocks did these people live under? No wonder they were unemployed.

But Tina wasn't like that. She'd done her research into the company. She had no problem with working shifts. She even spoke another language, French, which was rare amongst the candidates, some of whom could barely speak decent enough English even though they'd been born and bred here. The only fly in the ointment as far as Tina was concerned was that she didn't have a car.

'Not having a car, Tina, how do you propose getting to work for the four o'clock start early shift?'

'Oh am I am getting a car' Tina assured, with a big, wide smile. 'Well, my Dad is in the process of buying me one'.

'That's ... very good of him'.

'Oh yeah, he's great, my Dad. And it's what Dad's are for, isn't it?'

I wouldn't know, thought Julia. I've never had one. When I bought my car I had to penny pinch and save for weeks on end. There was no chance of getting a new one now, not with the wedding coming up.

'Sounds like he's very good to you?'

'Oh he is, we're dead close, my Dad and me, I'm a real Daddy's girl. My Mum feels a bit left out sometimes, I think. And when I came out as a lesbian he was fantastic. So, so supportive. Ooh sorry, have I got a bit personal there?'

'No' said Julia. 'Not at all'. There were plenty of gay people in the airline business. Liam's best man was gay. Julia wasn't homophobic in any way at all and didn't tolerate homophobia in others either. She thought it was lovely that their father accepted Tina's sexuality. She knew that some people had all sorts of problems with their families over that.

'Look, I'm supposed to tell you that you've to wait until you get the letter from us but seeing as it's my final decision anyway, I'm telling you now that you've got the job and you'll be starting the first week of April'.

'Oh that's great, thank you'.

'Just don't tell anyone on the way out' said Julia.

'I won't say a word until I get to my Dad's car. He's waiting outside for me'.

I'm sure he is, thought Julia. How sweet. How nice. How bloody unfair.

It had taken Julia a few weeks but now she was ready to take Tina into her confidence. She'd already told her that she was doing well in her new job and that the supervisors were all pleased with her. They'd become friends and been out for drinks several times and Tina had sometimes stayed over at Julia's flat. Tina and Liam had hit it off and Tina had filled in everything Julia needed to know about their father. Apparently he was something of a ladies man who Tina suspected of not always having been faithful to her mother, but he'd kept his looks and his hair and he had van loads of charm and he couldn't help himself flirting. A bit of a loveable rogue is how Tina once described him. But she also told of a loving father who was always there on sports day or anything else Tina took part in at school, the father who sorted out the bullies who blighted Tina's life when she was in her early teens, the father who'd always been there for her. It broke Julia's heart to hear about all the things she'd missed out on by not having Geoff Coleman, her father, in her life.

'He's my father too, Tina' said Julia.

'Sorry?'

'He had an affair with my mother but he refused to acknowledge me even after my mother died last year and I really needed him'.

'You're not making sense'.

'It's all true' said Julia. 'I'm not lying to you'.

'But if what you say is true then you have been lying to me all these weeks'.

'No' said Julia. 'I've just not told you everything until now'.

'Oh well excuse me for being picky! Am I to assume that you only gave me the job and became friends with me because you knew you were my sister?'

'It was like that at the start, yes'.

'Unbelievable! You've made me live a lie!'

'Our father has been living a lie as far as I'm concerned for the last twenty seven years of my life!'

Tina leered up close to Julia. 'He is not your father. Got it? If he's rejected you then he must have his reasons and from now, you stay away from me and you stay away from my family because you're not welcome!'

Julia burst into tears.

'Oh that's right, turn them on when needed' Tina snarled. 'But if you mess with my family you will regret it. Back off or else'.

The next couple of weeks at work had been excruciating whenever Julia and Tina were on the same shift. Liam had kicked off to Julia about not having told him about Geoff Coleman and for the way she'd acted with Tina all this time. He said he understood how she must've felt after her father had rejected her but that she shouldn't have played with Tina's life the way she had done. He couldn't believe that she'd done it all without telling him anything about it and that he'd had to find out through office gossip. He'd postponed the wedding and said he wanted a break from her for a month whilst he sorted out how he felt.

'But you can't make me out to be the villain in all this?' Julia pleaded.

'No' said Liam. 'But you kept something from me that was so personal about you and you did it for weeks on end knowing that we were making friends with someone who you knew was your sister. If you can deceive me about that, Julia, what else can you deceive me about? And is that how you want to spend our married life because it's not how I want to'.

'But Liam, you're the best thing that's ever happened to me. I love you!'

'Then you should've told me the truth from the beginning!'

'Liam, I can't lose you! I can't lose anyone else!'

'Yeah? Well right now it's fifty, fifty and you've only got yourself to blame'.

The next few days Julia slid into a dark downward spiral of drink fuelled depression. Both Liam and Tina were avoiding her at work and everyone else was being distant. How had it come to this? How had she become the one in the wrong? How come she was on the brink of losing such a good man like Liam? It wasn't fair! It wasn't right! She didn't deserve all this shit! She didn't deserve it. Well they were going to pay. She'd taken too many knock backs in life. She'd had enough.

Because Julia was the senior at work she had her own office and could more or less come and go as she pleased. So one morning she went into the staff locker room. She had a master key for all the lockers and she stole the set of keys that were in Tina's handbag. She then drove down to the nearby shops and had copies made before driving back and placing them back in Tina's handbag. One of the keys was for the front door and she'd know as soon as she put it in the lock.

A couple of nights later she drove round to Milton Crescent but parked just round the corner out of sight of number five. It was past midnight and in the darkness she stepped carefully round to the house and after trying two keys she managed it with the third one. She thanked God that they didn't bolt their door. As quickly as she could she gathered every cushion off the sofa and chairs, every towel in the downstairs toilet, every tea towel out of the kitchen. She was lucky that a wash had been done that day that was still sitting in a basket in the utility room at the back. She placed all the materials at the bottom of the stairs and piled them high. She poured every flammable liquid she could find all over the mound as well as the two cans of petrol she'd brought with her. They wouldn't be able to get down the stairs through this. They be trapped and they'd die. Her father who'd rejected her, her sister who'd rejected her, and a step-mother who'd probably gone along with it all. Well they were all going to pay now. They were all going to pay with their lives which seemed only fair considering they'd all conspired to destroy hers.

Then she threw a lit match at it all.

A week later

Liam lifted up a handful of soil and tossed it at the coffin after it had been lowered into the ground. All of Julia's workmates had turned up as well as all her other friends. Her Aunts, uncles, and cousins, none of whom she'd seen or heard from since her mother's funeral, were all there too, as were Liam's Mum and Dad who were there too to give him some support. Liam was so angry with himself for falling out with her in those last few days. He'd always regret not trying to understand better than he had done.

The fire fighters said that a 'back draft' of flames must've caught Julia after she'd lit the doused materials and engulfed her in the rapidly developing flames. There wasn't much of her body recognisable by the time they were able to get into the house. It was ironic that the Coleman family weren't even in at the time. They were all at a family party at Geoff Coleman's sister's house a couple of miles away which was why the bolt wasn't on the door.

The mourners were starting to disperse when Liam noticed Tina holding the arm of a man who must be Geoff Coleman. The sight of them made him angry and he marched up to them.

'What the hell are you doing here?'

'Please, Liam' said Tina. 'Me and my Dad just wanted to come and pay our respects'.

'Why?'

'What do you mean?'

'What I said. Why?'

'Because I'm her father' said Geoff.

Liam grinned with a look of sheer contempt and then grabbed Geoff Coleman by the lapels of his jacket. 'Yeah? Well it's a bit late for that now, don't you think? You fucking coward'.

TWELVE

KATE

Kate Hanson had always been known as something of a good time girl. She'd laughed with men, danced with men, talked with men about how their wife didn't understand them, she'd drank with men, been out to many dinners with men, and she'd slept her way into double figures. But none of the men she met stayed around. It was always 'the wrong time' or 'it's not you, it's me' or 'I don't want anything serious' without adding that 'I'm waiting for the right one to come along'. Oh and the bullshit excuse she loved the most which was 'the thing is, Kate, we'll have to finish because I love you so much that I just can't handle it'. Yes that was the one she laughed about the most before cracking up into tears over a bottle of Australian white once she'd been dumped. Single men never stayed around for birthdays and Christmas. Only the married ones stayed because they were the ones who could walk away without getting involved. And the latest in a very long line was Roger.

Kate worked as an administration assistant in the sales department of a large company in Bury, just north of Manchester, and that dealt with the manufacture of farming equipment. Roger Chambers was sales director for the north of England and was only physically in the office two days of the week. He was your average six foot tall man in his early forties, slim with receding black hair that had started to go a bit grey, married with two teenage children, handsome in that average man in the street type way. The type of man Kate would've loved to take home to meet her Mum and Dad if she'd ever had the chance. When he was in the office the rest of the staff always knew because Kate, ten years his junior, was always dressed up to the nines and always with a blouse undone just that little bit too far. But it seemed that Roger loved her breasts and she liked to tease him with glimpses of their shape.

They were indeed large and firm and when they'd first slept together he'd buried his face in them and licked his way around until he'd made his way down to her vagina. The rest of the girls in the office knew he gave a good licking out. Kate had told them many times, just like she told them about all their sexual exploits and they often had to avert their eyes the next time they saw him, knowing what they did about the size of his manhood and how much of a fan he was of the film 'Last Tango in Paris'.

Kate would often join him on those three nights a week he spent in hotels. Tonight they were in their favourite one in York. It was just outside the inner walled part of the city and it was where they'd first made love. This time they'd given him a larger room with a sofa and a low table and he'd ordered a bottle of champagne. They were curled up on the sofa. Roger was in the white bathrobe the hotel provided and Kate was in a black silk and lace slip. They both had their legs bent at the knees and underneath them. Kate was running one hand through all the hairs on Roger's chest whilst holding her glass of champagne with the other. Roger had one arm round Kate and with the other he was holding his glass of champagne.

'This is magical' said Roger. 'I look forward to these times we spend together so much'.

'Me too' said Kate.

'You wouldn't see anybody else? Would you?'

'Of course I wouldn't, darling' said Kate. 'I would never be unfaithful to you. You do know that, don't you?'

'Of course' said Roger.

'So what are you talking about? Or rather, who are you talking about?'

'Abdul?'

'Abdul? The security man from work?'

'I saw you having lunch together yesterday' said Roger. 'And I was jealous'.

'Roger, Abdul is a really nice man who's had to flee from his own country and he's now trying to make it thousands of miles away from home. He's had to leave all his family behind. He needs friends'.

'As long as that's all it is'.

'Of course's that's all it is' said Kate who wasn't entirely convinced that friendship was the extent of how she felt about Abdul. 'I'd never do anything to hurt you, baby. I'm yours for however long you want me'.

'Then we're in for a long ride' said Roger.

'You are silly'.

'I was just a bit afraid, that's all. It's hard to imagine anything this good coming without a catch'.

'We can go on for as long as you want us to'.

Roger then put his glass down and took Kate's glass out of her hand and put that down too. He took her in his arms and they kissed, slowly and deeply. Then Kate pushed him onto his back and tugged at the cord round his bathrobe.

'Come on, darling' she said as she slid off him. She passed her slip over her head and let it drop to the floor. 'Show me what we'd be losing if we broke up'.

'No problem there' said Roger as he stood up and took the bathrobe off. He was hard and proud. 'I'm always up for that'.

Kate was never usually late with her period. She'd always been regular as clockwork but last month it hadn't happened and now this month she was running a week late. She didn't want to think that she might be pregnant. She had no idea what Roger would make of it if she was but she had to face facts. She was late and she was feeling strange. It was time to buy a pregnancy test kit and keep her fingers crossed.

This wasn't a time to turn to her sister-in-law Beth for help but none of her friends were available that lunchtime and she needed someone now. Beth had answered on the first ring. She'd led a completely different life to Kate. Kate's brother Tom was ten years older than Kate and he'd married Beth when they were both nineteen. As far as Kate was concerned they were a boring pair of bastards. They'd never been to bed with anyone except each other and since Beth's uncle had died and they'd inherited thousands off him she really did walk around like she was little Miss perfect who was never wrong and it was all the fault of everybody else. Beth had acted as if she somehow had the right to look down on those who hadn't benefitted from the death of a wealthy relative. But they still hadn't lived. They hadn't been anywhere or done anything and yet they thought they were the moral high command. They'd had two children about whom they'd often boasted about having brought them up 'strictly'. To Kate that meant that her poor niece and nephew had never been allowed to be children but had been expected to behave like adults from the day they were born. If they so much as laughed too loudly in public Beth shouted at them so fiercely they flinched as if she was hitting them. And all they were doing, as far as Kate could see, was being children. But Beth and Tom had wanted to be 'seen' as 'strict' parents as if that was some kind of virtue. Kate would never bring up children like that. Her kids would be allowed to have fun and be kids. They wouldn't be shackled by what their parents needed to be 'seen' to be doing.

'You stupid idiot' said Beth after Kate told her that the test was positive.

'Not really the words I'd have chosen in the circumstances but I get your gist'.

'Well what are your Mum and Dad going to say?'

'Why, are they having the baby?'

'You know what I mean'.

Kate folded her arms defensively. 'No, explain it to me'.

'Well how are they going to tell their friends and the rest of the family?'

'Oh and that's what's most important as far as you're concerned, isn't it? What other people think'.

'Kate, you won't be there all the time to help them explain'.

'Explain? Explain what exactly?'

'That you're pregnant and not married!'

'Beth, what colour is the sky in the century that you live in?'

'And being sarcastic isn't going to change my view'.

'No, because you really believe that you're better than the rest of us, don't you, Beth?'

'Look, I know what's right and what's wrong and you may as well cut the clever talk because you're never going to convince me that you having this baby is a good idea'.

'And there's another example of your weakness. Try to cut the conversation dead when you think you might have to justify your own arguments. If you were at home you'd probably walk away and start hoovering or something to put me off pursuing'.

'Well at least I didn't have the stupidity to get pregnant when I wasn't married'.

'Yeah? Well if I have this child it will grow up knowing they've always got a mother to turn to who won't judge them'.

Kate didn't know what had happened to her mood but she was losing her temper like she was taking her breath. She'd known other women lose it like this over stupid, inconsequential things when they were pregnant and she'd often thought they were just playing for attention and using their pregnancy as an excused for their foul mood and rudeness. But now she took it all back. Pregnancy sucked as far as your hormones were concerned and if she had to argue that point with anyone she'd deck them.

By the time Roger came round to see her that evening she'd calmed down and her irritated state had been replaced with a knackered one.

'You look tired' he said as she came in and pulled her to him in an embrace. He kissed her on the lips and then started kissing her neck. 'I've not got a lot of time but I've got enough if we're quick'.

'I didn't invite you round here for that, Roger. Nice as that side of things is between us I do have other needs too'.

'Like what?'

'You have to ask? I'm a woman in my early thirties and you think that sex with a married man is all I need to keep me going?'

'What's got into you? You're never normally like this. I noticed in the office today that you were snapping at people for no reason'.

'I'm pregnant, Roger'.

She watched as the colour drained from his face. 'What? Fucks's sake. How?'

'Why do men always ask that in situations like this? It must've been one of the times you fucked me!'

'Yeah, yeah, okay, I get it, I was being your average insensitive man. What are you going to do?'

'What am I going to do?'

'Look, Maggie and the kids come first. You've always known that. You being pregnant changes nothing about my personal circumstances'.

'Oh piss off, Roger, just piss off!'

'You don't mean that. You need somebody to help you'.

'I'm getting an abortion' she declared. 'I've booked an appointment at a clinic next week'.

'You can't'.

'I can't what?'

'You can't kill our child'.

Kate screamed out in frustration. 'Oh, you want it all ways, don't you! Just like you've always done!'

Against her better judgement, when Roger crossed the space between them and held her she gave in and allowed some crumb of comfort to come through the feel of his arms.

'You don't need to get an abortion, Kate. I can't leave Maggie but that doesn't mean I can't take care of you and the baby. I'll provide for you both, of course I will, and you and I can carry on as before'.

'But it won't be the same, Roger' she said, tearfully. 'We'll have a child and one that will never come first as far as its Dad is concerned. He or she will never see you at Christmas and on your birthday it'll never be able to buy you a present because you won't be able to take it home. And what can I do with someone who has to watch the bloody clock all the time?'

'I know it won't be easy but Kate, please, don't go to that appointment next week. I'm begging you. Don't ... don't do that to our child'.

Kate was at a complete loss as to know what to do. This could end up being her only chance to have a child but how could she bring a child into the world in these circumstances? Yes, she knew that many others did but she still didn't see that as justification for her doing it. And she certainly wasn't going to be raising it on benefits. If Roger was going to support her it would need to be all the way. For a long time she'd thought of him as the best thing that had ever happened to her. So tall, handsome, strong, a real man in those places she needed him to be. But married to Maggie and adamant that it would always stay that way.

On her way back from collecting the post from mail room she

walked past reception and waved to Abdul who was on duty behind the desk. She didn't know what came over her after that. She must've fainted because the next thing she knew, Abdul was crouched over her and a couple of the other girls from the office were with her.

'What happened?'

'You fainted' said Abdul who looked so good in his uniform. His dark brown eyes, black hair, and olive coloured skin had made him very popular amongst the ladies at work. But he only had eyes for one and that was Kate. He was always asking her out and was determined that one day she'd say yes. 'How long have you been pregnant?'

'How did you know?'

'I'm a qualified doctor' he revealed. 'Back in Yemen I had my own practice'.

'Then why don't they let you be a doctor here?'

Abdul smiled. 'One of those things about being an asylum seeker' he said. 'Now have you been to see your doctor?'

'Not yet' said Kate who was embarrassed at the girls knowing she was pregnant.

'Then give me the number and I'll make the appointment for you. You need to see them as soon as possible. I will go with you if you like'

'Really?'

He held her hand. 'Of course'.

Kate then burst into tears.

The last thing Kate needed on nine-thirty on a Saturday morning was a visit from Roger's wife, Maggie.

'I take it you haven't come to tell me what's on offer at Tesco's?'

'I could rarely manage wise cracks when I was in the first few weeks so I take my hat off to you'.

'Am I being mistaken or are you being ... nice?'

Maggie smiled and said. 'You'd better let me in, Kate. You and I need to talk'.

Kate let Maggie into her flat and led her through to the living room.

'So?' said Kate. 'Forgive me but I can't imagine what we've got to say to each other'.

'Roger isn't the father of your child, Kate'.

'I beg your pardon? And before we go on, how did you know I was pregnant anyway?'

'I've got friends at the company' said Maggie. 'Look, Kate, I've always known about your affair with Roger. I've known about all his affairs, love. You're not the first and you won't be the last. I've accepted he had a wandering eye because you see, I'm the same. I love Roger more than life itself but every now and then, just like him, I need something extra'.

'And does Roger know?'

'No' said Maggie. 'Because despite how much I love him he is a chauvinist and he goes through life thinking I'm content with being at home and looking after the kids. His father is exactly the same. A woman's place is in the home and all that'.

'Except if you're his mistress, then you're expected to work as well'.

'That's what it comes down to, Kate, yes'.

'But I don't understand?' said Kate. 'Why does me knowing all this change anything?'

'Kate, Roger is not the father of your child because he's infertile'.

'You're lying'.

'I'm not' said Kate. 'Our kids aren't his. Their biological father is his brother Owen'.

'Christ! And does Roger know about this too?'

'No, he doesn't. We were having problems starting a family and we went for tests. Roger was stuck in a meeting and couldn't make the appointment when the doctor said that I was one hundred percent but Roger had such a low sperm count that it was almost undetectable'.

'And you didn't tell him?'

'I didn't have the heart! I knew what it would do to him. His brother Owen lives in Toronto now which is just as well because if Roger ever did find out he'd kill him'.

'Hang on, you get told that your husband is infertile so you just go to bed with his brother and let him sire you? Twice?'

'Don't make it sound like ... '

' ... like what? Like the way it is? Oh boy oh boy have you got some pretty explosive secrets to carry around'.

'And I'm asking for your discretion'.

'In return for what? I could just snap my fingers now and get exactly what I want'.

'We both know that if push came to shove, Roger would choose me over you any day'.

Kate couldn't help it. Despite everything she'd confessed, Maggie still had the nerve to look so fucking smug. Kate slapped her face.

'You may have the house, and the ring, and the kids who aren't even his. And you've got Roger. But you're no better than me'.

'Maybe not, but now you know the facts, who can you say is the father of your child? I'll leave you to ponder that one. Have a nice weekend'.

'If you were that good a wife he wouldn't have affairs!'

'And if you that good a mistress he'd have left me for you!'

'You've never invited me to your home before' said Abdul as he sat at Kate's kitchen table eating her roast beef and Yorkshire pudding. He didn't drink so they were on sparkling water which suited Kate in her pregnancy state.

'I needed to talk to you, Abdul' said Kate as she watched this gorgeous man from another world eat all the food she placed in front of him.

'This sounds serious?'

'Abdul, I think you're the father of my child'.

Abdul almost spat out his mouthful of gravy covered carrot. 'What did you say?'

'For a long time I've been seeing a married man and I thought that if I got pregnant it might make him do something about our situation' she explained. 'But the thing is I've since found out that he couldn't be the father of my baby because he's infertile. The only other man I've slept with during this period, Abdul, is you'.

'That night after the party when you were dead drunk I never laid a finger on you'.

'But we did get close the following morning when I was sober. Don't you remember?'

'Of course I do' said Abdul. 'So you're carrying my child?'

'I believe I am, yes' said Kate who wasn't sure how to read the expression on Abdul's face. 'There's no other possibility'.

'Oh my God' said Abdul. 'Well it's unexpected but ... it's not unwelcome'.

'It's not?'

'Kate, I've been sweet on you since I first saw you. I thought that if ever there was a purpose to me coming to this country then you must be it. I've tried telling you this a hundred times but I knew you were so wrapped up with this married man'.

'So what are you saying?'

'That we should get married and be a family for this little life we've created'.

Kate could hardly breathe. 'Are you sure?'

'Well it's a little quicker than I would've chosen but yes, I am sure. I want to marry you, Kate, and I want to be there for you and our baby'.

Seven months later

'Hello?'

Kate looked up and smiled at Roger. 'Hello, you'.

'I thought I'd come by late in the hope that Abdul wasn't here'.

'Well he's not so you're okay' said Kate who was in the maternity ward. Little Faisal was only a day old and his poor old

Dad had gone home to have some much needed sleep.

'I'm not intruding then'.

'No' said Kate. 'It's nice to see you'.

'Has Abdul been here throughout?'

'Yes' said Kate 'He was with me all through the birth. He's been great'.

Roger looked at the little baby boy with the light brown skin in the cot beside his mother's bed. 'He's cute'.

'Well I agree but I'm biased' said Kate.

'He's healthy?'

'Yes, everything is fine' said Kate.

'And his Mum?'

'His Mum has never been happier' said Kate. 'He's a beautiful baby and I've got a wonderful husband'.

'You've been through a lot'.

'Oh, you mean all those people who said he was only marrying me so he could stay in this country? Well damn them all to hell. Abdul is the most honest and genuine man I've ever met'.

'Ouch'.

'Oh you know what I mean, Roger, I wasn't having a go'.

'I know you weren't' said Roger who was overwhelmed with regret. 'I just want you to be happy, Kate'.

'I know' she said. 'And I want you to be too'.

'I know everything now' said Roger. 'Maggie told me the lot. We've had some terrible rows. I don't know if we're going to get through it'.

'Do you still love Maggie?'

'Yes' said Roger. 'Despite it all'.

'Then you'll find a way through it' said Kate. 'As for the children, Roger, you are their father and you always will be'.

'It's hard though, Kate, to think that my own brother ... '

' ... I know' said Kate. 'I know it must be. But it isn't the kids fault. You've got to act like the Dad they've always known'.

Roger held her hand. 'Thank you'.

'What for?'

'For helping me when I didn't deserve it'.

'We'll always be friends, Roger'.

'Do you think Abdul will be happy about that?'

'Abdul is a much bigger person than that' said Kate.

'You really are in love with him, aren't you?'

'Yes' said Kate, smiling. 'I really am'.

'Then I wish you all the best' said Roger. 'I'd better go'.

'Roger?'

'Yes?'

'All the best to you too' said Kate.

'Kate, I wish ... '

' ... don't Roger. I'm really glad you stopped by but don't spoil it'.

'Sorry'.

'It's alright' said Kate.

'I didn't mean to upset you by saying more than I should, really I didn't'.

'I know and it's alright, Roger. It's really alright. I just hope it's alright for you too one day'.

The next morning Kate woke up to find Abdul standing there

with a woman he'd never met before. She was wearing traditional Muslim clothing, complete with scarf over her head and nothing showing of the rest of her body at all.

'Babe?'

Abdul made no move towards her. 'Good morning. How is my son?'

'He's ... he's fine. Who is this?'

'This is Fatima. Don't try speaking to her because she doesn't speak English but you'll be able to communicate once you've learned Arabic. She's my first wife and she's just flown in this morning from Kuwait where she's been living with my brother. She's given me three children so you've a bit of catching up to do'.

Kate instinctively reached for her son Faisal and held him tightly in her arms. 'What the hell are you talking about, Abdul?'

'Well as soon as I'm allowed to go back we'll be going back to Yemen and we'll all set up home together with you, Fatima, our children , and whoever else might come along'.

'No way!'

'Darling Kate, don't try and fight me because you don't have a choice. We're married and you do as I say now. If you want to go back to your infertile British married boyfriend then please yourself but can you really say you'll be any better off with him? Can you really say that he can offer you more than me, your husband? You know the answer to that, Kate, darling, so don't try and make trouble. It wouldn't do you any good'.

THIRTEEN

JASON

Jason Matthews was sitting on the end of his bed eating his breakfast cereal. He tried to be as happy as he could in his little bedsit and at least it was preferable to going back home to live with his parents. At least here he had a semblance of pride and privacy. The bedsit was at the back of a converted old house so there was no direct sunlight but that was okay. There wasn't room for a proper sofa so he had to use the bed whenever he wanted to sit down. He had a dining chair in the window and a small table where he ate his main meals and aside from the wardrobe that was all he possessed in the way of furniture. And yet none of it was his. It came with the rental of the bedsit. His former wife Stacey had taken their house and all the furniture in it even though she hadn't paid for any of it. He'd paid for it all. He'd put down the deposit on the house out of his savings when he and Stacey had, he thought, been madly in love and looking forward to a shared future. Stacey hadn't had any money when they met. In fact she'd been in oceans of debt. Jason had paid off all her credit cards, store cards, and personal loans. A marriage, a mortgage and two kids later, she left him for a man who earned three times as much as he did and now he was in a bedsit that could've made him fall off the edge if he didn't love his kids so much.

She'd taken them too. Their two boys who Jason was missing so much it was almost like a physical pain. They say a grown man shouldn't cry but he'd cried a lot in recent months. He couldn't help himself. He was only human after all and there was only so much he could take.

Even though Stacey's new boyfriend could keep her in a style to which she'd always wanted to become accustomed, the court had still ruled that Jason had to pay for Stacey to maintain the lifestyle she'd had when they married. That meant that Jason's own lifestyle had been forced back into the single, unattached world. He couldn't afford to take his kids away on holiday, not even to Blackpool or to Cornwall where he'd spent many a happy childhood holiday with his parents. But Stacey's new boyfriend had just taken her and Jason's kids on a luxury fortnight to Florida, taking in Disneyworld and the Kennedy space centre. Jason's kids, Tom, aged seven, and Zach, aged five, would've loved all that. Stacey would've loved it too. She'd always had a taste for men with lots of cold, hard cash but Jason had really believed when they got together that she was in love with him. He should've taken more notice of the signs early on. After they were married and Stacey was pregnant with Tom she suddenly developed a disliking of him working shifts and working at weekends. But he was a fire fighter. He had to work shifts and she hadn't objected before they were married. It got worse after Tom was born. He felt like he couldn't do anything right and she subjected him to a constant barrage of criticism. But he took it on the chin and blamed it all on the hormones. She couldn't have meant some of the awful things she said to him. Then she got better and then she was pregnant again with Zach and she seemed to be back to her old self, the Stacey he'd fallen in love with. She'd never wanted a career. When she got pregnant with Tom she'd been more than happy to give up her job as an office worker. She'd only ever wanted to be a stay at home Mum. But after Zach was born she went back into the darkness of post-natal depression. Jason understood how hard that was on a woman. He wasn't some unthinking, insensitive macho idiot. He supported all the help women get when they're going through it. But where was the help for the husbands who have to constantly negotiate around the nasty, mean spirited creatures their wives become during post-natal depression? After all, it was like caring for anyone with any kind of depression. The ones who care need help and support too.

Jason was washing his cereal bowl when he heard the post coming through the door. He went to pick it up and saw that the familiar white envelope from his solicitor was amongst his delivery. He opened it and felt his insides plunge as he read the contents. He hadn't seen his two sons for almost a year and now Stacey had applied to the family court to prevent him from seeing them again until they were adults. Her reason was that it upset them too much to see their father for such short periods of time and for the sake of their emotional welfare she as their mother had 'decided' that it was better for them not to see their father until they were old enough not to be upset by having to say goodbye to him at the end of each period of access.

She had 'decided'.

She who'd walked out and taken their kids with her.

She who had seemingly taken away all his rights as a father.

So now he was going to have to fight her again. The court

hadn't enforced any of the visitation orders they'd made in Jason's favour and had let Stacey get away with keeping the boys away from him with all manner of flimsy, pathetic excuses. Now his solicitor was telling Jason that they would have to discuss what they were going to do about this latest bullet from Stacey. Reading between the lines Jason took that to mean that it would probably go back and forth to court countless times and it would be costly. It was another stab through his heart. What was a man to do in this day and age? How come he could have his whole life taken away from him by a woman and yet he's supposed to just stand there and 'take it like a man'. How come he could be made to feel guilty even when he'd done absolutely nothing wrong?

He looked around his bedsit and wondered how the fuck he got here. He'd never done anything to disrespect women. He'd never two timed any of his girlfriends. When he'd met Stacey he'd known in that instant that she was the one he wanted to spend the rest of his life with. He thought he'd given her what she wanted. He thought she'd been happy. He'd never messed her about or given her any reason to doubt him. So just what had she wanted? Every time she had told him she wasn't happy she hadn't been able to answer him or give him any hint as to why. They had a nice house, two great kids, friends and a social life. They'd had the usual problems over money from time to time but nothing serious. Why had she taken everything away from him? Why had he lost everything from their relationship when Stacey had been the one who'd had an affair and left him for another man?

Why did he feel he had to apologise just for being a man whenever he went to court over access to his sons? Why was it acceptable for Stacey to get emotional in court but when he tried to demonstrate his emotional distress and frustration he was warned that it wouldn't do his case any good?

Why did he feel so utterly powerless?

Why did Stacey have to be so damn cruel and merciless? Why couldn't they just talk about it and come to an agreement for the sake of the boys? Why did he have to go to court to fight to see his own children?

They found him the next morning. He'd taken an overdose of paracetamol washed down with a bottle of scotch.

Later that day his distraught parents went round to see their former daughter-in-law intending to have a frank exchange of words. But she'd taken the boys on holiday and in a phone call from the airport she told them that she wouldn't be allowing the boys to attend their father's funeral.

She also told them that she was cutting all contact between the boys and their paternal grandparents and she would use the laws on harassment if they so much a tried to contact them. The boys were no longer part of their lives.

Printed in Great Britain
by Amazon